I0581072

Also by Phyllis Wachob

Teachers Abroad Mysteries

#1 Revolution Revenge
#2 Oasis Assassin
#3 Turkish Delight Gone Sour
#4 Singapore Fling

Kern Kapers Mysteries

#1 Body in the Orchard
#2 Killer Kern

Killer Kern

Phyllis Wachob

Dedication

This novel is dedicated to all those hometown lovers
and their favorite places to eat and visit.

Acknowledgements

This series of mysteries would have been impossible to write and bring to fruition without the help of many friends and family members. The critique and change of cover design, contents, flow, and characters would not have been enjoyable, in fact, agonizing and slow, without their help. So, thanks to my Mom, my knitting friends, my Writers of Kern critique group members Srey Khoy and Bob Duncan, Maggie King (fellow mystery writer and critic), my cover designer Doug Thompson, my photographer Francisco Montesinos, and my proofreader Tere Swagler. A special thanks goes to all my fellow members of the Writers of Kern, who keep the encouragement coming.

Preface

Some of the places in this novel are real, for example the Sugar Mill, Dewar's, the Rice Bowl, and the Kern River. Also, Hart Park is real, as are the lake, the beaches, the adobe house, the former zoo and many other places introduced in this book. These places of Bakersfield and Kern County are easily found in histories, maps, guides and on the web. However, Darrell Pitt's office and the unnamed street where Very lives are fictional. In its essence, this is a work of fiction. Names, characters, places and incidents are either the product of the author's imagination or are used fictitiously, and any resemblance to actual persons, living or dead, businesses or establishments, events or locales is coincidental.

Cast of Characters

Vermilion Blew: retired school librarian and teacher
Frankie Monroe: Very's fiancé
Joey Sanchez: Very's best friend
Deputy Bobby Sanchez: Joey's husband
Darrell Pitts: Private Investigator
Michelle (aka Mouse) Malden: Kern River suicide
Deborah Malden Smith: Michelle's sister
Maria Hernandez: Kern River drowning victim
Gabriela (Gabby) Hernandez: Maria's sister
Carlos Hernandez: Maria's brother
Javier Hernandez: Maria's oldest brother
Pedro Hernandez: Maria's brother
Hector Fernandez: Maria's cousin and Kern River drowning victim
Cassandra Harger: Frankie's biological daughter
Father Sullivan: parish priest well-known in Bakersfield

Chapter One: Bodies in the River

"Killer Kern Strikes Again: 4 Bodies Recovered." Vermilion Blew stared at the headline in the local newspaper. Late spring was a difficult time on the Kern River. The weather was hot, the river inviting, but the water was like a frosty freeze, the currents pulled like powerful twists of a whip and the debris of branches and grasses tended to clutch like a two-year-old who didn't want mommy to leave. Four, though. Must be a record of sorts. And so soon after Mother's Day, what a time to die. Four grieving mothers?

Very hesitated to read the article. This could mean nothing but grief. Anger welled up at those so stupid as to go swimming in the river. At least half the year, and in most years, nine months of the year, the water was nonexistent through the city, but there was always water in the river at Hart Park and she had never heard of the river totally running dry there. Last weekend had been hot, unseasonably hot at 100 degrees, and the river must have been inviting, calling to those who had no pool to take a dip in.

Very refilled her coffee cup, gathered up the paper and went outside to the bright patio. Ah, almost summer.

She threw herself into a lounger, stretched out her long legs and kicked off her size 11 flip-flops. She loved summer, loved the heat, the dry crackling air that dried any sweat that gathered. Others complained. Some moved away and constantly whined about the heat when they returned. Others stayed and continually moaned about the hot summers while running air conditioners at full blast, thereby ensuring they felt immediately overheated when they ventured outside. Summer and heat came together in Bakersfield. She still had another six weeks before the worst began, so maybe she needed a haircut. She raked her fingers through her curly gray and brown hair to check the length. Maybe leave it for a few more weeks.

She skipped the front page and went to the obituaries. She scanned first, then began to read. When she got to the part about what a dutiful mother and grandmother Oma was and that she had devoted herself to her family and furry friends, Very closed the paper and swore. Was that all these women were, wives and mothers? But who was she to object to that?

Childless, Very had expended her maternal lather on her students for over 35 years. Mothers. Why did Very read these obits? Because her mother had, with a dedication that bordered on religion. What kinds of other things had Very taken on that her mother had done? No, do not start with the cross-word puzzles! Do not become your mother.

Today. It was one year ago today they had placed the slab on her mother's grave for the final time. It had lain there for almost 25 years, waiting for her. It had been engraved when her father's had been, a twin set. But it only had her mother's date of birth and was waiting for the date of death. After her passing, it was only weeks before it was ready and Very had gone to the cemetery to watch it relaid. The funeral director told her that it wasn't necessary for her to watch this, she could come later, but Very knew this was the closure of her mother's life. She wanted to be there.

That was one year ago. Now, here she was, still in her mother's house, using her mother's dishes, sitting on her mother's couch, reading her mother's paper and in the same order that she had done. Was it time for a change? She wasn't young and the thought that she could get stuck here for the rest of her life jolted her. She needed to think about creating her own space, finally.

She returned to the Killer Kern article about the victims of the river. Taking a deep breath, she began to read. One sentence in, she turned the page. She wasn't up to reading about these deaths. She let her eyes rove. "Police searching for beer bandits." Three 30-packs of beer were stolen from a fast food store. The in-store camera captured the images of two men struggling with the heavy weight of cheap beer, but the photo was so unclear the culprits were unrecognizable. Bakersfield beer bandits. Sounds like this dusty corner of the San Joaquin Valley. They wanted beer to slake their thirst, but couldn't afford it. Answer: steal it. At least they didn't shoot the cashier on their way out.

The Killer Kern article beckoned her. Who were these four confused and lost souls who took to the river last weekend? Ones who couldn't swim? Ones who thought they could swim out to the middle of a swollen river? Those logs floating by were not only things to hang onto, but also deadly spiders with multiple arms that reached to grab and pull under. A day so hot that the first bite of cold water didn't register as dangerous, only deliciously shocking and cool. Brothers and cousins standing on the bank, urging the non-swimmers deeper and deeper into the muddy waters and uneven bed of the river? What about those who came from out of town for the day, or the weekend, who didn't know that it was called the Killer Kern for a reason. Who were these?

Very closed her eyes, slurped her cooling coffee and then breathed deeply. She turned back to the front-page article. "Four bodies have been recovered from the Kern River and environs in the past three days. Fourteen-year-old Maria Hernandez and her twenty-five-year-old cousin Hector Fernandez disappeared from a beach in Hart Park on Saturday afternoon. Their bodies were found Tuesday morning not far from the last sighting. They were identified by the Hernandez family. The young girl was thought to have gone swimming, but experienced difficulties in the cold, swiftly-moving waters. The cousin, who shared the same address, presumably entered the water in a desperate attempt to save his young cousin."

Two from the same household, that was always a difficult one to digest. The newspaper had, every year, on the fourth of July, a small obituary that reminded everyone of the father, the young daughter and cousin who had lost their lives on that day to the river. How many years had the survivors paid to run the obituary? They said it was to remind everyone to take care. Perhaps this family hadn't read the paper, or they thought it was about someone else, strangers who had no connection to them.

And then again, there was the Merle Haggard song. "I'll never swim Kern River again." That summed it up. If you lost your one and only true love, well, who would try to swim in that river? Merle Haggard moved away, didn't even live here anymore. Really, it was the river that made him move? A powerful, mighty river.

Very rattled the paper in her face and went back to the article. "A third body, found washed up near the Rio Bravo Power Plant, belonged to a woman police have preliminarily identified as the owner of a car, found abandoned further up the canyon on Saturday afternoon. The Sheriff's Department have determined it to be a suicide. Investigations are ongoing."

Wait, suicides can't be included in the overall body count; the river didn't do it. And don't get started on the number personally known who have used the canyon as the site of their own self-inflicted deaths. There was no Golden Gate Bridge nearby, nor a deep gorge with a Suicide Rock to entice the melancholic and despair-ridden to end it all. The sweet smiling face of a high school classmate snapped into the forefront, a colleague of her mother, a teenage boy her sister had known. Could we use the moniker of Killer Kern to cover these as well?

"A fourth body was spotted Saturday afternoon by a group who were floating on inner tubes down the river. Near Choctaw Valley, less than a mile downstream from Hart Park, the swollen river that had risen in the past week, and had undermined a bank at the turn of the river. This had caused a collapse, exposing the roots of the brush that grew along the riverbank. As the group went by, one of them spotted a piece of cloth protruding from the bank. After making his way to the face of the collapse, he discovered the remains of a body. The rest of the body was found later in the day, washed ashore on an island just downstream. The Sheriff's Department suspect the remains of an historical body, preliminarily identified as an adult male. There is also suggestion of foul play. The Sheriff has asked the public for information. Please contact…"

Very's breath came quickly; a mild buzz started inside her head, a tinnitus that grew in strength until the entire patio resonated with a million mosquitoes. She felt her head go light and immediately she bent to nestle it between her legs.

"Don't faint now," she cried out loud.

She practiced her quiet breathing exercises and five minutes later, gingerly lifted her head. She allowed the paper to rest in her lap and she let her head loll back on the chair. Great rolls of emotion began to spread, until Very sat up and commanded them to cease. This called for serious thinking, not emotional roller-coaster rides. But the thoughts formed themselves; the questions poured out.

Was this, finally, the body of her fiancé? The one who walked out on her 38 years ago on the eve of their wedding? Could this corpse be his? Buried in the sands near the river, hidden from view, left to rot and decay? The paper said "foul play." That was just a polite term for murder.

Eight months ago, Very had been to emotional hell and back after another body had been discovered in an orchard. That had not been her Frankie, but an associate of his. Frankie Monroe's body had not been found after all, and those who might have been able to tell her had all died. But the unspoken thought remained, haunting Very every day. If his friend had been murdered and buried, what had happened to Frankie? That misguided drug deal gone wrong had enveloped Frankie's associate, so the only thing to conclude was that Frankie had been murdered and buried too. Either that, or he had run and disappeared.

Very had spent the intervening time working that angle as well, taking a job as a part time private investigator and spending her spare time trolling the databases of the US and Canada, hoping to find him hiding somewhere. A waste of time? In eight months, she had discovered nothing except there were a lot of Frank Monroes, or people with similar names. None could be her Frankie. So, where was he?

Very went back to the paper and reread the section about the historical, unnamed body. That was a serendipitous encounter by the kids on inner tubes. A cloth waving from the river bank? Bones? And what other remains had been found? No details there. Very shuddered.

Instead of calling the Sheriff's department and bothering the detective with questions, but no information to give, she elected to go in through the back door. She called her best friend Joey. Who else does a person call when they want to talk but their best friend? In this case, Joey's husband was Deputy Sheriff Bobby Sanchez and a person who kept up on all that went on in his department. If anyone knew any more than what was in the paper, he would.

"Joey," Very stated when she heard her friend's voice. "It's Very and I need to pick your hubby's brains."

"Good morning, Very," Joey answered. "Could this possibly be about the body in the river found this week? In the paper this morning?"

"Yes and yes."

"Very, you know that Bobby would let you know if there was anything to report, you know that. He takes you seriously. But I think there is not enough information on this one. You have everything in the paper."

"But that's nothing! An old body, adult male, buried in the fields out there! Just like the other body buried in the orchard."

"Not quite like the other one, that was in Wasco or Delano, somewhere out that way. This one is completely different. Very, calm down. Let this investigation go forward. Bobby knows, he told me so, that this would get you excited, but you have no reason to."

"Oh, so Bobby knows that it is like the other one. That it could be Frankie's body this time. That when those two crazy drug dealers did in Danny Boy Harger, they could have killed Frankie as well. They could have buried his body in the same way. Joey, please, please, tell me what Bobby said."

"Bobby knows nothing more than what was in the paper. A few details, maybe, but nothing definitive. I will tell him to call you. Maybe tonight, okay?"

Silence met this remark. Then Joey heard Very breathing heavily.

"Oh, oh, no, not again," Very's voice spoke weakly into the phone.

"Very, Very, are you okay? Should I call 911? Sit down, calm down. Very, answer me." Joey's voice screeched, trying to reach her friend.

"Joey, I'm okay. Just got too excited again. Breathing too hard. No problem."

"Very, you need to go see a doctor. And I don't mean a psychiatrist, I mean a medical doctor. You need to get checked out. Promise me."

"Okay, okay. But you promise me that Bobby will let me know everything, and as soon as he finds out. Bye, good friend."

Very sat in the chair and shivered as a cloud came over, blotting out the sun. She didn't need a doctor; she needed some answers. She needed to put all of this behind her. How could she go on with her life with the unanswered question? Where was Frankie?

Chapter Two: Investigating a Suicide

Thursday morning dawned warm and sunny. Before Very could get her act together, the great hot ball had breached the fence and trees and spread its pulsing heat onto the bricks of the patio. Before bothering Joey again, Very shook the paper and checked the local articles. No more mention of drownings, suicides or identification of historic bodies.

Very called Joey. "Hey, best friend. What news do we have?"

"Not much more than yesterday, but here are the latest details. Adult man was dressed in a red plaid long-sleeved shirt, like a Pendleton shirt. You know the kind, sturdy, almost indestructible, lasts for so long you don't need to buy your husband another one for twenty-five years. And a pair of jeans, also sturdy and long-lasting. Although, of course, they were torn up quite a bit. No shoes, socks, or underwear. No personal objects of any kind were found. The investigation now goes to experts because the local guys have done all they can. They are going through the missing persons reports to see if there is anything that might match."

"But will they consider that it might be Frankie? I, well, I haven't filed a report, so they won't have his name on any list." Very's voice dropped to a whisper as she admitted this.

"Very, no report, no consideration. I know that you have been looking, but what if he is dead, not alive? Those data bases won't give you any satisfactory answers if he was murdered and buried, will they? And, another thing, these investigations cost money. And if there is one thing we know, the Kern County Sheriff's Department doesn't have truckloads of money. They are always short of funds for things like this. If there is more money, it's for long overdue raises, more staff, new cars, not paying some fancy expert from LA to identify a body that has been sitting there for years. Kern County is full of these bodies. People fall down mine shafts, get lost in the mountains, run away from home and are never heard from again. If you want anyone to consider that this body might be Frankie's, you need to file a missing person's report."

"Thanks, Joey, for telling me off. I do know all of this, but I still need hope to resolve things. You will keep me informed of any news?"

"Yes, Very. You know there are three other drowning deaths that need investigating first, so I don't hold out too much hope for swift resolution of your body."

"Heavens Joey, it's not MY body. I don't really want it to be my Frankie, but it would be good if it were ruled out. Just saying."

"Hang in there, Very. I'll keep you up to date, don't worry."

Very punched the phone off and looked at the screen, as if the phone could tell her what to do next. It did. Darrell's name came onscreen. She answered immediately.

"Hello Darrell. What's up?"

"Wow, it didn't even ring. Are you psychic? How'd you do that?"

Very chuckled at Darrell's surprise. "I was on the phone and just hung up. Just checking in with the sheriff's wife to see if she would let me know what's happening with the Killer Kern body."

This was met with silence, a Darrell silence that indicated a loss for words. He used this tactic when he was confused, trying to figure out the situation, or unable to make stupid small talk, as he called it. He was of the notion that if you had nothing to say, don't say anything for fear of putting your foot in your mouth. Very waited, as she had learned to do.

Finally, Darrell spoke, "The reason I called is that I would like for you to do some work for me. It's not what you've done before; this isn't computer research work. It's more…delicate. I think it needs a woman's touch."

Very was quiet. Woman's touch sounded like busy work: stuffing envelopes, making phone calls to people who didn't want to be disturbed, brewing coffee, being unobtrusive, taking care of children and old people. Things that needed to be done that important men could not bother with.

"Well, let's talk." After all, this was Darrell asking and he had fewer hang-ups about what was and was not men's or women's work.

"Good. As soon as you get here, we can talk. This is your opportunity to do some real PI work. It's not really up my alley, so I thought you might like to handle it. More money…?"

"Darrell, I don't do this for the money. I'm retired and have a pension. See you around 10."

Very sat in the sun for a few more minutes, but when she began to sweat, heaved herself up with a grunt and a whoosh. Need to get into shape if getting out of a chair causes old lady noises.

At 9:40, Very climbed into her car and drove down the hill from her La Cresta neighborhood. She took Union to 24th Street, then turned on Chester Avenue and then 17th Street. Darrell's building nestled among others that contained offices of insurance agents, bail bondsmen and such. Parking was easy here.

Promptly at 10, Very climbed the stairs to the second-floor office. The door had not changed in the last eight months. It still had the gold lettering "Darrell Pitts – Private Investigator." She laughed as she pushed on the door. The first time she had been there she was looking for a Private Investigator to hire. Instead, he had hired her. He told her that she had the necessary skills to do skip-tracing, which is what she thought she needed to find Frankie Monroe. In the months since, she had done skip-tracing for Darrell in exchange for using his data bases to look for her missing fiancé. He had occasionally paid her, but it had evolved into an unusual relationship. Darrell was a man of singular interests and hard to get to know. And to think that she had imagined herself Bridget O'Shaughnessy in the guise of Miss Wonderly the first time she had entered his office. What fictional character was she today? Nancy Drew or Miss Marple perhaps?

"Ah, the other body, the fourth body that was found this weekend. That's what you needed the deputy sheriff's wife for." Darrell turned in his chair to face her. He pushed his thick glasses with black frames up on his nose and ran a finger comb through his thinning hair. A smile that showed teeth only on one side of his mouth indicated he understood.

"Good morning to you, too. Yes, I thought, well, maybe…"

"It might be Frankie? You are right. It is well worth finding out more before tossing the possibility into the trash. What do they know so far?"

The absence of a greeting didn't faze Very any more. It was just a polite way of speaking and they had gone beyond the necessity of the niceties. However, every time he was too abrupt, the urge came upon her to give him a greeting and a gentle nudge to return the politeness. She was still working on accepting him as he came.

"Joey told me very little. They need a specialist to find out more and they don't have the money for it." Very then filled Darrell in on what she knew. "So, what kind of work do you have for me, woman's work, was it?"

The snide jibe flew over his head as he continued. "It's a more active investigation than you have done before. I hope you are ready for it; I think you are. The sister of the suicide drowning on Saturday is not happy with the police's conclusion. They have said it was suicide and she doesn't believe that."

"Wow, what makes her think that? Was there a suicide note? Any reason to believe that something else happened? Accident? Or…worse?"

"Here," Darrell said, reaching over to fuss with his phone. "I recorded the conversation, just so you could hear it all. I made this recording yesterday afternoon, late. She called, and then I asked a lot of questions and I asked if I could record, and then she said she'd call me back. She talked to a lawyer, who told her she needed to make clear that this was for information only and it wasn't to go out outside the agency etc. etc. So that's the first part of the call, making sure it is all legal to record. Then she started talking. So, where do you want to start?"

"I want to listen to it all, including the legalese part. I want to know everything." Very took out her small notebook, but then reconsidered. She asked Darrell to wait until she found a fresh one in the depths of her oversized bag. Armed with a fresh notebook and a mechanical pencil, she sat forward to listen.

The first part of the recording was as Darrell said. Details and consent, limitations of use of the tape. Then the sister started to speak. She said her name, Deborah Malden Smith, and spelled it. She gave her address and continued, "I want you to investigate the death of my sister, Michelle Malden. She did not commit suicide as the police have said. She couldn't have. I don't live here, so I cannot know all the people and places that she may have known, or that could tell me anything more. But, I know this, she didn't do anything to herself. She couldn't have."

Very listened to Darrell's voice ask, "Why do you say that? What evidence do you have?"

"I have known her all her life, well, very well," Deborah's voice continued. "She is ten years younger than me, so I knew her well from the beginning. I saw her personality develop from a child. I knew her life. She may have been depressed, she had reasons to, but I am sure that she would never take her own life. She is a survivor, she is, or rather was, strong."

"Tell me about her personality."

"She was a little lonely as a child, I was so much older that I wasn't a playmate for her and it was just the two of us. The neighborhood kids weren't the same age, so she learned to be independent. Strong-minded and independent. And then..."

Darrell, the person who could wait, waited. Finally, he prompted. "And then what happened?"

"She was fourteen when my mother died of cancer. It wasn't a really long, lingering death, about two years from diagnosis to death, but long enough for everyone around her to pay even less attention. She was young and felt so bereft. She couldn't stop crying at the funeral and afterwards. She begged me to take her with me when I left. But I had just gotten married and I wanted to start my family, I was pregnant then. And I couldn't deal with her, too. My dad was there, so I knew that he would take care of her. He was very responsive to her, very close. But then, it was the first time."

A long pause in the tape made Very feel as though there was some glitch in the recording. She started to speak, when Darrell held up his hand. "Wait," he cautioned.

"She was sixteen the first time she tried suicide." Deborah paused and the recording picked up sniffling noises, agitation and shifting in a chair. "She obviously didn't succeed. That was when she came to me. I can't say that I welcomed the intrusion, but can you say 'no' to your sister? She needed me. After that, our dad just drifted out of our lives. He remarried and moved away. It hurt me that we meant so little to him. I mean, remarrying is one thing, moving away and ignoring us was another. But Mouse coped. She seemed better without him."

"Mouse?" Darrell asked.

"Oh, that was Michelle's nickname. Everyone called her that. It was what we called her when she was little. She was small, you know, like a mouse. And she had mousey-brown hair and she crinkled her nose, just like a cute little mouse. It's not a bad name, just a tad cute. And it really stuck. She would introduce herself as Mouse, and correct the grownups when they called her Michelle. I guess we could have tried to call her Shelley or something else, but she liked being called Mouse. Anyway, she came and lived with me for the last part of high school and then she went away to college. At least there was money for that and she stayed with me during breaks and so on. But I really didn't like having her around, young and sexy, you know. And my husband liked the young ones. It was about that time that I found out, how much he liked the Lolita types. I had to watch them like a hawk. One time, I caught them. That was it. Both of them said the other started it and it didn't mean anything, but I knew better. She went back to college and he was outta there! After that, she was more subdued, but she managed to finish college, and in four years. She was a little depressed from time to time, but nothing serious. I never accused her of anything with my husband, I forgave her. I knew it was him. She got over it.

"Then she got jobs, made some friends, had her own apartment. She didn't seem to do well on the boyfriend front, but I thought she was holding out for the right one to come along. She was young, footloose and was just being choosy, as a girl should. But she did have these little bouts of depression."

"Did she ever try suicide? I mean, after the first time? Or did she see a therapist or anything like that?"

"Yeah, she made another attempt. She had lost her job, they fired her and she felt it was unfair. So she called me and complained. I think I just thought it was another one of those 'someone else got the job, not me' kind of whine things. I encouraged her to look for something else, not to let it bother her. I think I said something like, 'We all lose sometime in life.' I mean, what did she think, that every time something doesn't go our way that we just give up? She was feeling really bad, though, and then I made her come to me for a few weeks. She got over it. It was one of those things where she took a bunch of pills. Didn't kill her, just made her really sick. It was a cry for help, no doubt about it. After a couple of weeks, maybe months, I don't remember, she had a friend here in Bakersfield call her and tell her they were hiring at her place and that she could get a job, no prior reference. The friend gave a reference and so she went back to work, lived with her girlfriend for a while, then got her own place again. She bounced back, she was a true fighter. She even had a boyfriend."

"Can you give us his name and contact? And maybe the girlfriend that helped her?"

"Sure, sure. The boyfriend I don't know, not even his name. It was a really new relationship, maybe just dating. But she was really cute when she talked with me one day. Very shy about it all. I knew that I shouldn't pry too much, just give her some space. And yeah, her girlfriend, I have the contact."

"Okay. And is there anything else you can tell me? You said she had therapy? Could I talk with her therapist?"

"Oh gosh, I don't know. I do know her name, but I'm sure she won't tell you anything. Client privilege."

"Well, if your sister Michelle is no longer with us, what the therapist can tell us may help to establish some motive. For suicide or not for suicide. And by the way, if your sister didn't commit suicide, what do you think happened to her?"

"That's what you need to find out! I know that Mouse would never succeed at suicide, even if she sometimes talked about it. So, what did happen to her?"

Darrell's voice was a trifle edgy, "But did she have enemies that would want to hurt her? Was she running away from someone? What about the boyfriend? What about the person who fired her?"

"Yeah, yeah, I get it. I'll get those names for you. And oh, there's the notebook. I have it. The police said that it wasn't of any value. Just the note."

"Notebook? Where was it?"

"It was on the seat of her car. She had left it there, with the note. It was torn out. I can get it to you. But I don't have the note, the police kept it."

"We are looking at two things here? A notebook?"

"Yeah, she wrote poetry, descriptions of places. She had gotten this idea she wanted to be a writer. Hey, maybe that is an angle. Anyway, the police returned it to me because they said it meant nothing to them. Just ideas, blah, blah. But they kept the original of the note. I have a copy, they let me have a copy."

"Could you send that to me? And what does it say?"

"Oh, it's a suicide note. But it was just torn out of the notebook, it wasn't a real one, I know. I believe that she had been jotting down notes, making phrases. It isn't a real suicide note. Here, I'll send you a copy."

Very listened to a click and a ping and then some more pings. Then Darrell spoke again. "This is her handwriting?"

"Yes. But it isn't what it looks like. You need to look into this. I will pay, no problem. We can't let this go on. We need to find what happened to my sister." The recording ended.

Very looked at Darrell. "And do you have the note?"

"Yeah, here's a copy." He produced a copy of a copy. It was legible though.

> This is truly the end. I can't manage any more.
> Goodbye. Mouse

Chapter Three: The Body in the Riverbank

Very looked at Darrell. "This really, really sounds like a suicide note. If she hadn't left a note, or if she had never been depressed, or if she had never tried to commit suicide before, I would say that it might be a good idea to investigate. But this? What are we doing with this case?"

"We are making money. Now, it is not really our place to make judgements on the validity of investigations, but on the moral way of carrying them out. I did try to argue with the sister, but she threatened to take her money elsewhere. If we can, do a thorough investigation, a couple of days should do it, and then write a report, take our money and we have a satisfied customer."

"Frankly, it sounds like a delusional customer. Will she be satisfied?" Very shook her head.

"Will you do it or not?" Darrell's voice betrayed his own frustration at the case. Maybe he had been hasty in accepting the case, before understanding the futility of investigating the probable suicide, and was now dumping on Very.

"Is it very good money?" Very ventured.

Darrell smiled. "Very. And now you know why I suggested you do it. This is delicate and we need to be able to investigate to the point of near certainty. We need lots of statements from friends and workmates etc. And it would be good if we could pinpoint a precipitating event, something like that. And then a nice report, subtle and muted, with the gossamer touch of a woman."

A gossamer touch? Was Darrell overreaching, or could she produce just the merest suggestion of...translucent, silky, flimsy, diaphanous, transparent like a spider's web? "Okay, I'll give it a try, as long as you allow me to tell the truth. If she did do herself in, then that's what the report will say. I'll be delicate, understanding of a sister's grief, but I will not lie."

"Fair enough, here's where to start." Darrell laid out a plan of research and interviews for Very to get started on.

Before she left, she asked Darrell about his contacts at the Sheriff's Department and what they might be able to tell her about the body found in the riverbank. "I'm going to get Frankie's daughter Cassandra to give a DNA sample. We're not positive that she is Frankie's biological daughter, you understand, but whoever meets her, and who knew Frankie as well, swears she is. And we will go with that, plus a description. I wish I could find dental records, it would make things easier. Everyone is familiar working with dental records and they have great gravitas, but DNA is still too expensive. They tell me that in ten years time, DNA will be within the budget of almost everyone. Think of what we could do with it then. In the meantime, if you find out anything, please let me know, asap."

Very called and then stopped by the motel where Michelle Malden's sister was staying. The conversation was brief and pointed. Deborah Malden was pleased that Very would be investigating the case and neglected to ask about experience at this kind of work. Very was prepared to tell a little white lie, but it wasn't needed. She was given the notebook found in the front seat of Michelle's abandoned car and Deborah showed her where the page that had been torn out. Very turned down a corner here to remind her where the page had come from, just in case it was relevant, or worse, crucial.

At home, Very changed into cool cotton clothes and went to the patio. Gingerly, she tried the water in the pool, just in case some kindly summer fairy had heated the pool early. No one had. It wasn't frosty, just too chilly for comfort. Was it the same temperature as the river? Very looked for the thermometer floating in the pool, a cute shark toy that clipped onto the round bobble head, and noted the figure on her notepad for the Mouse suicide case. As soon as she had written it down, she crossed it out. What difference did it make? People drowned in bathtubs of warm water and survived New Year's polar bear swims. She sat back on the lounge chair and promptly fell asleep to the sounds of birds, the pool pump and traffic streaming by on Panorama Drive just a block away.

Later in the afternoon, she called Frankie's probable daughter, Cassandra. The voice of a teenage boy in the middle of the awkward phase of voice changes answered. Very asked for Cassandra. "Mom," he screamed at the distance in at least three different octaves.

"Hi Cassandra, I thought this was your mobile phone, I mean YOUR phone, not the house phone."

"It is. This is my cell phone. I left it on the counter in the kitchen, and one greedy child answered it," she said.

"Doesn't he have his own phone? I thought they all did these days."

"Oh, yes he has his own. But he says he doesn't get enough calls, so he answers my phone. 'Go, now.' Sorry about that. So, almost stepmom, what can I do for you?"

"It has to do with that tenuous, almost stepmom, connection," Very answered. "I need your DNA sample. Soon. I need to file a missing person's report on Frankie Monroe and this is about the only concrete thing we have besides the one good photo. Can we do that? At least it's not painful."

"Yeah, sure. But why now?"

Very filled in Cassandra on the newest unidentified body from the river. "If we can get a partial match, then we will know something. Even if we don't get a match of any kind, it will rule out one more body from the past. I just can't stop thinking about the body in the orchard and all that brought up. It was complicated. The body turned out to be your father of record, one you had never met because he had disappeared and been murdered before you were born. But it led me to meet your mother…and you. But then, when those two scofflaws murdered each other in the County Jail, it left it all up in the air. I don't know if I'll be able to keep focused on other matters while we wait for identification of this one. I tried to put it all behind me, but with this newest discovery, I feel the upwelling of old emotions again." Very stopped and took a deep breath.

"Very, just stop. It doesn't matter, even if it is my dad. At least it will be done. But you don't need to be frantic. I'll see about the DNA first thing in the morning.

You know that it will not change much, our lives will go on, like they have."

"No, Cassandra, I think I will change. I will feel free of this burden. At least I hope so. I'm planning on it. Thanks so much for agreeing to do this as it means a lot to me. YOU mean a lot to me."

"I never thought about any of this before a few months ago, but I feel like so much has changed because I think I have found my biological father. It is important to me, and you are important to me. You are my almost step-mom. Even if we never find Frankie Monroe."

"Thanks again. I'm so lucky to have you. Let me know how it goes." Very pushed the red button and the phone binged.

She sat at the table in the breakfast nook, the one that had a view of the street. It was late afternoon, too early for the evening dog walkers and exercise fanatics, too late for the mail carrier. It was a quiet neighborhood, up here on the hill, above the winter tule fog and the pollution from the freeway through the city. The meandering streets went nowhere, except to intersect with the few major streets that funneled traffic to the community college just a mile away, and then more bucolic neighborhoods. This eastern part of town had fallen on hard times. The thrust of development had extended to the southern and western parts of Bakersfield. Her mother maintained that it was the flat ground that was easier to build on than the rolling hills and gentle slopes at the top of the bluffs. That left the northeast with fewer shopping centers, fewer services and aging neighborhoods. Even here the city had not extended itself and the street had no sidewalks, streetlights or city police services. It was a bit of county surrounded by city, but with the advantage of lower taxes. Why had her mother defended the deeply held belief that being county was better than being city? Aren't taxes that paid for services a good thing?

Very called Joey. They had known each other for almost 40 years and had been through Very's aborted wedding trauma together as well as years being teachers in the same system. Unlike Very, Joey had married and had family. There were times when Very envied the chaos and love found at Joey's house. At first, Bobby Sanchez seemed a bit dull and conservative. He wore his hair short and neatly combed, he didn't laugh much and he blushed if Very even mentioned anything off-color. But over the years, she had watched Deputy Sheriff Sanchez stand by his wife, his children and his extended family. He even changed diapers. He was a rock whose interests had consisted of Boy Scouts, playing touch football, helping cook mountains of tamales at Christmastime and being a member of the Knights of Columbus. His three sons and his wife were the center of his life, and only the nature of his job ever took him away from their concerns, their interests and their activities. He wasn't an intellectual, but he was well-informed, empathetic and an all-around good guy. Not that she wanted him for a husband, but she was profoundly happy for Joey. Could she dream of finding someone like that?

"What's up, Very?" Joey enthusiastically answered her phone call. "I'm working on dinner even as we speak."

"Just checking on the body in the riverbank, to see if there is any news."

"There is an interesting report on how the young man, a pre-med student, identified the body. He actually waded ashore and pulled on a bone that was sticking out of the bank. He dug it out with his hands. The shirt was in tatters, but recognizable as fabric. He had no idea that it was connected to the rest of the body. He was just so excited to check that he had correctly identified the bone, the head of a humerus bone. He didn't think about crime scenes or whatever. He just dug it up. The red shirt was right next to the bone, partially obscuring the rest of the arm. Oh, what a mess. I believe in the end, that the rest of the remains, minus the arm, were found on a little island, just thirty or forty yards downstream. The young men doing their inner-tube trip were impatient to get going, but he and his buddy stayed back and waited for the police. It is a real unknown how long it would have remained there, unidentified, if they hadn't come along. The rest of the skeleton was wrapped in a gunny sack or something like that and was extremely muddy. If the authorities hadn't been looking for it, they may have missed it altogether. A bit gruesome, I'm afraid. But all the pieces are now in the morgue, reassembled and ready to be examined. So, that's where that is."

"I just talked to Cassandra, and she is going to give DNA and I'm going to file a missing person's report, so when they have more information, they will be ready to see if it's Frankie or not. I hate to think of his body buried in a riverbank and his arm detached and dug out by an overly enthusiastic pre-med student. But it is what it is."

"Oh, Very, I have more."

"More on the body?"

"No, the other drownings. The young girl and her cousin. They, the sheriff's office, are investigating them as suspicious deaths."

"Nooooo? My, my, looks like more than the Killer Kern, huh? But I have news for you. I'm investigating Michelle Malden's death."

"The suicide? Investigating what?"

"Her sister has hired Darrell, and he hired me, to see if, or to prove it wasn't, suicide. She is convinced she wouldn't have killed herself; notwithstanding the note. I told Darrell it was a bit dicey, everything, but everything, points to suicide. But this was her kid sister, her only sibling, so she is desperate that it not be suicide. I tried to tell Darrell that it seemed unethical to take her money. But he convinced me that, because she was willing to pay well, as investigators, we were within our moral and legal bounds, to investigate. If we do a good job, and show that it was suicide, then we are within our professional sphere. I'm not so sure, but I'm willing to do some leg work. Talking to her friends etc. I don't even have my license. But it's just asking around, making some notes."

"I met her, once."

"What, you? How?"

"The one you really should talk to is my oldest. He ran in the same crowd for a while. She came by the house and I remember she introduced herself. 'My name is Mouse.' I had to ask her to repeat that. I couldn't believe anyone would deliberately introduce themselves with such a strange nickname. I mean, 'Hello, my name is Michelle, everyone calls me Mouse.' But no, 'My name is Mouse.' It was like she had psychologically become a mouse. And I don't mean a mouseketeer or something childish and fun. I mean, become a person who was small, afraid, wanted or needed to hide. But it was just the one time. She moved out of town after that, I think."

"I had heard that. About the name. Wow, so it's true. I'll put your son down on the list of persons to talk with, if he can shed some light on anything. He hasn't been in contact recently, though, has he?"

"What? That one? Thoroughly, completely, totally married and tied at the hip. He wouldn't dare even speak to a woman not his wife unless she is as old as his mother."

"So, he can speak to me?"

"Come tomorrow for dinner, he'll be here."

"En famille? I'll bring something. Oh, dinner, big or small?"

"Big, everyone, including the youngest and his fiancée."

"See you then. Oh, before I forget, if Bobby knows anything…"

"I'll have him call you. We know, Very. We know. See ya."

Very then called her sister. She tried to remember to touch bases more often since their mother had died. But Very had become enmeshed in the mystery of the body in the orchard and then building a relationship with Cassandra, who they both accepted as the biological daughter of her missing fiancé, that contact with Sissy had fallen by the wayside. She needed some prodding. The house had been left to Very, but their mother's possessions should have been divided equally. At the moment, Very had all of them. Sissy's reluctance to come from a long distance to claim old clothes, old-fashioned ceramic gew-gaws, out-of-date books, used furniture and miscellaneous family heirlooms was understandable. But Sissy needed to get these, as Very had no children of her own and Sissy could pass some of these things on. Sissy was adamant that her children cared little or nothing for antiques, as they preferred plastic and technological items to fill their lives and homes.

"Sissy," Very began when her sister answered the phone. "Come and get this stuff!"

"Coming, coming. Not right now, but maybe next month, or how about July?"

Very snorted in reply. "When was the last time you were in Bakersfield in July? You have forgotten, little sister. It is hotter than hell! And even though there is air-conditioning in this house, there isn't any in the garage. And going through stuff is hot work. I will try and do something in the next month or two, like throw out the old clothes that I know no one wants and the real garbage. Some of this stuff… well, you may feel like it is a memory for you, but I don't care. I can't do that to you. You may think that because I have no children that family isn't important to me, but it is. Stuff, Sissy, come and get the stuff."

"Message received, big sister. I do want some, but not the old clothes. And the kids, well, as I have said, they're not old enough to value family. Not yet."

"Well, okay. Oh, no, Sissy, gotta go. Talk later."

Very jumped up and yelled, "Cat!" On the table, where Cat rarely, if ever went, was Cat with a page of Michelle 'Mouse' Malden's diary clinched firmly in her jaws. "No, no, let that go!"

The cat obediently jumped down from the table, but skittered off with the white paper held tightly. Very leapt towards the table and retrieved the rest of the diary. There was only one page gone, but now there were neat cat canine teeth marks that had stabbed through a number of pages. Cat saliva smeared at least two other pages, along with green slime and some mud. The text was still legible, but why would the diary be dirtied like this? Wasn't it left on the seat of the car? Where did the dirt and green stains come from? Very looked at Cat who now sat on the tile floor, stretched out with the page clutched between her front paws. She tore the paper with relish and looked at Very with contentment.

"Give that to me," Very shouted and lunged for the page. The cat, startled, let go and ran under the sofa.

Very took the paper and smoothed it out. Still legible, but damaged. Why did the cat tear up the diary? What was that green gunk on the page? Catnip? Some other plant? Where did it come from? And why was it smeared on that page?

Chapter Four: The Suicide

Very showed up early on Friday morning at the 17th Street office of Darrell Pitts, Private Investigator. Very had a key, so it didn't really matter if Darrell was there or not, but in the case of this assignment, she needed the consultation time with him before he started work on other cases.

"What is our plan of action here, Darrell? What are the factors in choosing who and what to attack first? Sorry, I want to take back that expression, to explore first?"

"Take a notebook. Oh, you have one already. Maybe start from the back, or near the back. Make a list of all the people who may have information, prioritize them, check them off one by one. Check if you might want to ask additional questions. You know, people don't always tell the truth the first time around, or give all the clues they may have. I know you and I have listened to what the sister said, but she MUST have lots more to tell us. So, when we come across something that needs more explanation, make a note to re-interview the sister. And what we need to ask her. You can also do a spreadsheet, in fact, for a case as complex as this, maybe that's what we need. You can create one on that computer and then email it to yourself and keep it on your home computer too."

"You know what I really need is one of those small laptops that I can just slip into my purse. It's big enough, Lord knows, for a dozen little computers. Ummm. Oh, did I tell you about Joey and her son, knowing Mouse? Years ago."

"Good, write it all down. Anything useful?" Darrell leaned forward with enthusiasm.

"Not really, I'll talk with Joey's son this evening. We need to delve into her past a little more. I feel as though here are some answers there, or maybe more questions."

"Oh, I have done something for you. I'm sorry I didn't think to let you do it, but it was sitting here, with the phone number, so I called. The employer. She quit well over a month ago, said she had other options. Gave two weeks notice, then stayed on for one more week. Amicable. The manager had no idea what she was going to do. He wrote a reference letter for her, just a general one, but she neglected to pick it up from him. He hand-carried it to her desk on the last day, and she was polite, but didn't seem to care. Oh well, you can always get a reference later. It does appear that she wasn't going straight to another job."

"Her sister didn't mention that. It seemed as though she thought Mouse, sorry, Michelle, was still working at the same place. Sister knows less that she is admitting. Re-interview with that question. Why did she quit?"

"Her manager didn't know, and when he asked, she didn't answer. A bit cagey about it all. On the other hand, there was no ill-will, no fingers in the till, but no waiting around until…"

"Darrell, you are a poet."

"What? Poet?"

"No ill-will, fingers in the till, …until… Very clever, that."

Darrell blushed. "I didn't really try, I just, just…"

"It's okay. Let's look at the whole thing from another point of view. And I think the quitting the job might be worth pursuing. If she didn't commit suicide, was it an accident? Seems unlikely, to leave a note, not a lot of detail, appears to be written hastily, but, a suicide note. No accident, so was it murder? And who wanted her out of the way and why? I think we need to ask questions that might give us answers to the "murder" idea as well. I mean, are we trying to find out if she did commit suicide or that she didn't commit suicide?"

"Good questions. And if we look at it all from another angle, who benefits from her death? Who inherits? Did she have anything to inherit?" Darrell looked at a blank computer screen. "Does the sister know anything from that angle? We need to ask."

"Good idea. I mean, I don't look as if I am wealthy, but maybe my heirs, who are both rather young, might think inheriting $100,000 is worth bumping their aunt off. Gosh, Darrell, I've just confessed to who my heirs are. Don't tell. I've kept that a secret because frankly, I am a little fearful of greedy young people. Their mother tries to tell it as if they care nothing for family, just money. So, I don't want to let the cat out of the bag there. Maybe it is worthwhile to check into the financial angle, could learn something there."

"Then again, who else would want her out of the way? Rivals at work? Afraid she would get a promotion?

Was she climbing her way up the corporate ladder and got in the way of someone else?"

"That seems terribly unlikely seeing as how she quit her job a month ago, and left with no ill-will, so why kill her now; when she was out of the way of any competitors? Oh, a love interest." Very tapped her teeth with the end of a pen. "I know that her sister said there was a boyfriend, but no details at all. However, don't we keep our love interests to ourselves until we are quite serious? So, even though the sister thought there was someone, that might not be the case. Maybe Mouse was deflecting a sister's intrusive questions, pretending there was a special someone, when there was nothing at all? Has her sister looked at her apartment? Searched for something?"

"I think she may have mentioned checking her apartment, but that it looked clean and neat, not a lot of personal items there. And nothing to say that she was suicidal. Wow, we don't have much to go on, do we? Well, there's just a lot to discover. You can try to get an appointment to talk with the sister again. We need more leads."

"Here we go." Very called Deborah Malden and made an appointment for the following morning. They would meet at Deborah's hotel, then go on to Michelle's apartment. At the end of the short conversation, Very let out a whoosh of air. "I feel as though we are beginning to move forward on this case. Now, can I spend some time looking at data bases and maybe social media for Michelle Malden, aka Mouse?"

"Great idea. See who she has been talking with, what her trail is. Deborah was trying to get the password from a pocket calendar in her purse, so we should be able to tap into it all, eventually, if not today."

Very turned to her computer and started it. "Just thinking. You know the other two drownings, the same day, last Saturday. Or we assume they were on Saturday, bodies not found until Tuesday. A coincidence? Nothing more? Multiple drownings, suicides, on one day? Joey said there was something fishy about it and the Department was looking into it. I wonder?"

"Don't get distracted, eye on the ball. I wouldn't get messed up in that one as well. Yes, I heard some chatter about that. Gangs. Stick with Mouse."

They turned to their respective computers and worked steadily for an hour and half. Then Darrell turned to Very. "Anything to report?"

"Seeing as I don't have the password to her Facebook or emails, I can't check much. The other databases are thin at best. Addresses, a credit card rating. Nothing to link us to any other person or even get a feel for who she was. As dead an end as the search for my Frankie."

"Don't be discouraged. A lack of information tells us something."

"I don't get it, Darrell. How can a minus be a plus? I do get to put this hour and a half on my billable hours, don't I?"

"Yes, and we are a bit further than we were before. A break?"

"Coffee? Or maybe an early lunch?"

Darrell laughed, "I'm always up for food."

"I know just the place to go for more food than you can possibly eat, so you'll have some to take home."

"Don't tease me, Very. You take yours home as well."

"Best Okie food in town. The Sugar Mill."

"Never been there, where is it?

"My favorite suburb. On North Chester."

"In Oildale?"

"Darrell, don't be a snob. The food is good, like I said, best Okie food in Bakersfield, and that is saying a lot."

They took Darrell's car and drove north through town. Darrell seized up momentarily before entering the wide roundabout of the Garces Circle. A tall cement statue of the Spanish Franciscan missionary and explorer guarded the southern view. Saint or devil, depending on whose side you were on, the circle and statue were landmarks, such as they were. It was the only circle in Bakersfield, also one of the few in California, and every new driver practiced going around it. The Department of Motor Vehicles was only blocks away, on F Street, but Very admitted that she had never heard of anyone being forced to traverse this scary driving experience on a driver's test. But they could, that was the threat.

After they had gone half-way around the circle and exited, they drove further north where the Beale Memorial Clock Tower stood, now on the grounds of the Pioneer Museum. It had been built in the middle of town, in the street, at 17th and Chester and had been there for almost 50 years until the 1952 earthquake did it in. It was in a pseudo Spanish-style that was elegant, but who could imagine the thing stuck in the middle of Chester Avenue? Gracious in proportion, monumental in size, a lovely thing to look at, but it had caused no end of problems for the traffic of a growing city. It was rebuilt, with the old clockworks intact, when Very was a child. Much better where it was, although awkward as there was nothing else around that was comparable. A lonely monument from another century.

They crossed the river and entered Oildale. As they cruised up North Chester Avenue, Very pointedly did not look for Trout's, the old honky-tonk on the west side of the street. She had never been inside, but everyone knew its reputation. She had at one point contemplated entering it to look for informants. The dissuading factor had been a pair of local pranksters, practicing their mooning techniques. Just as well she hadn't gone inside.

Soon they were passing buildings that had seen better days. Not exactly run down, but faded, drooping, stuck in a previous era and not ready for the twenty-first century.

"Here," Very indicated and Darrell pulled into the parking lot of a shopping center. They parked beside a late twentieth century edifice that could have come from the Sears catalog. It was eminently unmemorable as a building, red tile roof, shaded plate glass windows, flowers and lawn. They entered and asked the girl behind the cash register for a booth. They were escorted to one near the front, with padded seats that poked them in the backsides as they sank into them. Menus with the thinnest film of grease were flopped onto the table, accompanied by a smile and a distracted hello.

Darrell avidly opened the menu and murmured the offerings to himself. Very went to the senior menu. Liver and onions. She shivered in disgust at the memory of the first time she had encountered this particular dish. She had been invited for dinner by a fifth-grade friend. Her friend's single mother proudly dished out a thin flat, dark red slab onto her plate and then covered it with wiggly-rounds of briefly fried onion pieces. A try-anything-once type of person meant Very had gamely picked at it, but gave up after five or six small bites. She never returned for dinner there. She had avoided this dish whenever possible, fearing that it would be even viler than her first try. No, no liver and onions. Catfish? Whoa, bottom feeder fish had the unhappy habit of tasting like the bottom of wherever they had been raised. And they had bones, lots of them, little sneaky ones. Yes, here it was, fish and chips. Fish, but hopefully no bones, nice white flakes of moist meat. But what about chicken fried chicken?

"Darrell, have you decided? It's all good, if you like that dish. And you get huge portions. I'm ordering off the senior menu, smaller portions, but still big."

"I'm not old enough."

"Order a dinner and take half home. You know you want to." Very smiled slyly.

They ordered and then sat, twisting around in their seats to view the handmade quilts that adorned the walls. Romanticized scenes of the origin of Oildale and the current state of the economy were created by the quilts. One was a triptych which included the name of the suburb, a gushing oil well with an old-fashioned wooden derrick, and a bucolic scene of the bluffs, the river and a trio of pumpjacks in the foreground. In Oildale, women created hand-crafted masterpieces of the simple surroundings while their men toiled in the smelly, dirty, dangerous, stark oilfields that fueled the economy. The air was scented with the smell of the refineries, the houses squatted in their shadows and children played in the front yards with these same views. It was sad, but it was the truth of life in the southern San Joaquin Valley.

Their food arrived, thick enormous platters piled with salt, fat and calories. Extra buttered bread appeared along with assorted bottles of ketchup and hot sauces, their outsides lightly coated with the contents mixed with previous patrons' sticky finger prints. Very eyed her piles of chips, at least two big potatoes worth of fresh, hot, oily, salty spears. Darrell looked at his healthy salad and murmured his envy.

Very took her fork and transferred at least one-third of the stack onto Darrell's platter. "Enjoy," she said.

Darrell began eating his food with the gusto of a starving man. Small grunts of pleasure, slurps at escaping sauce, plus mmmm's of contentment made eating with Darrell a challenge. Very blocked out the noise and ate at her breaded fish sticks. She squirted thick creamy tartar sauce from a small plastic packet, trying to be dainty and to keep her fingers clean. She failed. She reached for a fried potato and savored the heat and oil that her fingers felt.

"This could kill us. All this hardens the arteries, adds weight, pushes the creation of diabetes. Not the sort of food that promotes longevity." Very looked at her plate of half-eaten food.

Then she turned to the scene on the quilt. Just upriver from the place this picture portrayed was the bank in the Kern River where the years old buried body was found, and less than a mile upriver from that place was the scene of two more drownings, less than a week before. And a few miles upriver, was the place where they pulled the body of Michelle Malden from the river. The Killer Kern.

"I don't think this food will kill us today," Darrell mumbled between bites.

Chapter Five: Changing a Name

Very arrived home full from her lunch at the Sugar Mill, and was reminded by text that she promised to bring something to Joey's for dinner. Ah, dinner at Joey's. Joey was a whirlwind, had been for the forty plus years Very had known her. More than just an acquaintance, she had stood by when the wedding was aborted, through the loss of her baby a week later, and in the years and tears that followed. Joey teased Very about finding another husband, although Very never said anything about Joey's unsuccessful forays into the matrimonial race in her twenties. Joey said she was looking for her knight in shining armor, all the while becoming anxious and disheartened. Very's riposte to Joey's whines was to help her choose some activities that included men, unlike hanging out with her fellow teachers, ninety percent of whom were female. Joey's response was to ask if she was supposed to become a fireman's groupie. But she did join some clubs and had thrown herself into hiking, even though her short legs meant she jogged rather than walked to keep up. She had even tried skeet shooting, bless her little heart. Very had bitten her tongue as Joey added a pound every year to her short, but far from slender frame. Joey had other challenges in the attempt to meet men. She laughed too loud, cried too often and argued with a passion that scared most men who did not share her political and social views. What a gal. And she could also cook: huge cauldrons of beguiling soup, platters of nose-twitching enchiladas, trays of fresh vegetables, bowls of seasonal fruit, plates of cakes decorated like they had come from the bakery, but hadn't. She never seemed to get tired of doing errands for friends and family and always knew the right words to say in condolence or congratulation. She was everyone's friend, but no one's girlfriend. She was crowding thirty, when Bobby showed up in her classroom one day, a newly minted police officer on a mission to introduce the kids to bicycle safety.

Very found her mother's fruit salad bowl, shaped like a grapefruit cut in half, the one she had taken to every potluck. She ignored the little voice that tried to tell her she was repeating her mother's choices, again. Very filled it with fresh fruit and included a yogurt dressing to use on the side. She poked around in the bottom cupboard for a tray and found a large silver-plated affair with a "B" engraved in the center. A family heirloom. She then proceeded to empty the pantry of gherkin pickles, black pitted olives and cocktail onions. She cut up celery and carrot sticks. It was too much, but guilt about eating so many Friday night barbecue dinners and Sunday sit down affairs at Joey's house meant she always took too much food. Joey and Bobby's three boys, and now their spouses and kids, meant that hungry mouths always made huge inroads into whatever she offered. No food went to waste.

At Joey's house, she found she was the last to arrive. No one answered the ring at the front door, so she walked around to the rear and entered the chaos of a Sanchez family gathering. Joey's daughter-in-law #1 rescued her, taking the bowl in its carrier and the platter to the long table that served as a buffet. Very tried to count all the young people, testing herself if she remembered all the wives, and all the grandkids. They were moving around the yard, so she soon became confused. She waved at Joey who dangled a grandchild in her arms and approached Bobby, who stood, aproned up, at the barbecue.

"Hey, handsome," Very said in her most sultry voice. She gave him a poke in the belly and clicked her tongue. "I thought you had to pass a medical exam every year. Take care of that belly."

Bobby moved out of reach of her naughty finger. "I pass, the medical and the physical. That's not fat you are poking at, that is muscle. And hey, if you want to poke at a man, I'll find one for you. You know there are lots of single guys where I work."

"Yeah, yeah, and there are reasons why they are single, as am I." Very smiled sweetly at Bobby and moved towards the group of women on the other side of the yard.

Joey made a motion to rise, but Very waved her back, standing easily on the edge of the group. One of the young women, baby on her lap, nudged another with an indication that the newest guest was an older woman and that she should give up her seat. Introductions were made and the newbie turned out to be Daughter-in-law-to-be, or as Very noted, #3.

Hardly before Very was seated, a young girl approached, leaning her folded arms easily on Very's lap. "Hello, hello, hello, Aunt Berry."

"Hello, hello, hello, Clara." Very hoped that she hadn't confused this one with any of the others. Clara was her favorite and at age five, in the center of the scrum.

Very looked up at the group, "Aunt Berry? Maybe I should just change my name altogether. Chose something completely different. Linda, maybe."

"Why do you want to change your name, Very," asked Joey. The two younger women swiveled their attention to Very and waited for her answer. "And why now? You've had that name your whole life."

"I've never really liked it, I've just accepted it. It was my mother's joke on the riff of a red name like Ruby, Carmen or Rose, but not those. Something different. But you know what? I can choose my own name, or at least what people call me. Aunt Berry?"

Joey laughed, "Clara is just a little girl, she can't say 'v'."

"I know that, but you have to admit, Very is not the most attractive, or easy to remember name. An adverb? As a name for a girl or a woman?"

Daughter-in-law #1 ventured, "Could you change your nickname, not be Very for Vermilion, but be…Millie, for example?"

"That sounds nice," said the newest member of the family in a bright, helpful tone.

Very snorted in laughter. "Then everyone would either be confused, because they have known me all my life as Very, or if they are new to me, would think I'm a Mildred. Whooo, is Mildred better than Vermilion?"

"Aunt Berry," Clara sidled closer. "Don't you like your name? Why?"

Very stared down at Clara. She opened her mouth a few times, but failed to find words to explain to this child, with the lovely name, that hers was strange and she was tired of trying to explain to everyone what it was.

"But you can't change your name," Clara persisted.

"Oh, I can if I want to," Very explained.

"But you can't change your name. Your Mommy gave you that name because she loves you very, very much." Clara looked into Very's face.

"Out of the mouth of babes… Truth. However, I distinctly heard a couple of very clear 'v's. Who's going to tell her that I am not named after a berry?" She turned to look down at Clara.

"Aunt Berry, your name is beautiful, like a strawberry or a raspberry. Please don't change!"

"Ok. I won't change my name." She smiled and gave Clara a hug.

Bobby shouted, "Food's ready. Who's going to say grace?"

After a lot of eating, drinking and general merry-making, Very sought out Bobby Jr.

"Is that very precious little Clara yours?" Very asked.

"Yes, the most empathetic person I have ever met. I don't know where she gets it from. She cares about everyone and can't stand arguments. She tries to make peace with everyone. She has a bunny that she carries everywhere and when others are angry or sad, she comforts the stuffed animal by telling Bunny that it's okay. She thinks your name is short for Strawberry, so she is horrified that you might change it. Go figure."

"I can't help but notice that all three of you boys have chosen women who bear a remarkable resemblance, both physically and personality-wise, to your mother. Is that a coincidence, do you think?"

"Absolutely not. Who doesn't want to do the Oedipus thing? In reverse that is. We love her, so we want to keep that in our lives. Marry someone just like your mother." Bobby shrugged.

"But you three are very different, shy and quiet, loud and boisterous, intellectual or not, all so different, but you all found a wife that fit your ideal, your mother. What do the wives say about it?"

"Ah, they haven't noticed yet. They just think the world of her, and of their husbands. So far."

"You have good role models, all of you. Say, I wanted to talk with you about your friend Michelle Malden."

"Yeah, Mom told me that you wanted some information on Mouse. It was my last year in high school, so I was really busy with all kinds of things. I didn't have much time for friends except as buddies to "fart" around with. And I am not joking or being crude, really, it was a sad time in my life, because we would have contests. Loudest, most in a minute etc. I hang my head in shame for that one. Water under the bridge and I'd like to leave it there. But that was about the time that Mouse came into my orbit. We became rather good friends, and I don't mean that in a sexual way, just friends, someone to talk to about life, where we were going, what we hoped for."

"Why was she Mouse? I know that her sister said it was an affectionate childhood name, but when you are 16 or 17, surely you want to dump silly things like that?"

"She introduced herself that way all the time. I didn't even know her name was Michelle for months and then I just thought, 'oh, well.' And kept calling her Mouse. But she owned the name. I remember her once turning on someone, the only time I ever saw her angry, and corrected them when they tried to call her Michelle, or Shelly or something like that. No, she was Mouse."

"So how long did you know her? Just that year?" Very pressured.

"No, actually, she left before the end of that year, something about moving in with an aunt. I knew that she had lost her mother when she was a bit younger. She became nervous and jittery after a few months. I didn't have time for her starting around Christmas: proms, SATs, a girlfriend that objected to my friendship with Mouse and stuff like that. It was such a busy time. I had to distance myself from Mouse because of the new girl, you know, show loyalty. Even when it was totally innocent, I couldn't allow us to be seen together. We came here a couple of times, my mom met her. I don't think Mom was impressed. But I also thought that she thought I was interested in Mouse and that it wasn't a good thing. How do you tell your mother, at age 17, that this girl that you have brought here to talk with because you are hiding out from your real girlfriend, that your mother hasn't met yet, is an innocent relationship? Mouse was fragile, she needed my friendship, she needed support, she needed to be told that she was okay. Come to think of it, she was needy and I was being nice."

"That sounds a bit like Clara, doesn't it?"

Bobby stopped and looked at the sky.

Very hummed a response and then went on, "Do you know why she became nervous and jittery?"

"It was my impression that something happened. Family-wise. She had a sister that had already left home, so without a mother, she had no one to turn to but her dad. I gather that he wasn't good at listening to teenage girls. Just an impression. Remember, this was all 14-15 years ago. I haven't really thought about her much, I'm a busy man." He looked over to where his wife sat with a baby in her lap, five-year-old Clara plucking at her sleeve for attention and into another corner where a nine-year old boy loudly declaimed why his team was going to win big this year, quoting stats to bolster his argument.

"When did you lose touch with her?"

"High school. I never ran into her again. There were other friends to see at vacation time when I came home from college, but no one ever even mentioned her again. I'm surprised she was still alive."

"But she is your age, or a year younger. Why would you assume she wouldn't still be alive?"

Bobby sighed and hesitated before going on. "She was fragile, as I said. Life was difficult and maybe precarious. She didn't make friends easily. And I do feel guilty for not being a better friend all those years ago. I will put it down to being a teenage boy, trying to protect my own fragile ego. But now, I would definitely spot the signs. She wasn't going to last into adulthood."

"She was suicidal, even then?"

"I never knew that she attempted. No one ever said, and I think they would if they knew. Teenagers are horrible gossips, boys included. But definitely a tendency."

"The reason that you were surprised she lived so long was because…"

"We all knew that she would commit suicide some day. We wouldn't have been surprised to hear that she had. What surprised all of us was that she had lived so long. Surprised that she hadn't killed herself before now. It was always in the cards."

Chapter Six: Mouse's Story

Very arrived early on Saturday morning at the downtown hotel where Deborah Malden was staying. They met in the lobby and then sat in the restaurant where Deborah had a quick breakfast and Very another cup of coffee.

Very pulled at her knit top that she now could see had stains on the front, as she eyed Deborah's classy bright pink silk number that heightened the color of her cheeks. Slenderizing black slacks sat perfectly above black patent-leather pumps. She looked better than 99% of well-dressed women in Bakersfield. Very had a wardrobe that functioned well in the climate, on her tall figure, and for the events and demands of her lifestyle. But the well-dressed woman opposite intimidated her, making her curl up within. She sat up straight, squared her shoulders and smiled warmly. That felt better.

"How long do you plan to stay in Bakersfield? You must have a lot of things to do." Very sipped from her heavy white mug.

"At least until Monday. I might have to stay longer. There is nothing at home that commands my attention that can't be taken care of by someone else. I am taking some time to visit old friends as well. But obviously, Michelle's business is my priority. Whatever you need from me, I will be there for you."

"Thanks for that. Ummm…? Have you made funeral arrangements? I mean, it isn't too soon, is it?"

"I don't want to have a funeral as such. I don't want to bury her quickly as a suicide; that would be disrespectful and untrue. But I can't think what kind of ceremony we, or I, can have. I just haven't decided. I may have to go home and come back again. Oh well, I'll do whatever I need to do."

"Ok, can we go somewhere to talk, a little more private than here?" Very looked around the dining room as it began to fill up.

"Yes, of course. Let's go to Michelle's apartment. I haven't touched anything, I felt too bad, or scared or something to touch anything there. But I need to check for bank statements and things like that. And you can look for anything that might help you."

"The Sheriff's people didn't come and look?" Very asked softly, not wanting to attract attention.

"Yes, but again, they didn't touch anything. They had made up their minds what they wanted to see and if you don't look for anything else, well, the facts can suit the preconceived idea. Let's go."

Deborah paid for the breakfast and coffee. Very followed Deborah in her attractive Mercedes sports car. Very had chosen her Barcelona red Prius, but now she saw how the shiny expensive car was a symbol of the choices made by a woman who dressed and drove for success. Could Very possibly ask her how she got the money? Possibly not.

They drove up the hill to the northeast part of town to a cozy apartment complex. Guest parking places were at a premium, and Very looked around for something marked with a guest placard while Deborah parked in a numbered space. Mouse's. They walked together to a nondescript apartment door and Deborah unlocked it. She hesitated at the door and turned to Very, "You go in first, I feel spooked again."

Very, who had never met the occupant, had no fear as she walked directly into a small living room. A functional kitchen led off the room. Very peeked into the short hallway and saw a bedroom and the door to a bathroom. Nothing more. Although there were clean dishes in a dish drain, a toaster on the counter, two magazines on the coffee table in the living room and a colorful bedspread on the bed, it could have been set up for a realtor's shoot. Nothing personal betrayed the occupant. Very walked around and looked for more exclusive items. Deborah followed her inside, but stood near the door, her eyes searching for signs of her sister.

"She lived here, I mean, she actually spent time here?" Very slowly walked into the bedroom and opened the closet door. Dresses, slacks and skirts on hangers, rows of blouses and jackets neatly lined up in the small closet. Nothing strange, nothing out of place, nothing really intimate. In the small bathroom, the medicine cabinet contained the most mundane of medications and toiletries. The small trash receptacle was empty. Back in the bedroom, a small desk in the corner held a laptop, but nothing else. Very opened the drawer and saw pens and pencils, notepads, a container of paperclips and a stapler. In the back, she found a checkbook. She peeked at it, then handed it to Deborah with the comment, "Found a checkbook. This might be helpful."

Deborah flipped through the check register. "Rent, gas and electric, VISA. Nothing special."

"Boxes in the closet." Very pointed to two sturdy cardboard boxes on the top shelf above the clothes.

Deborah reached up and pulled one down. She placed it on the floor and took off the lid. "Bingo, personal stuff. Letters. Oh, my letters. Birthday cards, mine. Bank statements, going back about two years." She rifled through the documents, placed in the box in cheap manila folders, all labeled. "Nothing extraneous, nothing secret, nothing revealing." Deborah sighed. "I'll take these back to the hotel and look some more. If there is anything at all helpful, like a diary or an address book, I'll let you know."

The two women continued looking in closets and drawers, all neat, tidy, devoid of anything superfluous and nothing out of place.

"Would you say your sister was overly tidy or clean?" Very sat on the pristine sofa with the laptop in front of her. "A little obsessive perhaps?"

"OCD, you mean? Perhaps she was fond of clean lines, clean rooms, clean desks. But when she was young, no, nothing like obsessive behavior. I can see why you ask. This place doesn't look like it was lived in, just existed in."

"Do you have any idea what her log-in for her computer was? I believe you had it?" Very asked.

"mouse, or maybe MOUSE or mouse123."

Very typed the suggestions in. The third one resulted in instant access. "Didn't she know that you shouldn't use your name?"

"Mouse wasn't her name."

"Not strictly speaking, but I take it that she introduced herself that way."

"Lately, I thought she had gotten out of that habit. You know, working, being an adult. I thought she had gotten over the Mouse part of her life."

Very looked cursorily at emails and social media. There were two different email accounts, but there seemed to be few emails in either. Facebook page. Nothing. She had opened an account, put a note on a few categories, then never touched it again. Same with the LinkedIn. Opened, but never used. The emails revealed little. She bought nothing online. There were a few emails about a class reunion, but it appeared she didn't go. Her sister emailed. No boyfriends, no other friends. Bookmarks on a dictionary and CNN. "I'll take this, if you don't mind, and check more later."

"No, go ahead, just return it to me. I'll go through this box, but there doesn't seem to be anything private in here other than my correspondence. And that wasn't personal either."

Very closed the laptop and turned to Deborah. "Can we get some dates and names of places and people I can look up? An example would be high school and college places and dates. I know she went to high school here in Bakersfield, but did she graduate? And college, where and when? I can try alumni web pages."

Deborah ran through names, places, dates, all the while trying to reference them to her own stages in life. Mouse had graduated from high school while Deborah was in the hospital having baby number two, so Deborah had missed the ceremony. "I don't think my dad went either. Wife Number Two, you know."

"She was living with you at the time, right?" Very jotted this down in her notebook.

"Yes, it wasn't an easy time. Neither of us planned on it, but as I said, Dad wasn't big on providing a home for his little girl. Other fish to fry. Actually, he wasn't our biological father, but our real dad disappeared, before Michelle was born, so he was Dad. And he had always been a good father until this time, but…maybe it was understandable."

Very bit her tongue. Parental abandonment, such a complicated topic.

"Where's your dad now?" Very asked, in hopes that this might be a line of inquiry.

"He passed away a few years ago. Too many cigarettes, too much booze, a black heart, if you know what I mean. I hadn't spoken to him in many, many years. His current wife let me know, very casual like. And told me that I was not to inherit anything. Neither me nor Michelle were in the will. As if we cared, or needed the money. Water under the bridge." Deborah slumped on the couch as if the frivolity in the words she had just spoken were a lie.

Very wrote a tiny note on the top of the page, Dad? and turned to a new page. There was something there, maybe important, maybe not. She was not going to get more out of Deborah on that score now, but other friends or acquaintances might know. Step-dad.

"What do you know about Michelle's friends? Now or in the past. Who might know what was on her mind these past days and weeks?"

"Do you have something to write these down?" Deborah had made a list, indicating to Very whether these were her close friends or just acquaintances. Very noted that Joey's son, Bobby Jr., was not on the list. All of the names were female and there weren't very many. Well, Very could get more names from the ones she had, friends of friends.

"Do you have any idea of where she went or what she did on the last day of her life?"

"Not really. Her car, which is still in storage at a car place, was found late on Saturday afternoon. You have the notebook? It might tell you something more. No one else seems to have been in the car. The police checked for fingerprints, but only hers were found. So, she was alone, or someone or ones, were wearing gloves. I can't think straight on that one. Anyway, the neighbors didn't see her leave or see her at all that day. The groceries weren't new nor were there indications that she had a visitor at the apartment. They police didn't check for fingerprints here, because they said there was no need. They had that note, you see, and that was all they needed."

"I'm sure they looked a little farther than that, but it's hard when what they consider the truth is staring them in the face. Remember, they didn't know her, they have to go on the average or normal. Not that anything like this is normal, but if you look at it from their point of view?" Very tried to be conciliatory. "But they didn't know her like you did, so tell me more."

Deborah wandered around her life and Michelle's, relating incidents from Michelle's life as it intersected with hers. She had left home to go to college and never seemed to have returned except for the occasional Christmas dinner. Therefore, Mouse had only just turned eight years old when her sister essentially disappeared from her life. What could Deborah know about a younger sibling's life, especially her inner life, when she shared so little of it? Teenagers don't chat about boyfriends to a young child, nor are they interested in a youngster's doings and agonies. Deborah's concern for Michelle was affecting, but somehow not productive of the information that might explain what happened.

"Tell me again about when your mother died." Very said this softly, trying to keep Deborah talking, but also needing more information about this potentially devastating event in her life. If she had attempted to commit suicide after her mother died, then a current try would make more sense.

"Oh, Michelle was devastated. We both were. Our mother was such an angel. She had married someone her parents disapproved of, but she was a made-my-bed-and-I'll-lie-in-it sort of person. She tried to get my grandparents to be closer to us, and it was only after she died that they had much to do with us. My mother's sister took Michelle in for a few months because I wasn't in a position to do anything then. Later she stayed with me for a while. She got quiet after my mother passed, not that she was talkative to begin with. And maybe a little secretive. But teenage girls need to keep their secrets. And losing your mother, I know what it was like, she was my mother as well, you know."

Very was silent. How different was it to lose your mother at age fourteen, the youngest in the home, and being a married 24-year-old with kids of your own? Terrible at any age. Even as a mature adult, was it terrible? Maybe relief at a querulous old woman finally shuffling off?

Very continued the questions. "Did she have suicidal thoughts, or any actions in that direction? It is normal in the circumstances to be very sad, and have some problems adjusting, but more than that?"

"She was sad, she had trouble coping, she wasn't very happy and as I said, she became secretive. She started becoming like this." Deborah used her hand to sweep around the empty apartment. "Nothing personal, no pictures on the walls, nothing of Michelle here. That was when her personality changed. I always put it down to reactions to Mom's death. But you know," Deborah paused, "She was always Mouse, that nickname that my mother gave her. She was always shy and quiet and faded into the woodwork. She just became more mousey."

"What about the last day of her life? What about this notebook?" Very pulled the cheap lined notepad out of her purse. "Does this tell us anything about how she was feeling in the weeks and days leading up to the event? We know she quit her job, did that have anything to do with what happened that day?"

"I didn't know she had quit her job until late yesterday. So, I don't know if that had any impact. But that notebook just has poetry and descriptions of pretty rivers and trees. I think it shows that she was happy, not sad. I haven't read it all, just skipped through a few places. Doesn't say much. And she quit her job weeks ago. Maybe there is something about that? Maybe she had problems and someone… No, I will not go there. It has to be some sort of accident."

"But there is the note."

Deborah stood. "I don't believe that note. There is something wrong with it."

"But it is her handwriting?" Very stood as well. "Do you think she wrote it at the end, after she wrote things that day? The page was torn out of her notebook, but it wasn't the next page."

"That's another thing, isn't it? Why would she tear out a page in the middle to write a pathetic note like that? Not even a proper note. It could have been faked. She could have written it because someone told her to. Stood over her with a gun and told her to write the note, then killed her. She…this isn't…no, something is wrong with all of this. My sister did not commit suicide. She couldn't have." Deborah's voice rose in agony. "Please, you have to find out what happened."

"Okay, okay. Please just stay calm. We'll figure this out, don't worry. We can go to Hart Park, which is where these items seem to have been written and retrace her steps there. Her car was found just up the river a few miles and her body just downriver from there. Maybe there is a connection. Darrell and I can do that."

"Thank you, thank you. I can't cope right now. Please let me know if you find out anything and I'll answer any more questions that you have. Here, take the key and lock up. I can't stand to stay here any longer. Bye." Deborah rushed out the door, letting it slam behind her.

Very sat on the sad little sofa and looked around again. She had never met Mouse, aka Michelle, and this place where she lived did not tell her anything other than her shoe size and which toothpaste she preferred. There was no personality left. She opened the notebook and began to read, from the beginning.

The journal began six months before. The first page was dated, but subsequent pages lacked that clue. She had driven, by herself, to various scenic spots around the county. She had hiked, she had sat in parks, on wooden logs, on the ground, on whatever she could find. She had described scenes of natural beauty, from the smallest ant trails to the widest vistas, from brilliant sunrises to approaching storms. She had not related any of this to her own experiences, feelings or any particular choice of scenery or subject matter. Towards the end of spring, a month before, she had begun to write more, more poetic and more emotional without being more personal. The last page she had written described a serene riparian scene. Then she had scribbled. "Someone coming."

Very pulled out her phone. "Darrell," she said when her partner answered. "How would you like to go birdwatching tomorrow morning? Early?"

There was a pause. "Very, are you asking me for a date?"

"No, companionship only. I need to get to Hart Park, when no one is there and I need someone with me."

"Ah, I see."

"You have forgotten the bluffs, when I tried to call you and then got chased by a crazy man? Tomorrow, 7am. At the Peacock House. Do you know where it is?"

"Yes, I'll be there. It won't be a repeat of the bluffs, I promise."

Chapter Seven: A Walk in Hart Park

Very drove her car in through the monumental gateway of Hart Park and immediately slowed down. The speed limit was 25 here, not that it would be enforced at this hour in the morning, but the low speed limit was for a reason. The roads were winding, there were no crosswalks, no lights and few stop signs. The sprawling green space, at the base of the extension of the bluffs near her house, was built in the 1920's and 30's for the enjoyment of the growing population of Bakersfield and Kern County; it was built for people, not cars. Nostalgia swept over her every time she entered the unexpected green space. Beyond the bounds of the park and just outside the riparian ecosystem along the banks of the Kern River, the land was desert. But here, in the park, the great champion J.O. Hart had pushed through developments that created a peaceful green oasis accessible to all, all those with a car.

Very savored her trip along the southern main road, at the base of the bluffs. The first landmark was the pistol range, snuggled up next to the hills, with myriad small tracks leading to the top. The last vestiges of the spring grasses showed green. However, it would soon all be yellow, and then dry as the Mojave Desert. In late summer and fall, there were sure to be swathes of blackened areas, where wild fires happened. Happened was an odd word for the mixture of fires that sprang up: arson caused by teenagers or young men bent on experiencing the visceral thrill of flames, inadvertent sparks from cigarettes deposited by lazy smokers, or flares from lightening gone wild, whipped into a fury by whooshes of dead-dry winds that swarmed over the land. The steep hillsides boosted the updrafts that helped the fires fly upwards, just as they held aloft the red-winged hawks that glided and hunted the small animals on the hillsides or the hang gliders launched from above. This area was originally supposed to be a huge amphitheater with twice as many seats as the population of the city. A Hollywood Bowl in backwoods Bakersfield.

Further along was the lake. Carved out of the flat land and fed from the river by canals, Very had never been swimming in the lake, but she recalled boats. There was still a small building, a concession stand had been everything from food outlet to boat rental. An island in the middle of the lake was overgrown. Fisherpersons often lined the banks, especially at the points where cars could approach the lake. Sandwiches and fishing. Tall trees shaded large swathes of the lawn area, giving the place the feel of ancient forests, or at least of venerable age. Just beyond the lake was the area where the zoo used to be.

The tiny cages had been scattered among the trees and these smelly little spaces had seemed pathetic. Food was thrown onto the cement floors, mixing with feces. The odor of wild animals and the neglect from keepers was a bad memory. Very slowed and looked across the lawns, picturing the cages, but glad they were gone. There was a better zoo just up the river now. As she pulled out, up popped the memory of the hippo and she laughed. It had ended up at a local dairy; who knew why.

Across the road and further up the hillside stood a series of buildings. They marked the site of the Hart Park pool, now filled in. Very's mother had absolutely forbidden them from swimming in the pool, as she maintained that snakes from the river came into it. Very had always discounted this, but once she and friends had gone to check out the pool and saw a vast expanse of dirty water that smelled vaguely of rotting vegetation and perhaps eggs as well. Snakes or no, Very had preferred the local swimming pools or for a glorious occasion, the Union Avenue Plunge. Sulfur springs were one of the original draws to the park, but Very had never experienced them as the 1952 earthquake caused the spring to stop its flow.

But the pump station still stood. Constructed by the WPA in the 1930's, the material was river rock, large smooth granite chunks dragged from the nearby river. Cheap building material. Once, the river rock construction could have been found everywhere in the park, but as various structures fell on hard times, the river rocks disappeared. This round little building near the east end of the lake sat in quaint lonely splendor. A rendezvous point, a landmark, a magnet for graffiti artists, a marker for the frisbee course, what else could it be?

Very drove on until she came to a T intersection. To the right was the exit to the park on the Highway, to the left led her deeper into the park. Ahead of her lay her destination, but before she reached there, she passed the spot she had loved as a child. The street sign said

"Kiddyland Drive." Was that what they called it? The large area that had held the merry-go-round, the small roller-coaster and the Ferris wheel was the object of Very's fond memories. The last time she had been here was for the eighth-grade "ditch day" near the end of that school year. No one ditched as it was an opportunity to eat snow cones, caramel candy, cotton candy, greasy hotdogs with way too much mustard and then ride the dizzying mechanical machines. Throwing up, too. Adolescents.

Very pulled her car into the small parking lot around the adobe house, called the Peacock House for lack of a better moniker. Darrell was there waiting for her. She stopped her car and watched him watch the cats and peacocks. Three of the park's many feral cats sat looking warily at two pea hens who walked slowly, their voluminous tails swishing the ground behind them. Not as brightly colored as their male companions, they were still not going to be attacked by some snotty homeless cats. One turned her head and let out a screech, "Help." The cats bounded off in the direction of a pile of cat food left by the cat ladies. Feral cats, otherwise known as unwanted kitties, had been adopted by a sorority of cat lovers who made sure the felines were fed and if possible, caught and neutered. The theory was that if neutered cats were let loose into the same environment from which they had come, they would fight for their territory, but not reproduce. Fat chance.

Darrell had backed away from the strolling peahens and the house as Very joined him. "Don't like peahens, do you?"

"That yell, it sounded like they were calling for help. Really. I thought peacocks were, like prettier, with big, multicolored tails."

"The males are. These are peahens. You are a bird man, you should know that. Males are supposed to be prettier than females. And this is the Peacock House or perhaps more accurately, the Adobe House because it is made of adobe."

"As in southwestern, native American houses?"

"The same. There are lots of adobe houses in Bakersfield. Not tract houses, but individually built. Warm in the winter, cool in the summer, sturdy, if they are maintained. This one used to be a home, to an administrator or handyman or something. Abandoned now. But it could be nice. Maybe a visitor's center."

"Or a museum, or a wildlife exhibit. Lots of birds around here, we could do a nice exhibit with photos and stuff. I mean the Audubon Society. I'm sure casual visitors would like that."

"Yeah, this whole park used to be used a lot. So many things here, so many people. There was a swimming pool, a kiddies' ride area, boats for rent on the lake, a zoo. Everyone in Bakersfield came here. Family picnics, reunions, class get-togethers. It used to be so nice."

"I've seen people here on weekends, but it's kind of trashy and the toilets… We don't use them. But you said there was a swimming pool, in the river?"

"No, up on the hill," Very gestured to the south. "And some people swam in the lake. But mostly the river, they still do. That's where most people die. They don't swim in the lake anymore. It's too mucky. One little boy died there, about 30 years ago."

The two stood quietly for a few moments, a silent gesture to the drowning victims of Hart Park.

"So, why are we here?" Darrell asked.

"I have Mouse's diary, her journal." Very took it out of her bag. "The entries do not have dates, but they have good descriptions. I wanted to try and figure out where she went that Saturday. It's been just a week, so places should look and feel the same. It's not as warm as last weekend, which was a real scorcher, but the trees and bushes and the river should be the same. The river, not so much, as it was higher than normal and very cold, snow melt cold. But we can follow her footsteps because she stopped and described places. I want to find them. Then maybe we can try to figure out who and what she saw."

"Will that make a difference?" Darrell looked at Very directly, his small pack threatening to slip off his shoulder.

"I want to avoid homeless people or others up to nefarious deeds. I need someone to watch my back," Very said, pointedly not answering Darrell's question. She started off on the curving road to the north, towards the river.

For some minutes the only sound was the crunch of their walking shoes on the gravelly road. Then they came to a parking space, dirt only, but obviously one of the closest spaces to the river. Park and swim, or maybe fish. They walked towards the river, stood on the sloping edge and watched the water lap at their feet. It was shallow here and the beach was wide. Pacific looking.

"It's calm here, not dangerous?" Darrell reached down to dip his fingers into the water. "It's cold though."

"Right here, it's not dangerous. But it's so shallow that you can hardly get in the water. So, you go farther out, or you go up or down the river a bit. And look, that tree is dipping into the water. Looks like swimmers have used it as a launching pad to jump farther out."

"So, other than the river water being cold, what else could be dangerous?" Darrell looked around at the beach, so quiet now, in the early morning.

"Oh, there, there, do you see it? A branch, a big one, floating by? Most of it is under the water, so you can't see it, but think how easily a non-swimmer could get caught in that. It would pull you under in no time. That is why it is the Killer Kern. The unexpected. It's desert here, so how can you drown? Underrated."

Darrell stood and watched the big branch slowly float away. Suddenly, it stopped and turned so the branches upended into the air. The river tugged for a few seconds, then the branch slowly pulled away from the submerged object that had grabbed it. The water was blue where the sun hit it, but dark brown, full of rotting vegetation and debris in the shadows. Jekyll and Hyde. Pretty and deadly.

"She stood here, I think. She wrote a description." Very read lines out loud to Darrell, a combination of personal musings on the beauty of the spot, plus descriptions of the beach, the trees on either side, the cars parked and small children splashing in the shallows. "I think she was here after ten, certainly not as early as we are. But because she talks about children and cars parked here, I think it was nearer noon. People don't usually come early for swimming and picnics." Very wrote in her notebook as she drew a small map. "Back to the Peacock House. She described that too. She even chased a few into the back of the place."

Darrell lingered near the beach as Very waited on the road. Very watched him as he walked towards her, his head hung low, staring at his feet.

"I can't believe that anyone could drown here. It's so peaceful and beautiful," he said as he turned to cast one last glance at the open stretch of river. "Oh look, a heron!"

They stood quietly to watch a great blue heron land and then walk into the water, his feet pulled up at every step as he gingerly waded into his element. A bird's environment, not man's.

Chapter Eight: Sunday Morning in the Park

"Where did she go from here?" Darrell turned away from the river to ask.

"She writes about the Peacock House. She saw the peacocks and some cats. She had some interesting ideas about the house. She said the kids had called it haunted. What kids she doesn't say, but just like me, she probably came here as a kid and we all had our ideas about the place."

"What kind of haunted? It doesn't look like there is any way in, except to break down the door. Maybe we can get around to the back. Did Mouse say anything in her journal about that? The back way?" Darrell started walking around to the back of the building, Very following slowly.

"No, she doesn't say she explored, but that doesn't mean she didn't."

The undergrowth had not been cleared well here, although there were tire marks through some of the long grass. A fenced-in area forced the explorers to skirt around the series of outbuildings. The yards of the buildings were lush with green mixed with dry grass, which indicated that no one had mown or cut anything recently, certainly not since the fall. Sharp grass seeds clung to their socks and threatened to worm their way into the flesh. Soon the road and the House had disappeared behind them as they pushed further into the brush. The river noises ahead urged them on.

Suddenly Darrell stopped. Ahead was a pile of wooden planks in a pool of murky water. One set of boards outlined a giant wheel, now crumbled into the depression.

"The old water wheel," Very exclaimed. "I've only seen photos of it; I had no idea where it was, except that it was around here. Wow, what a find."

A small fence kept them from approaching any closer. The ground was uneven and overgrown. Very was just as happy to find an excuse for not going closer.

"This water wheel brought the river water into the lake in the park. You will notice there are canals everywhere for the water to run into the lake. But when the dam at Isabella was built, the flow wasn't what it used to be and a flood brought the wheel to a stop, never to be restarted. And there it has sat, falling apart, or fallen apart. What a lovely building it must have been."

They stood at the fence, examining the picturesque wreckage. Finally, Very turned to Darrell, "Let's go, this place can't tell us anything." They retreated the way they had come.

When they emerged into the parking lot, Very stopped and stood on the east side of the road. "She was here, right here, that morning or at noon. She described the picnic area. The crowds. The families. The noise. There it is, the huge picnic area. If all the tables that are scattered throughout the park are taken, you can always find a place here. And there is a lot of parking around here."

"I just love this place, no curbs, just grass verges, so anyone can park anywhere they like. I mean, people don't park on the grass, do they, just near it? Weird place, so old-fashioned, so early twentieth century. It just hasn't worn well, has it, into this century? I wonder when they'll decide to sell it for a fun park with water slides and go-carts?" Darrell sighed.

"Don't go there. I don't often come here, but I have such nostalgia for the place. My dad and my mom talked about coming here, so it is so, so, so… Bakersfield. Everybody has memories, different ones, but scratch any old Bako person and you get loads of, 'My favorite animal was…' and 'I loved the…' And maybe that's what Mouse was doing here, reliving something from childhood."

"But the question is, was she doing it because she was going to jump into the river later, or was it an accident, or did someone follow her and…?" Darrell hesitated to murmur the hideous word, murder, and left it dangling. Even though neither of them had ever met her, she was beginning to take shape as a person. To think that someone would deliberately force her exit from this world was becoming more and more unthinkable. Darrell didn't normally deal in murder, and Very loved murder mysteries, but the real thing was not sitting well with either. Ignore it, sweep it under the rug, sling it far, do not deal with it.

"Listen," Very said. "She wrote a silly poem about the picnic area. Okay, here it is." Very cleared her throat and read aloud.

> The picnics, the barbecues, the feasts
> All are invited, even our relative beasts
> Cousins, brothers, girlfriends and boy
> Break out the beer, the margaritas and joy.

"That was the first verse, the second one is all scratched out and not finished. Does that tell you anything?" Very shook her head at the mangled lines.

"I can imagine her thinking of those quaint lines as she stood here or sat somewhere nearby. Good evocation of the weekend scene." Darrell looked sideways at Very.

"And she also evoked the smells in the second verse; it's all about the smell of chili and bubbling tamales. Maybe you can finish it for her?" Very whispered under her breath, "evocation" and shook her head.

Darrell heard her and blushed.

"So, let's see what else she saw that day. This all seems to be on the weekend, the Saturday. Here we go, heat; she writes another poem about the heat. Want me to read it?" Very waited for a reply.

Finally, Very began to read without waiting for confirmation or assent.

> The scorch of unseen fire, bubbling on my skin
> Sucking life like an incubus
> Heat waves dancing on air, squiggles in ether
> How can life go on, with… (rhyme bus)

"Whoa, 'how can life go on'? Did Mouse's sister read this stuff? Actually, I think Mouse was thinking about how people in Bakersfield can live with the heat. You know it was almost 100 degrees last Saturday? When it gets that hot, I just wonder how and why anyone lives here, so maybe she was thinking the same."

"How can life go on… and then rhyming with bus?" Darrell tried to look over Very's shoulder to see what Mouse had written.

"See," Very pointed to the poem. "I think she was trying to find a rhyme with incubus. Maybe you'd like to try?" Very held out the page to Darrell who backed away.

"No poetry for me. Why was she writing anyway? What was her purpose?" Darrell turned away and looked around, as if the trees and grass could give him an answer.

"Remember, she had quit her job. Maybe she was searching for the next thing. Maybe she wanted to try her hand at writing. Sometimes people try to write when they have something burning inside and want to express themselves. 'How can life go on…' Maybe she was writing about what her life should be, trying to find a new way to live life. 'How can life go on this way?'" Very closed her eyes to think. She sighed. "Maybe she was just talking about the heat."

"Where did she go next?" Darrell tried once more to look over Very's shoulder.

"The river. She went to the river. 'The water calls, the gurgle, the swish, the hum.' And then about the trees and the quiet and the absence of people. So where is the river from here?"

"Well, there are only two directions. One of them is back that way," Darrell pointed north, towards the parking lot by the sandy shallow beach.

"No, too many people there. They would have been swimming and shouting. You wouldn't be able to hear any swishing of water. No, not the little beach. Another direction."

"This way," Darrell said, swiveling and heading determinedly to the south. Very followed. As they walked, she took note of the road, the bushes, the trees. At one point, she stopped and called to Darrell. "Wait a minute. Along with the sounds, she mentions trees overhanging the water, peacefulness. Where can we find that?"

"All along here," Darrell waved his arm to the east. "The river takes a turn to the north right here. Although a lot of it is blocked off with the fences, like we saw at the water wheel, there are a lot of places where you can get to the river that are quiet. Fishermen and birders know about these places. If we take this path, it will take us to a lot of those quiet places."

"Yeah, I see what you mean," Very looked towards the east, but she couldn't see any river, only riparian trees, brush and bits of overgrown land. "She mentioned a log where she sat to write. Maybe we should look for a log with a view of the river?"

"Lots of riverbank here, but we can look." Darrell strode at a determined pace and Very, not wanting to appear to be a wuss, followed swiftly.

At first, they tried to reach the river directly from the road, but soon came across a fence. Just a few feet from the fence, a small path, untended and unused, ran to the south, following the line of demarcation. Suddenly, they reached a place where they could hear the rush of the river. Very hesitated to push through the bushes saying, "She didn't write about having to bushwhack here, just that she sat on a log and listened to the river sounds. Maybe we can find that place?"

"Ok, let's look for a place where we can approach the river more easily," Darrell said. They continued to parallel the river along the footpaths, choosing the one closet to the river when there was a choice. They could see the road at times, and also the river through the trees. They slowly made their way south along the river.

At one point, Darrell said he could see the river and took a small path to go look. There was a three-foot break in the foliage, a tiny beach, but no log to sit on. Very sighed, "This is shady now, but it would have been in the direct sun in the early afternoon. No, too hot and open here. And no log. We should look some more."

They poked their noses into small breaks in the trees and realized that there was an island just a few feet out in the river at this point. A low mound covered with grass and brush, it might be underwater in a flood. It was not inviting.

Then the path turned slightly to the left and curved around some trees. They approached slowly as the atmosphere darkened when they went through the trees. As they emerged nearer the river, Very called out, "The log. There it is. Perfect for sitting on, away from the crowds and right near the river! This is it, I'm sure of it."

She raced over to the log and examined it. She turned and sat down, wiggling her backside to make sure it was a comfortable sit. She lifted her head and looked at the river, now directly in front of her. "Darrell," she said softly. "What is that?"

Darrell joined her and looked in the same direction. At the edge of the river, a small beach opened up, facing the overgrown island. Branches of trees closed in on the small space, just big enough for a fisherman or a person entering the water. They both stared at the tape, crime scene tape, that draped across the space. The crisscrossed tape read "Police Line – Do Not Cross."

"What does it mean?" Very asked softly.

"It means many things. It looks a little old, one or two weeks maybe; it's drooping. I don't think it has anything to do with Mouse, er, Michelle. Her car was found miles away up the river. Her body was pulled out of the river miles from here as well. I can't imagine the police knew that she sat here, that this was a place she visited on the last day of her life. They don't care about her journal; they have ruled it suicide and have washed their hands of it. No, this isn't about our case."

"Then, what case?" Very sat on the log, reveling in the comfort of it. "It couldn't be the body found in the riverbank, could it? The old body, the one that might be my… Frankie?"

"No, I doubt it. That was found downriver, maybe a mile or mile and a half. And things don't drift upriver, they go down. No, no reason for tape here for that body."

"There were other drownings that day." Very said quietly. "Maybe this tape has to do with that."

Darrell walked directly up to the tape and looked at the small beach. It had been churned up and little could be deduced from footprints or any other clues that might have been there. He pulled on the tape, but it clung to the tree branches and gave no answers.

"She sat here," Very said. "She wrote another bad poem about the water, the river, the bushes and trees, the peaceful scene. Wanna hear that one?"

"No more bad poetry," Darrell answered. "Anything else?"

"Oh, yes, I'd forgotten. Yes, yes. Right here, the last thing she wrote, very small and quickly. 'Someone coming.' That's all, just scribbled. I knew that, it was what brought me here. How could I forget? There were people everywhere but here. Here was peace. But then she noticed someone coming. Someone who drowned?

Something about the family, two who drowned, and others who went in after them. This tape. Joey said that Bobby mentioned there were complications with that drowning. Sorry, drownings."

Darrell continued to pace and look, while Very sat on the comfortable log and thought.

Finally, Very announced. "If she saw them, they must have seen her. We need to talk with that family."

Chapter Nine: Another Chat about Mouse

"I'm starving. Are we done here?" Darrell said suddenly, ready to move on.

"Yeah, that's it for the journal. And here is where it ended. I just wish I knew what that tape is about. And I know who to ask. And yes, food." Very heaved herself to her feet and acknowledged that she was hungry. The cup of coffee when she first got up had worn off.

"24th Street Café, my treat. Or rather, on the expense account. Meet you there? Know where it is? Park around the corner, it's easier." Darrell headed for his car.

They walked back to their cars, just a short jaunt away and Very realized that the picnickers might have seen Mouse, that is, if anyone was paying attention. Would anyone remember her? If they did, would they be able to discern her mood, her intentions? Was it even worth a try to ask anyone?

Darrell left first and Very drove behind him, slowly, as they headed west out of the park. The vast lawns were quiet, waiting for the day's visitors. To her right, Very glimpsed stretches of the river. When she reached the great arch at the end of the park, she noticed that Darrell immediately sped up as the road changed from the two-lane meandering street to a divided highway. Before she left the park, Very pulled over and got out. She saw the brush was in her way and that she couldn't get to the riverbank to see forward the half-mile or so where the historic body had been found. She got back into her car and realized that she had lost Darrell. Oh well, it was straightforward to get to the café. She could see the river off to her right as she drove up and out of the park. In the past when she had driven by at sunset, the river here appeared as liquid gold, reflecting the setting sun.

The road was wide, well-maintained and, at this time of day, devoid of traffic. Anywhere else but Bakersfield, this would have been a well-used highway. It had been built in the day when there was money and Hart Park was a going concern. It wasn't the fault of the highway builders that the Park had fallen on hard times. It had started about 1965, and the decline had been steady. The train went; too many accidents caused by small boys derailing the thing. And loss of ridership. The Kiddyland rides disappeared and the speed boats on the lake went to the newly built Lake Ming further up the river. The money for repairs of the toilets and the picnic areas dried up. Now, it was down-at-heel, a faded jewel, a dangerous place with the Killer Kern running alongside it.

The bluffs loomed on Very's left and as she took the turn to climb the steep hill. Her dad had talked about the road, the one-way road, up and down. Too many accidents, he had said. Too many beer-fueled Saturday nights with a carload of friends who had crashed head-on with another car, similarly laden. She had never heard details. But it would have taken only one significant crash to push the county to demand a better way, two-ways really, one up and one down. Still scary on a Saturday night with a beer-fueled driver, but safer.

Very drove up the cliffs on a road named China Grade Loop and turned right on Panorama. She drove within one-half block of her home, in the La Cresta neighborhood, but kept going on Panorama to the wide curve onto Union Ave. Soon she was negotiating the tricky on, then weave and off from Union Avenue onto Hwy 178 and onto 24th Street. She made a left turn off the one-way street onto K Street and found a parking place in the first block. She walked back to the restaurant.

She found Darrell waiting for her at the door. There was a line, but Darrell ushered her ahead. "I have table already."

When they were seated, Very opened the menu and in reaction, her stomach growled. Soon, coffee came and she gratefully poured creamer and added sugar to the hot aromatic liquid. She slurped, "What is it about coffee that we love so much?"

Darrell launched into a discussion of why we like the bitter flavor of coffee and what that means for coffee consumption. "The more sensitive a person is to caffeine, the more coffee they drink. And then there are the other things in coffee…" Very tuned him out and studied the menu.

The smell of cooking fat, and especially the heavy odor of bacon in the air, made Very salivate. She had to swallow a few times before she was able to get on with the perusal of the offerings. Ordering pan fried potatoes and eggs seemed a waste of time, she could cook them at home. But what about a steak? Ah, she had sworn off red meat, not good for her heart. But was any of this on a good diet? Probably not, so eat what you want.

Bacon, she never bought bacon anymore with the thought that it was not good for her. So, now is the time. Today, one day. Eggs. She loved eggs, but the same with bacon. Oh, here, Bacon and Avocado Omelet. That would combine her eggs and bacon and besides it had avocado, which was good for the body. Bad, bad, good. Or maybe just the eggs and bacon?

Darrell was muttering to himself, weighing his options. "How about a sandwich, English Muffin Sandwich? Or maybe a TriTip Scramble? With biscuits and gravy? Maybe too much."

"You can always take it home," Very said, sotto voce.

The dining room sang with laughter, the platters clanged as they landed on Formica-topped tables, forks and knives rang when they met the heavy stoneware, salt and pepper shakers pinged when they struck the tables. The walls were covered with old Coca-Cola signs, fly-fishing rods and other paraphernalia.

When their food came, plonked down by a harried waitress, Very sighed in appreciation. Yellow-yolked eggs, a deep orange-yellow, not pale like morning sunshine, stared up at her. The pan-fried potatoes lay neatly, one edge touching the glistening eggs, while a sprig of parsley peeped out from the other side. The Japanese prided themselves on presentation, and this was the Bakersfield equivalent. The bacon slices looked perfect. Very reached.

Before she had demolished her plateful, Very's phone rang. Joey. "Hi, Very, come over this afternoon and talk with Bobby Jr. again. He has more to tell you. We're having a grandma-taking-care-of-kids afternoon, so the wife won't be here. Stay for dinner if you want."

"Mumph," Very answered. "Maybe. I'm having one of those Sunday breakfasts at a café now, so don't know if I'll have an appetite. See ya later."

When Very got home, her bed called her. It hadn't been made, so use it again, she thought. She woke at two and had a quick shower. Off to Joey's.

"Your neighbors will think I have begun to live here. I was here just two days ago." Very said as a greeting.

"Never mind the neighbors. Clara wants to play with Aunt Berry. In the back."

"I really do need to change my name. Berry is so much worse than Very."

Clara greeted Very with a book, which she proceeded to demand be read to her. Very read with one eye on Bobby Jr., playing catch with his oldest son. When they both came to a stopping place, they rendezvoused in the kitchen. Bobby popped the top on two beers and they sat at the table with a view of the back yard.

"I felt constrained with my wife here, for fear that she would overhear my conversation. And I also remembered a few more things about Mouse, I mean Michelle."

"Call her Mouse, everybody else does. What things?"

"She looked like a Mouse. Her hair was always stringy and this funny mouse-brown color. All the girls were wearing long hair then, but hers just didn't, I mean it just stayed neither long nor short. Mousey. Now that I think of it, looking back, I think she may have been pulling it out. Like she was stressed or traumatized. Working with teenagers now, I see so much more than I did then. Seventeen-year-old boys are the most clueless creatures around. I told you that we weren't boyfriend-girlfriend friends, just friends. But everyone thought otherwise. Actually, my then girlfriend and I were also just 'friends'. I mean we did the occasional making-out, but no sex. It wasn't that we didn't want to, raging hormones and all, but I felt like I would disappoint my parents somehow. Well, really, recently, I heard she had come out, and then I began to look at that whole year differently."

"You mean, your girlfriend came out of the closet? She's gay?" Very prompted.

"Yeah. Like I said, seventeen is a clueless year. I'm not sure what she felt. Maybe she felt safer with me, because I didn't pressure her too much. I don't know, she has never talked with me about it. She skipped the class reunion, surprise, surprise, and so no one really knows. She left town and never came back. Again, surprise, surprise. But I started to think some more about how she reacted around Mouse. At first, I thought that she might be jealous, but then I realized how much time we all spent together. And, in fact, the two of them used to pal around. I couldn't possibly object to that. But now that I think about it…"

"Do you think Mouse was a lesbian too?"

"No, I don't believe that. But maybe she felt safer with another girl and not a boy, or boys. And when she was with the two of us, we could protect her. I was like a big brother and my girlfriend was a sister. She was troubled. Oh, Mouse was a mess as a teenager."

Very laughed. "Who wasn't a mess? I thought that was what being a teenager was all about, being troubled."

"Were you troubled? You are one of the most together women I know. You know exactly who you are, what you want and you go out and get it. Always have." Bobby Jr. smiled at her, taking her hand in his.

Very squeezed it, but shook her head. "I'm so glad I give such a nice impression. But I felt so differently when I was young. I couldn't wait to get out of Bakersfield. I couldn't be my own person while I was here. I was my parent's daughter. I had this name, this last name, and everyone knew it. I felt pigeon-holed. I felt that I was expected to do this or that. I had this social status, and I had to maintain it. But I also couldn't get too far above my roots."

"Absolute nonsense."

"It's easy to say that now, but that's how I felt back then. I got really good grades, so I knew that I could get out and go to college. I couldn't wait. I loved Santa Cruz, the hippie haven. Even though it really wasn't as far out as it was portrayed. I got a good education, an opportunity to remake myself, find my true self and then when I came back, I was so much stronger. Maybe Mouse was like that too."

"Maybe, but remember, I wasn't in touch with her at all. I haven't seen her since she left at the end of that year, actually, it was a bit before the end of the year. One Monday morning, she looked awful. My girlfriend spoke with her, I do remember that. And she didn't come back to school for a while. In fact, I don't know if she ever came back except maybe to clear out her locker. She was really upset, and she wore a long-sleeved blouse even though it was hot, it was probably May." Bobby put his head back and closed his eyes. "She had red eyes, like she had been crying and that long-sleeved shirt and she…was…traumatized."

Very sat and let Bobby think. He was quiet, trying to find the words that would describe what he saw.

"I think she had tried to commit suicide. Maybe I knew it at the time, but blocked it out. That is pretty radical, especially for us middle-class, stable family types. Because she disappeared after that, I couldn't think more about it. It wasn't my place to say or do anything. Just wonder. And remember, busy, eighteen and clueless, I couldn't involve myself. My girlfriend, too, couldn't do much. We said goodbye at the beginning of the summer, 'See you in the fall' sort of thing. We never did. I think I put those relationships into a box, locked it and threw away the key."

"And now? What can you say now?"

"Well, Mouse's death has opened it up. I have been thinking about it a lot the last few days, trying to make sense of it. I've tried to figure out my part in it. I don't think I really had a part, except as a safe person, but not so safe that I could be confided in. Just an accepting person. But it has dredged up other things. Now, I want to reconnect with my old girlfriend, just to see if she's alright. A little like you trying to find your Frankie Monroe. I need to resolve some things."

"I know how that feels. And now, this newest body. I don't know whether to be hopeful or not."

They sat at the table, watching his three children playing outside.

"I'm so lucky," he said, "I have family, stability, a good job, friends. Mouse had none of those, at least when I knew her. She was the most broken person I've ever met."

Chapter Ten: The Therapist

On Monday morning, even before Very got to her second cup of coffee, her phone rang. Deborah Smith was on the line.

"Hello," Very said. She hoped she wasn't being asked for a report yet. If that was the case, she needed to scramble in her brain for a reply.

"Good morning, Miss Blew. I have just spoken with Michelle's therapist who has agreed to talk with you. She went on and on about confidentiality, blah, blah, so I don't know how much she is willing to divulge. I told her that she could talk with you. I'm in a real hurry this morning, and frankly, I don't want to know anything about what my sister was doing with a therapist. I really think it was her own business and in some ways, I want to leave it at that. But please go talk with her and if she is able to fill you in on anything that might be useful, please take note. She said that she wasn't busy right now, but would be later. So, if you can do it now, that would be great."

Very grumbled quietly to herself. She might want to talk with the therapist, but somehow the timing was awkward. She had not asked the therapist for an appointment, but Mouse's sister did. Was she doing the investigation, or was she being manipulated? She took the number.

A short phone call verified the time and place. Very quickly changed clothes, sure that the casual pants she had thrown on this morning would have been inappropriate for interviewing a professional. Darrell didn't mind, working on the computer in the office, but Very knew what professionals wore and what they didn't. She found a silk scarf and wound it around her neck.

She drove downtown and then made a right onto Truxtun Avenue, heading west. The neighborhood to the north of Truxtun, once a middle-class haven of single-family homes of moderate size, was almost all professional offices now. Who would want to live in a house with a doctor on one side, an accountancy firm on the other and all the other houses in the neighborhood transformed into business offices? It wasn't that it was busy, although the streets during the day had little parking, but that one couldn't borrow a cup of sugar, or have a good gossip with the dental assistant or physical therapist. Even though the houses still had the appearance of single-family dwellings, few were.

Very found the address and parked on the street near the office. She entered the front door to find a tiny waiting room with two doors. One said 'Restroom' and the other was unmarked. Very was about to knock, when the door opened.

"Rita Shaw?" Very asked, surprised at the casualness of the office.

"Yes, Ms. Blew?"

As Very walked behind Ms. Shaw, she took in the clothes, the office décor and the layout of the small house converted to an office. Very had changed clothes, chosen her best silk scarf to wear and was trying hard to be a big city girl. But Rita Shaw was dressed in a cotton-linen dress that was wrinkled, slip on shoes, albeit ones with sparkles, and her hair was in a super casual bun, the ends sticking out. Her makeup was minimal and the necklace that jingled around her neck was an outsized collection of shells, beads and bells, strung together in such a way as to make outlandish noises when Rita moved. The presentation was pure Bakersfield dress casual.

She led Very into an office full of colorful prints on the walls and a number of green plants. The light that came in was soft and the entire impression was comfortable. Rita indicated a chair for Very and she took one opposite.

"Now, I just want to let you know that as a licensed therapist, my position is clear. Client confidentiality is taken very seriously in this business and as such, Michelle Malden's files are not open to you or to anyone. Even now that she is deceased, the client-patient confidentiality still holds. So…"

"So, why am I here, if you can't tell me anything? I think I am wasting my time. You do know that Michelle's sister hired me to find out if Michelle really committed suicide. The police have said she did, but Deborah Smith believes she didn't. I am not absolutely sure why she needs to know. Closure, I guess. But now I am beginning to wonder. Well, I'll not take more of your time."

"Oh, I didn't say I can't tell you anything. As the representative of my client's nearest relative, you are able to receive information on her behalf. And I do have some information. And then there is this," she said, taking a photocopy off of her desk. She handed it to Very.

It was short and to the point, dated about three years before, and gave the therapist the authority to divulge information to her sister. "Is this legal?" Very was surprised that there could be or would be such a thing.

"Not sure. But I told Mouse, sorry Michelle, what confidentiality was, and that if she wanted to talk with her sister, she could do it for herself. But she said, 'Just in case.'"

"Just in case, what?"

"Her death or disability I assume."

"Why did she feel she needed this? As you said, if she wanted to talk with her sister, she could do so. And if she planned on committing suicide, she could have written a suicide note explaining what happened in her life to make her do it. I mean, isn't that what we usually do when we plan on suicide?"

"That's the theory."

"It isn't true?"

"Not everyone wants to lay it all bare. Some just want to get it over with. Some see an attempt as a cry for help. Suicide is not straightforward and it is not the same for everyone." The therapist sat back in her chair and folded her arms as if she was bored with explaining this simple psychological event with an amateur.

"So, what can you tell me about Michelle, I mean Mouse, whatever."

"Let's call her Mouse, that's the name she used. She introduced herself to me as Mouse; she called herself that. She felt close to her mother, who died when she was fourteen, who gave her that name. It made her feel safe and valued. She had a small collection of mice at one time in her life and she brought a mouse cup here to drink tea out of. It's in the cupboard. Would you like to have it to give to her sister?"

Rita jumped up and retrieved it. She handed a small cup with a line drawing of a mouse on the side to Very. Unlike Mouse's apartment, the sterility of which defied Very's vision of the dead woman, this unlikely piece of ceramic spoke to Very. She could smell the faint odor of mint that clung to the cup and she noticed a tiny chip on the top of the handle. "Thanks. This is an unexpected… gift. I'll see if Mouse's sister wants it." Very cradled the mug in her hands and smiled at Rita.

"There are some things that I can tell you that are not confidential that might be helpful to you. If you want to know if she committed suicide or not, you need to look at the facts, that's all. But I can tell you about her life, her friendships, her personality, many things like that. First of all, life was very smooth and happy until her mother got cancer. Then it took two years for her to die. So, I would say that starting about age twelve, her life took a tragic turn. Her sister had already left home, and even though she was supportive, it was terrible for Mouse. Her aunt took her in for a while after her mother died, but when she was in high school, age fifteen or so, junior year I guess, she came back to Bakersfield. But at the end of that year, she went to live with her sister. That didn't work out too well, either, but by then she was old enough to go away to college. Sacramento. Found a good place to stay, finished college, got a job, and eventually drifted back to Bakersfield. She's always kept in touch with her sister, staying with her during vacations and things, but wasn't close with her dad. He eventually remarried and moved away, far away. Left his two daughters behind, so to speak. So there is the short story, bare outlines of her life."

"So, it appears that, even though she felt really bad about her mother dying, she managed to get on with life?" Very felt unsatisfied with this thumbnail sketch. It was the kind of thing you could get from a Facebook page or LinkedIn biography. What she really wanted to know was her inner life. How was she going to ask about that?

"Okay, okay. I know that doesn't really tell you much. But because I have that release, or paper or whatever you want to call it, I believe there is much more I can tell you. Her personality, her hopes and fears and something of how she lived with the fears of her life. Okay, personality." Rita stopped and took a deep breath. "Well, she was a self-avowed Mouse."

Very sat still, waiting for Rita to explain what she meant. The crazy decorations on the walls and the tinkling of her necklace as she rearranged herself were a momentary distraction. What's a Mouse? Like Mouseketeer or like the animal? A description of her personality?

"She acted scared and timid so often. Like a Mouse. A stereotype. Life was scary for her. She often refused to buy new things because she couldn't make up her mind what kind, what color, what size, anything. She let her friends select clothes for her, tell her what kind of car to buy, things like that. She was not one full of initiative. On the other hand, she was a survivor. She had amazing resilience. If you think of all the terrible things that had happened to her in her life, well, she managed. She managed not to be a substance abuser, not to abuse or take all of her life's downturns out on anyone else. She wasn't friendly, if you mean having lots of friends, but she coped so much better with life than lots who had no reason not to do well. If you have two parents and a happy childhood, then we can, sort of, expect to be successful in coping with things. But if we've had trauma, well, then, it is no wonder that life turns out shitty."

Very felt bamboozled with this statement. She was beginning to feel as though Rita Shaw was a bit off as a therapist. Even though Very was of the mind that it takes all kinds to make up the population, this woman was scary. Did she mean to imply that Mouse was easily led, but then resilient? Not a substance abuser? Well, no one had ever said she was. If you say that someone doesn't drink to forget their sorrows, well, what sort of statement is that? Very listened to five more minutes of the same.

"Mouse had no friends, her workmates were nice to her, but she never went out to lunch or dinner with them. She was a moderate eater, not a strict vegetarian, but rejected red meat. She refused to say that she had a particular taste in music, saying nothing positive or negative about popular music, country, classical or any other kind. The same with sports or art or anything else. She had no favorite in anything."

Very hesitated to stop the flow, as any minute, Rita might just say something useful. She sat and listened as Therapist Shaw became more and more general and farther and farther away from specifics about Mouse. Finally, Very stopped listening to Rita and began to listen to questions in her own head.

"That's about it," concluded Rita, jerking Very back to the present. "That's about all that seems relevant. You know how it is, we talk about the same thing over and over and nothing seems to get resolved, but we do get closer to acceptance, maybe closure even."

"So, that is all you can tell me? These things are a little more general than I had hoped, but I do understand that you are under legal constraints. Thanks for your time." Very began to stand up.

"One more thing," Rita said.

Very sat down. She looked at Rita with an expression of interest and concern, a conglomeration of facial expressions and tics that she had cultivated for years as a teacher. "Yes?"

"There was one incident. It was important. Mouse seldom talked about it, but it colored her life. Somewhat. I think."

"What was this?" Very felt like strangling the woman.

"You know that I cannot discuss details, that would be breaking my client's confidentiality. That would be illegal."

"Can you tell me some outline or a brief story?"

"Seeing as how Mouse had given her permission to mention things, she didn't specify what, I can tell you this, briefly."

Very said nothing, but waited.

"She wasn't an adult, but not a child."

Very sat still, feeling the weight of the coming statement.

"She was…molested…sexually… And she never said directly, but I believe it was by someone close to her. There, I have said it. No more, no questions." Rita stood in dismissal.

Very opened her mouth to ask for more, but realized that she had gotten far more than Rita had meant to say. The best course of action was to take her nugget of information and leave. She picked up her purse and hung it over her arm. She stood and turned smartly towards the door.

Rita bustled out to the small reception area and then leaned closer to Very. Rita gripped her upper arm in a pinch that Very tried not to show hurt her. Rita leaned her head towards Very in a conspiratorial gesture. "Don't ever say anything to anyone about this. If you do, I'll deny every word. I never said this."

Very nodded in a numb fashion.

"As you know, as professionals, we need to talk things over sometimes. And this case, well, we discussed it. Some of my friends. No names, ever."

Very had been paralyzed into inaction. She desperately wanted the vice to let go of her arm, but she also wanted to hear what Rita had to say.

"We all wondered what took her so long."

Rita Shaw released Very's arm and retreated to her office.

Chapter Eleven: Mouse's House

Very felt drawn to return to Mouse's apartment. She had been prevented from snooping, rather, looking into the drawers and the boxes in the cupboard.

She still had the laptop, and she had started on that. But she needed to get the key again to Mouse's apartment, and go without big sister looking over her shoulder. It was a clean, neat place, but there were still many clues to the woman there. Why had she returned the key to Deborah? Very called her.

"Sure, come by and get the key. I'm sure you won't find anything else there, it's a barren place. But you are welcome to look again. Just don't think I'm going to pay loads of extra money to explore a place that has no information. By the way, I'm off for a few days, but please do keep in touch by phone."

Very did a little jig. Deborah didn't know how much could be revealed in a person's kitchen, medicine cabinet and stash of books. Of course, she had already looked into her search history on her laptop, but that hadn't revealed much. She sped off to Deborah's hotel, fearing that Deborah might leave before she got there. Wonder where she was going, and why? She was so desperately keen on ferreting out whether Mouse committed suicide, but now seemed to have gone sour on the search. "Don't think I'm going to pay extra…" Never mind that now, Very was sure she wanted to continue the investigation, pay or not. She had become fascinated with Mouse and her personality and how and why that might have led to suicide, or not.

She got the key, still dressed in her nice clothes, and went to Mouse's apartment. When she let herself in, she stopped at the door to listen to the rooms, to see if they had anything to say about their former occupant. She gently smelled the air and tried to identify the odors. Cleaner, stale air, a funky smell as if the air conditioner had cycled on for the first time in the summer. Dirty filters. She closed the door and listened to hear any outside noise, traffic or neighbors. It was quiet here, even though the apartments all shared walls and were small. Lots of singles, maybe. Couples with kids wanted houses, not apartments.

She sat on the couch and looked around the room. Ikea furniture, second hand bookshelves, a few prints on the wall, but generic, nothing particular. The bookcase held two shelves of books, and some souvenir trinkets from local places and one miniature sombrero from Mexico, or just LA? Very made a mental note to look at the books, and in the books.

She went to the kitchen. She had looked before, opening a few drawers while Deborah hovered and looked to see that Very didn't take anything. Now, she did a methodical look, starting on one side, opening each cupboard and drawer at a time. Functional kitchen utensils, nothing different or interesting. Dishes, a set of four, yellow and blue. Serving dishes, ditto. She went faster, deciding to leave the drawers for last. Everyone had a junk drawer, didn't they? What was in Mouse's? Secrets would hide in these repositories of daily detritus: receipts from stores, recipes, elastic bands from exotic vegetables, practice suicide notes?

Very found the junk drawer. She pawed through it with practiced abandon, looking for the things that were out of place, unusual or would speak to her. She found a receipt for a notebook and a book from Barnes and Noble on California Avenue. What had taken her there, searching for the book, or to buy the notebook? The vague description on the receipt matched the notebook that Very still had. It was dated just about the time she quit her job. Whatever her intentions were, a notebook to record them were on her mind. Very saved it and put it in her voluminous bag. Finished with the kitchen, she turned to the bedroom.

The boxes on the upper shelf. Deborah had looked at one of them, but pushed the other one aside quickly, the one she said was the children's things box. Now, Very was going to look in them again, in detail. She easily reached the first box, the one with bank records and such. Cradling it in her arms, she took it to the living room. Sitting on the couch, she dipped into its contents. She took things out, carefully keeping them in their various manila folders. Manila folders, who filed things alphabetically and time-wise in neat little folders anymore? Very blushed at her piles of papers. She had had trouble after her mother's death to find the relevant documents, as opposed to the extraneous receipts for services rendered ten years before. But wait, some of the more recent receipts were in the junk drawer, not here. Aha, not the total neatnik she was espoused to be.

Very methodically looked in every folder. Mouse's life was very straightforward. She bought and paid for the normal stuff: gas and electricity, phone, cable TV, clothes, groceries, medicines. Nothing out of the ordinary, nothing to indicate she was other than a dull as dishwater thirty-year-old. Nothing here indicated anything special, all was humdrum, routine, standard. But, did that tell Very anything? She knew that Deborah had taken the file with letters that Deborah had written to her, that also contained birthday cards and other things. She said she would take some recent bills. That made sense if she wanted to cancel things, the numbers on the bills were always needed. She put things back into the box and returned it to the shelf in the closet, but not before she rescued the second box, the one Deborah had said contained childhood things.

Very looked into the box before she sat down. Beanie Babies? Is that what these little, bizarre toys were? She had, of course, heard of them, and yes, had confiscated a few that appeared on desks and had caused problems for those with low attention spans. But keeping them for posterity? Deeper in the box were more souvenirs of Mouse's childhood. Three T-shirts with camp logos were neatly folded at the bottom to one side. They contained the name of the camp, a year and were three different colors. A different color for each year, but otherwise all the same. The newest one was a size bigger than the other two.

On the other side at the bottom was a box holding a Barbie doll. It was pristine, apparently never opened. This was something Very could relate to, although she had never owned one herself. The very first Christmas that Barbie came out, Very had asked for one. But come Christmas morning, there was no Barbie under the tree.

By the time the next Christmas rolled around, Very had outgrown dolls. Later, Sissy had gotten a Barbie doll, but Very never, ever played with her. She turned her back on the clothes, the accessories, the whole worship of everything Barbie. Just a few years ago, before her mother died, she had asked her mother why she hadn't gotten a Barbie doll for Christmas that year. Her mother mumbled, "Expensive, too expensive, probably." How could Very have communicated that she would have given up all the other toys, clothes, presents from everyone that year, for the joy of having the latest, newest toy doll? The disappointment welled up in her, looking at this never-played-with doll. Could Mouse have gotten this too late, last year's desire? The upshot was to never play with it. Would Very have done the same, had she received a Barbie the year after she wanted it? It couldn't have been the doll herself that she wanted, but perhaps the feeling of having your parents give you whatever your heart desired? The show of unconditional love?

Very tucked the doll back into the niche that Mouse had chosen and stuck her hand into the far corner, pulling out two miniature trophies, both with gold-colored soccer balls. A year inscribed on each indicated participation, nothing more? No first, or runner-up, only a year. Also in the corner was a stack of ribbons, and one lone plastic case with a silver medal. The sport or activity was not indicated. A manila folder tucked up on the side held certificates. Soccer, swimming, arts participation, and volunteer work, they were dated and in order. They stopped abruptly. Nothing for the year, or later, that Mouse's mother died.

Very put everything back into the box and carried it to the bedroom. There was nothing else in the cupboard.

Photos? Didn't everyone have photos? In the last few years, people had become more used to using their telephone for photo-taking, but lots of people had photos printed and of course, no one had digital cameras in the old days. Where were the photos? She needed to ask Deborah. Maybe there had been another box, or maybe Deborah had taken them along with the letters.

Very checked the bedroom once again, concentrating on the nightstand drawers and the dresser. These were private places, where a person would put photos, mementos, souvenirs, scraps of life to remember. But Mouse had nothing here, nothing personal. Very looked in the bathroom. The same. But, hang on, would five different shades of pink lipstick count? Or maybe, just trying out which one was the one she preferred and not throwing away the rest? Very noted the colors in her notebook. A clue?

The last thing that Very had to look at was the shelf of books in the living room. The two shelves of books were tightly packed, two were even stored sideways on top of the others as there was no more room. Very sat on the floor in front of the books and looked at the spines. She took out her notebook. A person's reading material was an excellent judge of character. Did a person spend hours reading mindless romance novels, cozy mysteries, or, heaven forbid, graphic novels? No, no, Very was a fan of cozies, and some of the classic ones as well. Agatha Christie wasn't mindless, surely? But a person's bookcase was revealing.

She sat in front of this one and pulled books from the shelves. One was a photo album, not a book per se. Very squealed in delight at the find. It was a chronicle of Mouse's life, starting with her birth certificate and baby pictures. She had, or perhaps her mother had, labeled them all. Parents, grandparents, sister, cousins, friends. Birthday parties, Christmas, day camp, last day of school. Mouse appeared in them all. She was a tiny child, seemingly smaller than her classmates and fellow campers. That, coupled with her habit of standing behind someone else, rendered her shadowy. Only in the school photos of herself, portraits of a girl in braids, curls on top of her head, braces, wearing a Brownie uniform, did the individual personality emerge. Her smile was coy, with a soupcon of naughtiness, and that recognition made Very understand why she was 'Mouse.' Small, cute, but a real presence, a diminutive bundle of real desires, ideals, wants and needs.

As Mouse grew, she took over labeling the pictures. "Me, Sandy, Debbie" read one that contained a girl of the same age and her older sister. The photos ended abruptly. The first day of high school was included, and a few others, but sometime during that year, the photo-taking and collecting ended. Then Very turned the page and found the last picture. It was not stuck into the album, nor was it labeled. It was a dark photo, and did not contain Mouse in it, unlike all of the others. It showed a coffin, surrounded by banks of flowers.

Very flipped through the rest of the album and found nothing else. Was it of her mother's funeral? She died when Mouse was fourteen, about her freshman year in high school, so it fit. And everyone said she was devastated by her mother's death. It was the album of a person who had died with her mother. Very hesitated to take the album, but Deborah did indicate she could look for anything. Oh well, it didn't have much to tell her. Very left it.

On the bottom shelf were more serious books. Some college textbooks, with notes in the margins, self-help books on determining the right profession such as "Finding Your Parachute," books on life changes and growth, spiritual searches for a person at each stage of life such as "Passages." She tried to reshelve these, but they resisted. There were a few stuck in the back. Very reached in and pulled two books that had been stuck behind the others.

They were small, and had handwritten notes on many pages. Very's hands began to shake as she read the notes. These books were not meant to be found by anyone, they had been hidden and now Very understood why. "Suicide Survivor's Handbook" and "Why People Die by Suicide." Suicide, Mouse definitely thought about it. And judging by these books, hidden in the back, and with the marginalia, she thought about it a lot.

Chapter Twelve: The Body in the Riverbank

Very spent the evening watching TV, reading parts of two books, playing with the cat and went to bed early. The day brought more sunshine; it was already bright on the back porch. As Very stepped outside on the Tuesday morning, she felt the gathering heat. The fateful weekend, now ten days ago, had been unseasonably hot, but since then, the weather had gone back to normal. Today the spirit of summer threatened to engulf them again, setting the precedent for the coming months. Heat was never a problem for Very, unless the thermometer reached the triple digits, so she stood for a few minutes soaking up sun. Then, she prepared for a day at the office. She wanted to consult with Darrell.

As soon as she entered the cramped office, Darrell greeted her effusively. And then, "We have news. About the body. We can definitely date it to after 1971."

"What, how, why 1971? And you are talking about the body found in the riverbank, aren't you? I thought we were working on the Mouse suicide. But, whatever."

"You need to speak to Deputy Sanchez. He called here, looking for you."

"That sneaky so-and-so. He knows my home phone number, or if he doesn't, he can ask his wife. Why relay the message through you? Is this one of those 'guy' things? Women are too delicate to hear the bad news? Or the interesting news? They will faint dead away if we tell them something sad, or difficult? Is that you, Darrell?" Very stood, arms akimbo, staring at Darrell in his chair.

"No, no, no. It's not like that. He was at work, and he called here and I told him that you would be here shortly, and you were probably driving, and that I wouldn't say anything, but that there was news, and that I would get you to call him. I would never presume you were too delicate for bad news, or any kind of news." Darrell shook with indignation, or was it fear of Very's retribution.

"Oh, so he just now called, did he?"

"Yes, just now. Please call and talk to him. It's interesting, and I know that you can take it."

"I'm glad you approve of my fortitude in the face of bad news. Since when do women automatically faint, have hissy fits or accuse someone else if they happen to be confronted with other than the best of information? Women are, contrary to your old-fashioned beliefs, quite strong and resourceful. I promise I will not faint or throw a tantrum. Okay?"

Darrell looked off to the tiny window at the end of the room, not daring to meet Very's pointed gaze. "Yes, I understand. You will be calm in the face of whatever news you hear."

Very spent fifteen minutes playing telephone tag before she was connected to Officer Sanchez. "Thank goodness, I finally got you. What news, Bobby?"

"Well, Very, this is limited information, you understand. We are only doing the small bits that we can do with our limited budget. I mean, if we had the bucks, we would do DNA, but that costs money, so we are trying to do as much as we can with low level analysis, dental records, analysis of the skeleton and so forth. You understand that?"

"Okay, Kern County doesn't have the resources to do the real work of finding out who this guy is, I get it. But tell me what you can. Darrell said it was post 1971. Is that right? How can you tell?"

"1971 or later, okay, we'll include 1971. But it's the jeans."

"His jeans, as in his pants?"

Bobby chuckled. "I know, weird, isn't it? Well, the body was only wearing two items of clothing. No underclothes, no shoes or socks, just the red lumberjack type of shirt and a pair of jeans. The tag in the shirt was cut out, so that is more difficult, but the jeans… How can I say this? The manufacturer of the jeans, the real things, not any of those knock-offs, has put lots of clues in lots of places. They are not easy to counterfeit. And for good reason. Anyway, there is a particular way of stitching the pockets and other things. You know the grommets on the pockets? Well, if you find a pair of jeans with the grommets still on, they were manufactured before a certain year, when they took them off because they were getting caught on things, and scratching chairs. Anyway, over the years, the manufacture of the trousers changed and some of them were very subtle. This one, that identifies it as 1971 or later, is involved with stitching on that little red tab thing. It's to do with the size of the stitching and the color. Amazing that the tab lasted so long. Anyway, the jeans tell us that the body, or rather the jeans covering the body, couldn't have been buried before 1971. On the other hand, there is significant wear in the knees and seat, so the guy in the forensics lab says that it is likely to be at least, at the very least, two years later than that."

"So, you are telling me that this person was likely buried in 1973 or later?" Very said.

"Yes. Therefore, we will be looking at databases of missing persons from 1971 or later. No earlier."

"That, then, includes my missing Frankie Monroe?"

"Yes. Bringing you up to date then, this is what we have, almost certainly. Male, aged 25-45, buried no earlier than 1971."

"That's it? Nothing else? Height? Come on, that one is easy. Hey the stitching on the jeans was difficult!"

"Very, I want to remind you that we are short on money and expertise. We are a small outfit here. We need to get experts from LA or some big department in on this one. It costs money and takes time."

"What about DNA?"

"I've told you, too expensive. And besides, we don't have a great data base, yet. In another ten or fifteen years, it will be cheaper and more people will give DNA and then, it will be super useful. But, it takes time, and it's big bucks. Right now, this is not a priority."

"It is to me!" wailed Very. "It's at the top of my list."

Bobby stayed silent, waiting for Very to calm down and return to her usual serene self. She fell silent and let serenity envelope her.

When there were no more sounds at all coming through the telephone, Bobby continued. "We might be able to get an artist to help with facial reconstruction, you know, draw a picture of the face. But again, it's the money. Anything else for now?"

"Yeah, I want to know if he drowned."

"That is a difficult one. It is not obvious, but it could be the way he died. There don't seem to be any blows to the head, bullets to be pulled out of bone or anything like that. So, we can't say. The skeleton has been there for years, it appears. He could have drowned, or been thrown into the river, or buried."

"But the skeleton was found in the river." Very stated this as fact.

"But it does appear that he was buried in the ground, not far from the river. As you know, the river has moved over the years. And right at that point, there is a significant bend in the river. We haven't had time to reconstruct the flow of the river, but the most likely scenario is that he was buried in among the bushes, maybe not too far from the river. But as I said, the river has changed course over the years, and with the latest heavy water flows, the river ate into the bank, causing the side to fall and exposing the body. And well, also tearing it apart, but that doesn't help now, does it? It could have been buried twenty feet away, or maybe more. Whoever put him there did not expect the rain to wash it all away like that. In the old days, before the dam, maybe. It used to flood in the spring and early summer, but after they built the dam, no one would ever expect the river to change much."

"So, the deterioration that might be expected if he was covered with water, or dumped and remained in the river or at the bottom of the river, is not there, or minimal. In other words, the body is well-preserved?"

"Not really, but we have bones. On the other hand, it wasn't put there a year ago. It's unclear when it was buried, but no earlier than 1971. So that brings us full circle. You know everything I do now."

"So, you will consider that it might be Frankie Monroe?" Very's voice rose in frustration.

"We will go back to missing persons starting in 1971. We will even consider a wider scope than just Kern County. So, when Monroe's case file comes up, we will consider him."

Silence hung along the wires.

Bobby spoke. "You have filed a missing person's report, haven't you?"

Very whispered, "No."

Bobby's voice crackled over the phone. "Then we will NOT even consider him!"

"Look, we've got DNA. Or we will have. Cassandra says she'll get it. And then…"

"Very, this is unlike you. You are not usually ditzy or forgetful or neglect things that need taking care of. I will put this in the strongest of terms. We will not consider this body to be Monroe's until and unless we have the paperwork. You have been a bureaucrat. You know how these things work."

"Yes, I do. I'm sorry. I should have done this a long time ago. But when there was no possibility, it was easier to put off. You have never done this?"

"Of course I have, I understand. Now, the DNA. First of all, I've told you that this is a cost thing and we don't have the money. And secondly, Cassandra is a long shot for DNA. What is her relationship to Frankie Monroe based on?"

Very let dead air lay between them. He knew very well that there was no sure thing about Cassandra being Frankie's daughter. Cassandra's mother died before she could tell her daughter who her biological father was. But when Cassandra saw Frankie's picture, she recognized her face in his. Upon meeting Frankie's adoptive mother and sister, they, too, confirmed the uncanny resemblance, not only in her looks, but in her peculiar husky voice, and a few mannerisms that must have been passed down through genes, not nurture. The women had accepted that Cassandra was Frankie's daughter. How and when still remained a mystery, but it must have happened before Very and Frankie met, based on Cassandra's birthdate. Only a man could throw up such questions.

"Are you going to tell me the story about Danny Boy Harger's widow blowing herself up with a cigarette and an oxygen tank, and trying to tell her daughter on her death bed that she wasn't Harger's daughter? That will not stand up. No, no…"

"But DNA will, won't it?" Very's voice came out more forceful that she had planned and she muttered, "Sorry, I didn't mean to be so, so strong. It's just that years ago, we didn't have this wonderful tool, but now that we do, we need to consider it."

"And I'm telling you that we don't have the money. You need to accept that and practice patience." A grit had entered Bobby's voice.

"'Patience is a virtue, keep it if you can. Always in a woman, never in a man.' The nuns taught us that."

Bobby laughed, a series of huge howls and ha-ha-ha's. "Vermilion Blew, you are a hoot!" He hung up.

Chapter Thirteen: Preparations for a Visit

Darrell and Very sat, consulting about the Michelle Malden case.

"I think we need to talk to the Hernandez family." Very clenched her teeth after saying this. They both knew why it might be a good idea, but the spoken idea was another thing entirely.

"How can we do that? They are in mourning; it's only been a week or so. They must be devastated. Two people in their family, a young daughter and the cousin. How can we talk to them?" Darrell stared at the floor as he said this, not daring to look at Very.

Who was the investigator here, anyway? Darrell took the job and then practically foisted it off on her, leaving Very to do all the footwork so far. It was Very who talked to the sister, led them to the park, looked at the notebook, photo albums, everything so far. This was the obvious next step, wasn't it? Gut instinct told her that more was needed. And this was it, didn't Darrell see that?

"Well, Professional Private Investigator Pitts, if we don't talk with the Hernandez family, what do we do next?" Very's words came out sharper than she anticipated. "I mean, Darrell, what else is there to investigate?"

"I know, I know."

"She was there, where that tape is. You know that, there were her very words, and that log, that seat. It was just as she described. Everything was just as she wrote it down. And then, within what, an hour, there are two drownings, right there. And she says, 'someone coming.' Could the 'someone' be the Hernandez family? Could they have seen her? Maybe they can tell us something."

"Maybe."

"Maybe they can say she was acting funny, or she looked depressed, or that she was scared, or that someone was following her, or that she wasn't alone, or… something else. Maybe. Something."

"Wow, Very. You have quite an imagination there. I guess we could try. Let me find the address and phone number." Darrell turned to his computer, first looking up the article in the paper, then trying the directories. "Whoa, do you know how many Hernandez's are in Bakersfield? It's got to be one of those names like Smith or Jones for Hispanic surnames."

"Not surprised, half of Bakersfield is Hispanic. How long is that going to take you? I could try my secret back door to goings-on in town." Very offered this half-heartedly, but she saw Darrell give her a look that she took as his personal challenge. After all, he honed his skills on skip-tracing and using his databases was his forte.

Very turned aside and went back to her notebook. She tried, unsuccessfully, to connect with two of the friends, or acquaintances, of Mouse's. She left messages. If they didn't want to talk with her, there was nothing she could do. She looked again at the notebook that Mouse's sister had given her. She turned the pages carefully and used her own notebook to make notations rather than making marks on the margins, which is what she wanted to do. Occasionally, she glanced over at Darrell, who was beginning to sweat with his efforts.

Then, a few grunts erupted and Darrell wrote a series of names, addresses and phone numbers on a sheet of clean paper. He then crossed a couple out, lightly. "There, that is the address and phone number. A landline, but should do it."

"Are you sure?"

Darrell grinned. "Do you want to bet on it? If I'm wrong, you can skewer me. If I'm right, you buy the next lunch."

"Deal. This is really a test of your skill, isn't it?" Very took the paper and looked at the lone standout address. She recognized the street name in East Bakersfield. "Okay, now what do I do? Cold call?"

"You'll have to, unless you want to just go and knock on the door. If no one answers, you may have to do that. Pardon me, WE may have to do that. It's best to plan what you want to ask, and think of ways to approach this. Remember, my first impression was that they were a family in mourning and this wouldn't be a good idea."

"You're right, let's construct a method of attack. No, attack is not the right word, more of a stealth invasion. Let me see, this is a community tragedy, anyone could come to the house and pay their respects."

"That's disingenuous."

"I know, but we need a way to get a foot in the door."

Darrell heaved a sigh of acceptance. "And then what are you going to say?"

"Condolences, condolences, blah, blah." Very stopped. She needed time to think, to plan. He was right, Very couldn't just walk in, say "sorry" and then launch into Mouse's story. "I am not going to lie, that just compounds the untruth, but what can I say?"

"Let's get prepared with all the info we have to trigger remembrances. So, do we have a photo? One that would be recognizable? Hair length, clothes etc. And do we know exactly what she was wearing that day?"

"The clothes she was found in, presumably. Let me see. Here, jeans and a pale-yellow tee-shirt. One shoe was lost, but little sneaker things, white. Her bag, an over-the-shoulder brown sac-like thing that could be changed into a backpack. No one has mentioned a hat or how she was wearing her hair."

"Here is the selection of photos we have." Darrell handed her a number of snapshots. They prepared a couple to scan and copy.

"Am I going to do this by myself?" Very looked directly at Darrell, challenging him to commit himself to the encounter ahead.

"I think that's the best idea. You are less provocative. It's easier for a woman to go into a stranger's home and ask questions. You can certainly be honest with them, we are just looking for information about Mouse, and we don't care about their movements or whatever. Not that we don't care, but what happened to them, while tragic, is not going to impact our investigation. We don't think it is, maybe not."

"You know, there is a history."

"What history? Whose?"

"Drowning in the park and intrusions. And I think it was minority. Let me see if I can find it." Very searched for a few minutes, then hit "print" for a page. "Yeah,

1985. I remember that. A child drowned in Hart Park Lake and a photographer was there as they were searching for him. Romero was the kids name, Edward Romero. And this guy took a photo of the kid in his body bag, with the family around, screaming in agony. You can quite easily see the child's face. Look here's the photo." Very handed him the page as it peeled from the printer. "And the photographer was told by the police not to take photos, but he did anyway. Printed in the paper. Ugly, ugly."

Darrell read the accompanying article which was written by the photographer, justifying the photo and publication. "He won an award for it," Darrell remarked. "I see what you mean, this kind of intrusion with ethnic overtones."

"We, of course, will do nothing of the kind. We will take no photos, we will not intrude on their grief, except to ask some questions about another person. We will be sensitive."

"You will be sensitive."

Very responded by dialing the number given to her by Darrell. "Hello," she said, as there was no answer from the other side. "Hello, is this the Hernandez house?"

A kerfuffle ensued, but no one hung up. Finally, a girl answered in a smooth authoritative voice. "Yes, this is the Hernandez house. How may I help you?"

Panicked, Very stumbled out her explanation. She had not prepared what she was going to say, contrary to what she and Darrell had agreed. "Hello. I would like to extend my condolences. I want you to know how sorry I am to hear about the tragedies in your family."

"Yes, thank you." The girl's voice came through with much less confidence than her previous statement.

"I would like to speak to the rest of your family. To extend my condolences to them and ask them to help me with something. I'm not a reporter or police or anything. I don't want to cause any interruptions."

"Who are you?" the confidence had returned.

"My name is Vermilion Blew. Ms. Blew. And, I'm a…" Very's hands had started to shake. She had not prepared herself. Darrell had warmed her. The textbook he had lent her had emphasized preparation. "The Complete Idiot's Guide to Private Investigation" had a whole chapter on techniques of interviewing. She had highlighted the relevant passages, words and phrases like "be prepared" and "completely familiar with all the facts." What had caused this lapse of judgment? This investigator needed to think quickly, and to activate her nerves of steel.

"I'm a teacher. I'd like to speak to your family. If that is possible?" She had been a teacher, that much was true, but she wasn't anymore. And she certainly wasn't a teacher of any of the Hernandez kids. Lying was becoming habitual, was it?

"I guess so. But you have to come after school. The kids will be in school and you can't come before they get home."

"That's fine. About 3:30 or 4:00?"

"Yeah, yeah."

"See you then. Bye." Very hung up. She had jumped the first hurdle. Someone in the household had agreed to her visit.

"Have one foot in the door," Very said to Darrell. "And I owe you one. But instead of lunch today, I've brought a sandwich, I'll treat you to a sundae at Dewar's."

"Is it the same? I mean, a sundae?" Darrell stuck out his lip.

"Okay, a banana split. And a quart to take home!" Very offered. "And a box of chews. That's more than a lunch. And you were very good about that phone number and address, I'm impressed."

"Thanks, you should be. That's the one thing I'm really, really good at."

They both went back to work, stopped for a few minutes to eat sandwiches and then wrapped up work when Very suggested it was time for ice cream.

Very sneaked into the last off-street parking spot next to the store on Eye Street, while Darrell parked on the street. They met at the door under the pink awning and walked in together.

Very stood just inside the door and took a deep breath, smelling the aroma of the place; frozen metal with a heavy dollop of sugar. She knew that all good ice cream parlors smelled like this, but Dewar's smelled better, maybe because they made the stuff here as well.

Darrell stood beside her and stared. "You know, I've never actually been in here. I've eaten the ice cream, and I've been in the other store, but never this one, the mother ship as it were." He looked at the end of the counter and his eyes focused on the stag's head and his impressive rack and then at the big horn sheep, enormous horns curling around his head. He reached his hand out to caress the bright red covering of a counter stool. He hoisted himself onto it and turned to show Very a gigantic goofy grin.

"Quintessential childhood memories!" Very sat on the stool next to Darrell and said, "Menu's on the wall."

They both tilted their heads to read the offerings which consisted of a long list of flavors, both ice cream and ice milk, a long list of toppings, and another long list of shakes, malts, sundaes and banana splits. Very watched as a classic Black and Tan sundae made its appearance and was placed in front of a young woman at the end of the counter. The woman looked at it, giving reverence to its beauty, composition and impending demise at the end of her spoon.

"My mother grew up down the street and she remembers getting ice cream cones for five cents. She always complained about the prices, but she sure did like the ice cream. What are you going to have?" Very turned to Darrell who was still perusing the menu.

"That sundae is huge, I'm not sure I can eat all of that. It will send my cholesterol skyrocketing and use up all the calories for the day and in to next week. And the sugar, oh no," Darrell said with dollops of dejection.

"Okay, here's what I'm going to do. I'm having a two-scoop bowl, one of Peppermint Stick ice milk and the other of Butter Rum ice milk. You know what you can do? Just eat this instead of dinner." Very chuckled. "You know how people say, 'it was better in the old days'? Well, the Rum Butter was. It was yellow, like butter and there was a soupcon of rum in it. It was naughty, it was smooth and alluring. And then they couldn't put alcohol in food fed to children, so they renamed it Butter Rum. It still tastes good, but not like the old days. And let me tell you about the Peppermint. The color has gone weird, like some day-glo pink, but the flavor is still fantastic, my favorite, all-time favorite. What's yours?"

"I like vanilla. But I like the chocolate sauce and the peanuts and the whipped cream and the cherry on top.

But maybe you're right, ice milk." Darrell put on a sad face and stared at the menu.

Very laughed. "I've got stories about this place. I told you about my mom, but my dad grew up just a few streets over that way," Very leaned her head in the direction of the west. "And he had stories of getting free or cheap ice cream. He told me that on Saturday mornings, the neighborhood kids gathered at the back door. It cost five cents and they could eat all they wanted of the old ice cream, because they'd made a new batch or something. Can you imagine a store giving away ice cream these days? Not allowed, I'm sure."

Very ordered from the counter girl and looked over at Darrell, who spit out his decision to throw caution to the wind and ordered a Black and Gold Sundae with peanut butter topping. He avoided Very's gaze.

"I used to come here with my great-aunt. I can't imagine that she liked sitting on these stools, they are a trifle uncomfortable, but I loved the smell and the ambiance. And it was so very special to have my own ice cream sundae, not sharing it with my sister or cousin. There is this feeling of sound bouncing off the walls and floors, the squeal of children eating ice cream, the bustle of ordering chews, which kind, how much… It is my childhood, a good part. I love this place. Ah, here it comes, such a huge two scoops!"

Before they left, Very bought a box of mixed chews and a quart of ice cream for Darrell. She also got two half gallons, one vanilla and one chocolate, to go. She had a visit to make.

Chapter Fourteen: A Visit to the Hernandez Family

Very set her phone's GPS system to find the Hernandez family home. It was in East Bakersfield, the older section of town with classic street names like Niles, Monterey, Jefferson, Lincoln, Oregon, among others. She found the street and drove down, looking for street numbers and listening to her phone, talking quietly to her in her car's cup holder. The houses were all small, mostly clapboard, mostly old. Some were obviously owned by the occupants, those with yards full of plants and flowers, with well-kept lawns. No one would bother keeping up a yard unless they could afford the water bills and what kind of landlord would tell a tenant to use as much water as it took to keep the palm trees green and the roses in bloom? Some yards were so overgrown that the house was invisible from the casual driver along the street. But then the next one sported a totally bare front yard, tufts of Bermuda grass trying to reach any drop of water along the edges where a leaning post from an old chain link fence still stood, or from the next-door neighbor's largesse. Some had made attempts to claim a share of the middle class dream of a front yard by planting a few bushes along the edge of the house. Some houses had fences that blocked the driveway and were decorated with signs about vicious dogs or security cameras. There was no sign of either beyond the signs. It was a neighborhood where people knew who lived next door, knew who to watch out for, and who would watch out for them.

There were copious signs of children and pets: broken plastic tricycles in the front yards, headless dolls in the dirt, dust baths made under the bushes and trees for dogs trying to escape the heat, uncollected dog feces along the fences. And vehicles. They were everywhere. Most parking spaces along the street were unoccupied this time of day, but the driveways were full; almost all had at least one car or truck and the lawns in a few yards held more. The alleyways, where there were any, would hold more. Bakersfield was a city of cars and trucks and everyone needed one for him or herself and to give rides to the older generation whose vehicle had broken down, or was lent out to a grandchild or had been stolen and not yet replaced. The car represented not just transportation, but a generation, or a gender or the identity of a person within the community. Cars, the ultimate California identity.

And this neighborhood also represented the divide between city and county. Just driving down the streets one could tell where the city stopped and the county began. It wasn't where the people lived, because there were a lot of people who lived in this neighborhood, and the one that Very lived in. No, it was the tax base, and with it, the amenities of a city. Here, there were no cement curbs, no sidewalks, no street lights, and no city police. Just the county, the sheriff's patrols, in dark streets and alleys, and poorly serviced by garbage collection.

Very found the house and slowed down, cruising past and looking closely. Who was it that she talked to? A young woman, maybe a sister of the one who drowned. She knew enough to make sure others were at home when visitors came calling. The yard was small, and empty. Clean swept, but no grass, no plants, but also no trash or abandoned toys. Very continued and parked two doors down. The house next door sported a lawn and a big shady tree, one of those that had leaves all year round. It gave a friendly tone, not just to the house, but the neighboring houses as well.

Very parked, picked up her purse and the heavy sack of ice cream, locked her car and slowly walked back to the Hernandez home. A broken-down truck stood in what she took to be a driveway. The graveled area did not lead to a garage, so this was one of those seat-of-the-pants, ad hoc driveways, better than going all the way around to the alley to get the truck into a parking space. Chances were that there wasn't any space in the back either. She walked up to the front door. There was a miniscule porch with a tiny roof, just enough to get out of the rain. Except it so seldom rained in Bakersfield that it came across as only a suggestion of a porch. Very knocked on the door.

A scuffle ensued behind the door and soon it was jerked open by a barely teenaged boy. He looked at Very with supreme interest.

"Hi, I'm Very Blew, I called earlier. I think someone, maybe your mother, should be expecting me. I came to pay my respects. I'm so sorry for your and your family's loss." Very stood at the door, waiting for some action.

A commotion erupted behind the boy and he was elbowed out of the doorway by a girl of approximately the same age. "Yes, yes. We are expecting you. You are Ms. Blue, right, like blue skies, or blue jeans? What a nice name, very unusual. I like that. Not an everyday name. Not Hernandez-like. Too common. Oh, yes, please come in." She pushed the screen door open, which forced Very back. She stepped back and down, completely off the porch and into the sunlight of the front yard. Yes, the porch was only a suggestion. Then, Very stepped into the front room of a small house. Three kitchen chairs were tucked up under a clock and a Sacred Heart of Jesus picture on the front wall. A two-person settee took up the other wall. A much-used coffee table graced the space in front of the couch.

An older woman appeared in the doorway that led to the rest of the house. She wore a uniform blouse, blue jeans and a short apron over all. Her long dark hair spilled around her shoulders and she grabbed at it, twisting it into a bun at the back of her head. "Are you the one who called?"

"Yes, I'm Very Blew and I want to extend my condolences. I am so very sorry for your loss. Was it," Very dropped her voice, "was Maria your daughter?"

Tears pooled in the woman's eyes and she nodded. She clenched her jaw in a vain attempt to keep the tears in her eyes and not dripping down her face. "Sit down." She jerked her head towards the couch.

Very stood, unable to negotiate the next step. This was not a good idea, not a good move. Very gritted her teeth to keep from tearing up herself. "Oh," she said, holding out the bag. "I brought something and well, it needs to go into the fridge, the freezer. It's ice cream."

Mrs. Hernandez jerked her head at the two youngsters. The boy took the ice cream and the girl sat on one of the chairs. The mother jerked her head again and the young girl disappeared into the back room as well. Very listened to excited whispers and then the clink of spoons, bowls and giggles. The ice cream, it turned out, was a very good idea.

"I'm sorry to bother everyone. I realize that this isn't a very good time, mourning and all, but I am looking for information." Very stopped and looked at Mrs. Hernandez's face, trying to judge her reactions. "I know that your family was at Hart Park a week ago, the day that your daughter and cousin… went to the river."

"Went to the river," was that a new euphemism for drowning? How many other ways were there of saying "died" without saying it? Careful how these things were said; the information would not be forthcoming unless the words were correct.

"I'm looking for this woman, or rather, I'm looking for anyone who saw this woman last week. You see, she was there and I need some information about her." Very took out the best photo they had of Mouse and showed it to the woman.

Mrs. Hernandez looked at the photo and shook her head. She had allowed Very to show her the photo, but made no attempt to hold it, look at it closer or study it. "I don't know. There were lots of people at Hart Park that day. Lots."

"I have a map here, could you show me where you and your family were?" Very showed a map of Hart Park with the wide arc of the river on the north and east side. The roads were marked, as well as the big barbecue area, the restrooms and the two lakes. The woman looked at the map and tried to turn her head to orient herself. It was obvious that she didn't think of Hart Park as a map. "Well, here is the barbecue place, the big one, were you there?"

"No, but not far. It was too out in the open, I think, too hot. And other people were there, we just took a table near there. We had our own stuff anyway. I don't know where we were, just near the big table area."

"But did you see this woman? We know that she was there, not far from your family, from the place…where…"

"I don't know anything. I wasn't there. I came out with some stuff, some food and stuff, and then I left. I had to work, so I wasn't there. I wasn't there when my baby…drowned." She put her head down and began to weep, a soft blubbery escape of tears, grief, and the pain at not being there when a good mother would have been.

Very let out a soft sigh. This was hard. Maybe too hard.

Suddenly a man walked into the room. He was a short, wide man with jet black hair, going gray at the temples. He wore jeans and a soft cotton work shirt. His boots thunked on the floor as he approached his wife. He bent and spoke softly, so soft that Very could only hear that it was Spanish.

He turned to Very, "My wife wasn't there, she left early. You are looking for someone?"

Very felt weird. Had he been listening at the door? How did he know what Very wanted? "Sir, maybe you can tell me. Did you see this woman? She was there and I really need to be able to know where she was, trace her movements, find someone who saw her."

He approached Very and took the photo in his rough, calloused hands. "No, I didn't see her. I don't know anything. I was off at the bathrooms. One of the little kids wanted to go and I couldn't let them go alone and then I saw some friends and didn't come back. I didn't see anybody like this." He handed the photo back. "Maybe Mama saw something. But she doesn't speak very good English. I don't want to ask her."

Mrs. Hernandez had recovered somewhat and sat up in her place on the old couch. "Why do you want to know if we saw her?"

Very had hoped this question wouldn't come up just yet. She had hoped to have more time. "Well, you see this woman went into the river that day as well. There were a number of people that day. And we think she was there, at the river."

"But, she didn't have anything to do with us, did she?" Mrs. Hernandez asked, a hint of anxiety creeping into her voice.

Mr. Hernandez reached for the photo again. "This one? She died too? The same day? But, I remember they told us. There was another one, who drowned too, the same day, but she…she wasn't drowned. She committed suicide. This one?" He held out the photo to Very.

Very bit her lip. "Well, the police say she did. But we have reason to think she didn't. That maybe she died some other way. Maybe she did commit suicide, maybe she didn't. We are really not sure. But we are sure she was in Hart Park that day. And maybe you can give us some information about her."

Mr. Hernandez looked at the photo again. "I can't help you, I didn't see her."

Mrs. Hernandez shook her head. "Maybe the kids know something?" She looked up at her husband. "Maybe they saw her."

"The kids?" Very's voice sank. Kids weren't very perceptive. Kids were not the ones to ask. "Thanks for your time. I think…"

"She means us." The young girl who let Very in appeared at the open doorway to the back part of the house. Over her shoulder appeared her brother, two siblings if ever there were. Very suddenly recognized the voice on the phone, the one that told her to come, but wait until the kids got home. Here were the kids, after school. But where was she when she answered the phone if not at home? Precocious, perceptive, sassy smart-aleck? Maybe more than Very had bargained for.

Chapter Fifteen: The Twins

Mr. Hernandez nodded and the young girl took Very's hand. "This way, come in here, it's quieter." She led Very to a small alcove that contained a dining room table. At the moment, it was spread with books, notebooks and pencils. "Charlie, clean this up, and bring a chair for the guest." The brother turned and fetched a chair, while the girl cleared the table of the homework debris. Had she forgotten that she had commanded her brother to do this?

The boy returned with a kitchen chair and wiped it with a dishcloth that had seen cleaner days. Very took the chair, while the two children sat in the places they had been occupying.

"How's school?" Very asked, sensing the need for a neutral conversation starter.

"School's okay, you should know that. You're a teacher," the girl responded.

"How do you know that?" Very asked, a tiny jab of fear creeping into her voice.

"You said so. It was me you talked to on the phone, you know."

"I know that now. I thought it was your mother."

"Well, I told her, that you were coming. I don't think she understood. I think she thought it was something to do with school." The girl looked at Very through narrowed eyes. Two could play at this game. "You brought ice cream. Why?"

"It's polite. I came to visit."

"But Dewaaaars! That stuff is really nice, really expensive. And two cartons. Wow. Do you want some?"

"No, I had some at the store."

"I know where that is. The one across from BHS?"

"Yes, that one. How do you know Bakersfield High School?" Very looked at this young kid, so cocky, so smart-mouthed, so sure of everything.

Her brother Charlie answered, "Maria went there, she was a freshman. We would go with her sometimes after school or to games and things."

How old were these kids? Asking them wasn't a polite thing, they were too old for the "how old are you" question, but still too young to be hanging around a high school. Could she ask?

She did. "Maria went to BHS, but isn't this East Bakersfield High School territory? How did she get to go there?"

"Father Sullivan made it happen. Do you know Father Sullivan? Everybody does. He's such a good guy, looking out for everyone. He said that there are fewer gangs at BHS, EB is just so full of them, that Mary would be better off there. I don't know how, but it is something about where we live. We're not supposed to tell anybody where we live, because we don't live here, we live down the street because that's BHS, but this end of the street, well, this is EB. So, if anybody asks, we don't live here, we're just here for the night, just visiting, Mary is, that is, she was…"

"Shut up, Gabby," her brother snapped. "You talk too much."

"So your name is Gabby?" Very stifled a chuckle with a snort and bent her head.

"My name is Gabriela, but everybody calls me Gabby. And I see that you got the joke. That's a special kind of joke, you know. That one word means different things. Like I talk too much and my name is Gabriela, so that is gabby for short."

"Yeah," Very commented. "It's a pun, that special kind of joke."

"A what? A pan?" Gabby grabbed a notebook and whipped it open. "It's a what?"

Very explained the meaning, the spelling and Gabby wrote it down as the last in a long list of new words. Very peeked at the list and a short conversation ensued as to where the other words had come from.

"We're in seventh grade and maybe we're going to BHS too, when we get to high school," Carlos said, intruding into the girls' conversation.

"We're twins," Gabby contributed. "Not identical, but born on the same day. Mom said it was the last. Two at once, too many. I don't think I ever want twins. Waaaay too much trouble. Especially Charlie here."

"Maria was worse. And my name is Carlos," he retorted.

"No, she wasn't. Mary, she liked to be called Mary. And she was no trouble. She was wonderful, she was beautiful. She had spirit, she had, had, had…" Gabby bit her lip so hard a drop of blood began to ooze from her clenched teeth.

"I'm so sorry. Your sister sounds like a really nice person. You need to remember her like that. Wonderful and beautiful. She will always be full of spirit and love." Very tried to smooth over the momentary awkwardness.

Carlos hung his head shamefaced. Very looked in his direction and tried to think of something to say. "I'm sure you miss her too. It's hard to lose someone. One day they are there and the next, gone. And the best thing to do is to remember good things. If you think bad thoughts, it makes it worse. I know. My mother died last year. It was hard."

"Your mother?" Carlos said. "You're old, so your mother must have been really old!"

"Yeah, she was, really old. But you still have to remember the good parts. Even if Maria wasn't always the best, she still had good traits."

"Yeah, she liked us." Carlos hung his head.

"What he means," a recovered Gabby said, "was that some members of this family resent us. That we are so many, that there were two of us and we eat too much and we wear too many clothes, and we take up too much space. If our Mom hadn't had twins, but just one baby, or if one of us would have died when we were born, then there would be more for the rest."

"But Maria knew that we are special. Twins are special." Carlos looked across the table at his twin and crinkled his nose at her. She crinkled back.

"But, you have to do your own work, teacher said. And she said that next year, you're going to be in a different class, so I can't do your work for you." Gabby crossed her arms and scowled at her brother.

"I can do my own, don't worry. Or I can find someone else to help me. My brother, so there." Carlos sat back and scowled.

The squabbling twins were getting Very farther and farther from her intentions here. What would it take to bring them back around to the awful day and Very's burning question? Maria, she needed to ask about Maria again. Mary, Gabby said that she liked to be called Mary.

"So, how did Mary like Bakersfield High? You know, 'Once a Driller…'"

Gabby jumped up and threw her hands in the air, "'Always a Driller.' Yeah, Mary liked it, she loved it. She wanted to be a cheerleader; she even tried out, but she didn't make it. She was always such a dreamer."

"You mean she wasn't born here? She came later?"

"No, she wasn't that kind of Dreamer. No, no, Mary was really, really American, she was born here. No, what I meant was that she always dreamed of being a great dancer, and a singer. She could be anything. She was beautiful and talented." Gabby leaned in towards Very and said in a conspiratorial whisper. "She was going to be a star."

Carlos snorted from his side of the table. "No, she wasn't. She was nothing. She couldn't sing, she was too skinny to be a dancer. But you are right, she was a dreamer. Dreaming big stupid dreams. She was never going to be a star. And neither are you."

Gabby stood. "Yes, I am. I'm going to be a star, just like Marvelous Mary. Or, as she liked to call herself, Mag Mary. That's Magnificent Mary. She is somebody. She's talented, she's going to make it." Gabby was shouting in desperation.

"Was, was, was. She's dead. She's nothing now." Carlos' eyes filled with tears as he shouted back at his twin sister.

"She still is. As long as I remember, she still is. She would have been fabulous. Better than Selena." Gabby's voice was hard, sharp, insistent and full of truth.

"Tell me about her," Very said gently, looking from one to the other.

Gabby reached for her purse, hung over the back of her chair. She dug into the wallet and pulled out two small photos. "Here, this is Mag Mary."

Very saw a pretty girl with long, curly dark hair, looking directly into the camera. She smiled, but didn't show her teeth. Her skin was a warm brown, with delicate make-up that made her cheeks shine and her eyes sparkle with a hint of rebel. Very looked up at Gabby and saw the same delicate bone structure and mischievous eyes. The second photo was taken in a cheerleader's outfit, showing her bare legs with arms tucked into her waist and her saucy attitude. A hopeful freshman cheerleader.

"You're right. She was set to be a fabulous dancer. How old was she?"

"Fourteen, she was going to be fifteen this year. So mature."

"Was she going to have a quinceanera?" Very blushed at her butchery of the word, but figured that Gabby knew what she meant.

"Of course, she had it all planned out. She chose the colors and she was working on her dress. Red, she was going to have a red dress."

"She was not!" Carlos stood and tried to tower over Gabby. "She was NOT having a red dress. It's not allowed. Pink, it's got to be pink. Or maybe white, but red, no!"

"No, she had it all planned. She was going to have what she wanted."

"Papi was never going to let her. She was crazy." Carlos sat.

"Were you going to be in the ceremony?" Very asked, aware they were talking about plans and a celebration that was never going to be.

"Yes." "No." They said looking at each other.

"I was," Gabby answered. "I was definitely going to be in the ceremony, one of her damas. But this one, this Carlos brother, he was refusing. Didn't want to wear the suit, didn't want to practice the dances. He'd have to dance, with a girl, and he didn't want to. But I was going to dress up, and join with all the other girls. We had started practicing. We were going to be great."

"But not anymore, no quinceanera now." Carlos said under his breath, but loud enough to be heard. "Anyway, where was it going to be, in our backyard?"

"No, we're going to have it in a nice restaurant, in a nice place, a big place, a beautiful place, with lots of flowers and all the traditional things, the bouquet and the doll and the shoes, the big limo, the videos, the best dancing, everything. She was practicing you know. She was going to be just like Selena, she was practicing her song and she is going to sing it herself. She is going to BE Selena!"

"Selena's dead!" shouted Carlos. "Maria's dead. It's not going to happen."

Gabby sat still, her eyes red, but her mouth firmly held back the tears. The switch into present tense was a giveaway, a dip, not quite a fall, into a fantasy that Maria was not dead. A dream that she would live on, if only Gabby kept her alive. Her spirit was alive; her sister would make sure of that.

"She's going to wear Selena's dress, her red dress, her special dress. She is going to get someone to do her make-up so she looks just like Selena. And then she's going to come out from behind the stage and come on and dance and sing just like Selena. She's going to sing Selena's song."

"Mami won't let her do that! It's stupid, it's, it's…not right. She's just a little girl, she shouldn't be so sexy." Carlos took on his sister's intensity, and verb tense.

"Mary's going to do what she wants to do. She is going to be a star. She is going to be famous, so famous she won't even know you!" Gabby spat out the words.

"Listen, guys, I don't want to interfere in a family disagreement. I think it's great that Mary, or Maria, was going to do wonderful things. I'm sure both of you would have been proud of her. She sounds like a high-spirited, adventurous young woman. She obviously knew her own mind. That's something to be proud of. She must have been a wonderful sister to both of you." Very reached out her hands to both Gabby and Carlos. Gabby took one. Carlos looked at it, but shied away from some imagined impropriety. It wasn't a hug for heaven's sake. Very let it sit on the table, available, if wanted.

"She was a good sister," mumbled Carlos.

"She was the best. She was…"

"Your only sister," Carlos concluded.

Very pulled out the photo of Mouse and put it on the table between the twins. "I would really like to ask you a question. I know that it was a sad day, and you might not remember this, but I am looking for anyone who saw this woman that Saturday. She was at Hart Park, we know that, but we are not sure exactly where and we want to know if anyone saw her?" She placed the photo down and took out the other photo, taken from farther away, and not quite as clear. The twins were doing a good job of distracting her with all their talk of Maria, but maybe it was a good way of gaining their confidence. Very waited while they looked at the photos.

Carlos pushed the photos away from himself. He looked at Very, intensity and interest in his eyes. "Maybe Maria saw her."

Chapter Sixteen: What Maria Saw

Very's hand went quiet as it rested on the photo. "Why do you say that?"

"She left and went to the river," Carlos said.

"How do you know this woman went to the river?"

"Didn't she drown too, the same day? So, maybe if she was at the river, then Maria saw her." Carlos paused.

"Yeah, she did drown, yeah, that day, she died too." Very stopped her mouth running on, unable to form the right words.

"I didn't see nothing." Carlos sat and again crossed his arms.

Gabby had been sitting motionless, her eyes still brimming with tears, but now she came alive. "Give me that picture." She stared at it, then asked, "What was she wearing?"

Very searched her brain. "She had on jeans and a yellow tee shirt. She had on white shoes and maybe a hat."

"I don't remember anyone like that." Carlos repeated his earlier denial of knowledge. He scrunched up his nose into his eyes and cocked his head. "What kind of car was she driving?"

Very sat, a bit startled at the question. "A white one, a Toyota, not old, not new."

"That doesn't help very much, everybody's got one of those," came Carlos' answer.

Gabby had been looking carefully at the photos, "I think, maybe, I did see her, but there were lots of people that day." She pushed the photos back at Very.

Very sat and watched the twins, both taking peeks at the photos, sliding their eyes sideways to get a better look. Why didn't they look directly at the photos? Was it because she had died too? Too much death, too much looking at the face of a dead person could bring back memories? Or was it because if they recalled her, they needed to recall the tragic events of that day all over again? She needed to be careful, tread very, very lightly, use the calmest of words she could muster.

"After Maria went missing, maybe she was there?" She had said it, she had said Maria's name and had used a euphemism for dying. Would that be enough to elicit more information? Knowing that this woman was dead, like their sister, maybe that could cause them to dredge up anything about her.

"Maybe Maria saw her," repeated Carlos.

"Charlie, why would you say that?" Gabby then turned to Very. "Mary went swimming. So maybe she saw her there, at the river."

"Mary, I mean Maria, went swimming. When was that?" Very began to feel confused. Did Mary go swimming or not? She drowned, so of course she went into the water, went swimming.

"No," said Carlos. "Yes," said Gabby.

Very waited. Someone was going to explain; the air of denial and obfuscation hung heavily.

Finally, Gabby blurted out, "She wanted to. She didn't bring her swimming suit, so Mom told her she couldn't go. She was mad."

"She couldn't go in her clothes, Mami wouldn't allow it. She had to wear a proper swimming suit, not clothes, not one of those bikini thong things, and not in her underwear. Mami said it was inapp… not a nice thing for a young girl. You know, she didn't think she was a kid anymore, but Mami was afraid for her. She was acting too old. And she wouldn't do what anyone told her to do." Carlos was firm.

"That's exactly why she would go. She did what she wanted. She never let Mom, or anyone else, tell her what she could do. She was free and did like she said she would." Gabby almost shouted.

"Like the red dress?" Very asked.

Gabby looked at Very, "Yeah, like the red dress."

"So, did she go swimming?" Very felt confused, very confused. Where was this conversation going? A waste of time to ask kids, they kept changing their answers, or maybe they were the answers to different questions. "Of course, she went swimming."

"Yeah, she drowned, didn't she?" Carlos said quietly.

"Did she go in her clothes? Her mother told her not to, but she went swimming in her clothes?" Very asked, puzzled at the obfuscating answers coming from the twins.

"What do you think?" Gabby asked her.

These answers that turned into questions were not getting her closer to finding out what happened to

Mouse. She sat back and let the air clear. The twins sat looking down, trying to avoid her questions.

"The reason why I'm asking this question is because we believe this woman was near the place where your sister drowned and we are concerned about how she was feeling that day. Her name is Michelle and we know that she drowned, but not at that place, she went further up the river and then she…died. We want to know, that is, her sister and I, want to know if anyone saw her and can give us an idea about what she was like that day. Was she happy or sad or something else. So, if you saw her, we want to know what you saw. So, do you think Maria saw her? Really?"

"Maybe she killed her!" Carlos blurted out.

Very looked at Carlos with fear and suspicion. Who was 'she' and who was 'her'? Very waited a full ten seconds, "What do you mean?"

Carlos hung his head, "Nothing, I don't mean nothing."

"Anything. You don't mean anything," Gabby corrected her brother.

"Shut up!" Carlos shouted in return.

"Sorry, I don't mean to cause you pain or disrupt your mourning. I just want to know if you saw anything. That's all." Very began to reach for the photos which still lay on the table between the siblings.

"Maybe I did, I don't remember," Carlos said. He hung his head and closed his eyes. Maybe he was trying to recall or picture Mouse in the scene? Or was he only trying to escape the scene of his sister's death?

Very looked at Gabby for confirmation or an alternative answer.

"Maybe my brother saw her, but he's gone. I don't know how you can ask him." Gabby sat, not looking at Very.

"You have another brother?"

Carlos answered. "Yeah, two."

Very waited. Let them tell the story in their own time.

Gabby couldn't wait. "My brother was there, that day, my other one. And maybe he saw her, maybe he knows something."

"What might he know? Where is he now? Can I talk with him?" Very said.

"Pedro's gone. I think maybe, everything that day. Well, he's gone and I don't know where. Who tells us anything?" Carlos added.

"Petey's been a bit…" Gabby started.

"Don't call him that. He's Pedro, or you can call him Pepe. Pepe is our name for him. He's grown up. He's eighteen and it's time for him to go." Carlos sat up straighter. "And now, there is more room. I don't have to share with those big guys. Hector's gone and Pedro. Now, well…"

"How can you say it is time for him to go? He didn't graduate. You're not grown up if you don't graduate." Gabby stated this with utter conviction of the righteous.

"Who says? That's stupid. He has a girlfriend and maybe she's going to have his baby. And he's got a tattoo."

"He doesn't!" Gabby's mouth hung open in surprise. "Pop will kill him!"

Carlos leaned forward and lowered his voice and said in a conspiratorial whisper, "It's a '13.' You know what that means?"

Gabby's face said everything she felt. Fear. Surprise. Anxiety.

Very said very quietly, so as not to alert the rest of the household. "Gangs?"

Carlos looked knowingly directly at Very and nodded his head slightly. "And that Hector…"

"Do you know where I can find him, Pedro, that is? To ask if he saw this woman?" Very asked.

Both looked stubbornly down at the table, at the photographs lying there. Finally, Gabby looked up, touching one corner of a photo. "Sorry, I can't remember her. There were a lot of people there." Gabby leaned forward and whispered like a conspirator. "But if she was there, maybe Mary saw here. Maybe that's why she left, she felt safe with a woman around." Gabby looked down at the table and twirled the picture of Mouse around.

"Mary left? When? Where did she go?" Very tried to keep her voice from becoming a grating, angry one. Why were these kids playing around? Did they know something, or didn't they? And why toy with the facts, or the suppositions of where Mary was?

"She went swimming," Carlos stated in a flat voice. "We told you that, everyone knows that. She drowned."

"Where did she go swimming? Did she go by herself? Did she have a swimsuit? Did she go in her clothes? Did you see her go?" Very felt frustrated by the questions with no answers. She waited for some sort of hint or clue to these answers.

"Was your friend really nice?" Gabby asked in a bright voice. Deflecting the questions by asking another question, this Gabby was one smart cookie. Needed to be watched.

Very was backed into a corner. Now, was she going to tell Gabby the truth, that she had never met Mouse, or was she going to continue the charade? But was it a charade? Mouse would have been a friend, maybe.

"I think you could call her that, really nice. I think she would try to be…protective of a younger woman."

"Yeah, Mary would've like that. An older woman, not her mother, not always telling her, 'you can't do this, you can't do that.'" Gabby smiled as she got into the mother talk. "'You can't have a red dress for your quince, too old for you. You can't have fourteen damas, too many. You can't have a grand party. A restaurant, a ballroom, you can't do that.'"

"It never woulda happened. Never. The dress, the party, the quince, it was never gonna happen. None of it," Carlos grumbled.

Gabby flew to her feet. She planted both hands on the table and shouted at her brother across the table. "Yes, yes, it was going to happen. It has to happen. It's her right. It's her right as a girl. She was going to be fifteen. She's a Mexican girl. It's her right to have a quince, she can't grow up without it. Her family owes her. It's always been that way, fifteen and you have a quince. You can't deny a girl her quince!"

Behind Very the door flew open and a deep powerful voice said, "She's dead. No quince."

Very turned around and would have quaked if she wasn't so startled. Standing in the doorway was one of the biggest men she had ever met. He was fat, but he was also superbly muscular. His torso fit the door frame and brushed against the door jamb. He was the size and shape of the sumo wrestler Very had met in Japan. Human, but only just. He had been shaved bald, although the black hair on his head stood out against the pale scalp. His eyebrows hung over his eyes, creating a hawk-like cast to his face. His broad nose sat above thick red lips, that glistened with a sheen of moisture. Cheeks bulging with fat and flesh belied the strength in his taut gaze.

A camouflage colored undershirt, cut out to expose his arms, revealed huge well-defined muscles, too well-defined to be natural. His legs stood like tree trunks; a pair of shorts revealed his massive thigh muscles. His feet were clad in running trainers split at the sides. Feet too big to fit into a normal pair of shoes, even big ones.

The twenty-something man stood holding his body in readiness, to fight, to flee, to stand his ground, whatever life was going to throw at him. An aura surrounded him, a force field that encompassed the people in the room with him and anyone who attempted to penetrate it wouldn't stand a chance to defy whatever he wanted. A guardian, a fighter, a protector, an annihilator? All at once?

He waited for a reaction from the three in the dining room. Very waited for an introduction or an explanation.

"She's dead. No quince," he repeated.

Chapter Seventeen: Brother Javier

Gabby stood. "My brother Javier, call him Javi."

Very sat tongue-tied. A small tremor went through her body, but she soldiered on. "Hello."

A long pause, then, "Hi."

"I just wanted to ask," began Very.

"I know why you're here. C'mon, let's leave the kids to their homework. They need to get working." He narrowed his eyes, the hawk's hood exaggerated, and pointedly stared at the two.

They quickly picked up pens and opened their books.

Javi jerked his head, indicating Very should follow him. They entered the kitchen, currently occupied by two women banging pots and cutting boards, with food stacked on table tops. They ignored Javi and Very as Javi led the way through and out the back door. Two steps led down to a bare strip of ground, a small garage on one side, a fence along the other.

A dog house sat next to the fence and upon Javi entering the back yard, a large dun-colored dog leaped out. Two sharp barks greeted Very. Then a wild lunge was truncated by a chain that rattled on its way out of the dog house. Javi's right arm snapped out and a fat index finger pointed directly at the hound. "Dog," he said with quiet authority.

Dog stood down. He quickly dropped onto his haunches and lowered his eyes.

Very had stopped and now stood rooted to a spot on the bottom step. Javi kept going, walking slowly towards the garage. He looked over his shoulder and nodded to Very. "Dogs are pack animals. They know alpha. I'm alpha. You're safe. This way." He continued walking towards the small one-car garage. He opened a door and stepped inside. Very followed.

The wide door to the alley was open, and fresh air blew in. Used gym equipment sat on one half of the small space and the other half was taken up with a machine of such glorious magnificence, that Very drew an involuntary breath that stuck in her chest.

It was big, like Javi. Every inch of chrome shone, reflecting from the overhead light and from the open doors to the outside. Black leather, faux leather actually, panier bags hung from the back, just below the high extra seat. The seats were all covered in shiny black leather decorated with chrome studs in neat rows. The handlebars were tilted to the left and high mirrors rose like insect antenna from the shiny bars. There was not a single speck of dust, not a particle of rust anywhere.

Very bent forward and stared at the insignia. She gingerly reached out her fingers and caressed the wings and name, clearly-seen. "It's real. It's the real thing. It's a Harley."

A low rumble preceded the chuckle that arose from Javi, who stood back and let Very admire his machine. "Yeah, it's real."

"It is magnificent, just a wondrous, marvelous thing. I'm impressed." Very turned to Javi and let him see her wide smile.

His face crunched up, his eyes disappeared in the folds of flesh of his cheeks and a grin spread slowly from his mouth. He nodded silently, accepting the praise.

He strolled to the back of the garage and pulled out a kitchen chair that had been stuck in a corner. "Have a seat."

Very felt that she couldn't refuse, although this was the only place to sit in the crowded space. It didn't match any of the chairs inside, but they didn't match each other either. Which was more important, some mismatched kitchen chairs or a superb, shiny motorcycle?

Very sat, and then reached to pull out the photos from her bag. As she bent down, she noticed a cot stuck into a cubby at the very back of the garage. Neat corners were revealed as a clean white sheet showed at the top. "You sleep out here as well?"

"Yeah, quieter, some privacy. Too crowded in the house."

"Those are very nice corners."

"Military. I was in the Navy for four years."

"Yeah, I learned those corners at Girl Scout camp during the summer. A good skill to know." Very smiled again at Javi.

He smiled back, leaning on some of the gym equipment in a familiar way. He was the alpha human here, but, like the dog, Very was willing and able to allow him the designation. After all, she was on his territory, she was the one who had invaded.

She pulled the photos from her bag and held them out to Javi.

"Don't pay attention to those two. Maria wanted a party. But we couldn't pay for it. Look at this place. Do you think there is money around for that? And she wanted the whole thing. She wanted…too much."

Very looked around the garage. The gym equipment was shabby, the garage was shabby, the backyard, the front yard, all needed work. She looked wide eyed at the Harley.

Javi saw her glance. "Well, yeah. Got out of the Navy, had some money. But now, well, chrome polish and elbow grease are cheap. Can't afford the gas to drive her anywhere."

Very stopped looking at the machine, now a useless piece of vanity. Even if Javi sold it, would it be enough for the night of partying? The clothes, the food, the place, the gifts? Five thousand, ten thousand, how much did a quinceanera cost? She knew that sponsors, friends and relatives, helped a lot, but that created obligations that stretched into the limitless future. An undertaking of this massive nature could not be committed to lightly by a family of limited means. And there was another girl, waiting in the wings for her quinceanera in just a few years' time. Would Gabby make it to her quince?

"But I guess that every fifteen-year-old wants her quince," Very said. "She wants a day for herself. It's tradition."

"Not our tradition. Not my mother, not my grandmother, not my aunts, none of my cousins. None had it. It's just here, in America. It's just the American dream. A quince. American. No." Javi grumbled.

"But I thought it was an old Mexican, an Aztec tradition." Very said very timidly. After all, what did she know about it? The girls at school had talked and a couple gave presentations about their upcoming parties for a class project. She had prided herself as being well versed in the traditions surrounding the custom. And yes, very American, but what was this pushback really about? Was it the money?

"In Mexico, the girls get married at fifteen, not have a big party that bankrupts the family. It's for the rich, the people who think it gives status to throw a big party." Javi fell silent after this pronouncement. It was his last word on the topic.

Brittle silence hung in the air for a full minute. Very clutched the photos.

"You have a question for me?" Javi broke the quiet of the late afternoon.

Very held out the photos. "On that Saturday, you know, the day of the…tragedy, did you see this woman? The reason why I am asking is that she died that day as well." Very gave an explanation of Mouse's sister's request, not mentioning that it was a paid request. It would not be a good thing with this man to reveal the monetary nature of the transaction and why she was doing this. When she finished, she looked up at Javi and noted his reaction to the photos.

Javi squinted and looked closely. "What kind of car was she driving?"

What was it about these men, this fixation on cars? Cars, and trucks, were the modes of transportation in Bakersfield. The public transportation system was crap, even when she was young, the buses ran only to the major places in Bakersfield. If you were poor, well, the bus didn't come by your place. You'd have to walk half a mile to find one, and then go downtown and transfer, if you wanted to go across town. Very's mother talked about the street car, but the tracks had been torn up long ago. Fewer and fewer rode the buses and now, well, pathetic was the word used. But cars, and more and more lately, trucks, took over the needs of transportation in the town. Besides, why ride the bus, when you have a big truck to take you anywhere you want. Status symbol? Oh yeah, big time. The bigger, the noisier, the more monster-looking it was, the better for generating prestige.

Very repeated her description of the car. "I know, every other car in Bakersfield is the same."

"Yeah, I saw her, I think, maybe. But just for a minute. Just saw." He handed the photo back to Very.

This was the first bit of information that she had received that confirmed what she had suspected, that Mouse had been to Hart Park on Saturday, the day of the drownings. But how much of a confirmation was it?

"About what time was that?" Very ventured timidly.

"Afternoon."

"Early or late, a time?"

"Later."

"Where was this? Where were you? Where was she? Close, or far away. What was she doing?" Very held her breath, hoping Javier would answer the questions, preferably all of them, but two or three would be good.

"It was by the road. And she was heading away, walking towards a car. That's why I asked what kind of car."

"Was she walking towards her car?"

"Couldn't tell."

"How was she? Fine, agitated?" Very needed more information, not just these snippets of vague sightings.

"She was walking. I was looking for my sister. She had gone, disappeared."

"And so you were looking for her. She went swimming, didn't she?"

"They said so. That's why I was looking."

"Because she wasn't supposed to go in her clothes and she didn't bring her swimming suit?"

"The water was cold. She could swim, they all can swim. It was hot, but the water was too cold."

"So, you went looking for her? Was your brother Pedro there as well?"

"He was somewhere. I don't know where he was." Javi turned away and shrugged. "I don't really know where he is now. Gone."

"That's what the kids said. Do you think maybe Pedro saw this woman?"

Javi turned and looked at Very, his eyes narrowing. "I have no idea. I don't know what he saw or didn't."

Very sat still, trying to let the air clear and become calm. It hadn't been a calm discussion; Very asked too many difficult questions. Had she forgotten that the family was in mourning? Maybe they really, really didn't want to talk about it.

"What about Hector, your cousin? Maybe he saw her, but now…"

"He's dead." Javier's tone of voice was like that when he had talked about Maria's death. It was final. Nothing could be done. And of course, no one would know if he had seen her either.

"The kids said that maybe Maria had seen her. But we can't ask her either." Very stopped. Was Javi willing and able to talk more now? Maybe later?

"What difference does it make if Maria saw her or not? She's gone, your friend is gone. They are all gone. Dead or run off. Who cares? Now? It's too late." Javi stood with a finality that Very recognized as end-of-interview.

"Thank you for your time. I want to extend my condolences one more time. For your sister Maria, for your cousin. It has all been so tragic."

"My sister Maria," whispered Javier, crossing himself. "Hector, my cousin…" He spat on the floor and used his foot to erase the spit, grinding it into the cement with a vehemence that was unnerving.

Javier looked at Very. "It's gone you know."

Frightened, Very croaked out, "What, what is gone?"

"The ice cream. Didn't you hear the noise? They came, it's like a bird flying up and down the street, letting everybody know. They ate it all up."

Very looked puzzled.

"The whole neighborhood came. They all wanted their share. They wanted to know who brought it. Greedy."

"Maybe the neighborhood knows your family is generous, that of course you would share."

"Vultures. You know vultures? They look for the sick, the weak, the dead ones. They fly around and around. Big ugly birds."

"No, I'm sure you're wrong. I'm happy to bring ice cream to everybody."

Javi let out a breath of pent up air. He closed his eyes and forced himself to relax: his face, his hands, his massive thighs. He opened his eyes and looked at Very.

"Maybe you're right. 'Something sweet takes away the bitterness.' That's what my abuelita says."

Chapter Eighteen: Retracing Mouse's Movements

"And who do you think I met going into the house as I left? Father Sullivan."

Very was seated across from Darrell in the office. She had arrived early, unable to sleep late, and unable to get interested in any of the chores that she should have been doing, such as sorting through old magazines, organizing cupboards and cleaning out her mother's junk.

"Gabby, the twelve-year-old, had mentioned they knew him, helped get Maria into Bakersfield High School instead of EB, too many gangs at the local school, he said. And presumably they are Catholics, so it should not be too surprising that they are acquainted. I wonder if it would be worthwhile to talk to him? Probably not, unless he was there at Hart Park that day. As Gabby said, everybody knows him."

"And does he know everybody?" Darrell said. "Does he know our Michelle, the one we are working on here?"

"Don't know. He could, I suppose. It's not outside the possible. But…not probable. Okay, leave that."

"Unless she was a parishioner of his." Darrell's chair squeaked as he twirled back and forth. "That's not outside the realm of possibility. Maybe we could ask her sister. Often, troubled people turn to the church or to religious organizations for help."

"But does that really sound like her? Has anyone even breathed a word of 'getting religion' or 'joining the moonies' at all? Ooph, I wish I could figure that one out."

"Well, if she didn't turn to religion, what did she do?" Darrell said.

"Don't forget the therapist. She had been seeing a therapist for a while, but she quit. Hmmm? Did she quit the therapist to get religion?"

"No sign of that."

"Everyone has said that she committed suicide. No one was surprised. But here we are, trying to prove the opposite?" Very pounded the chair arm in frustration.

They sat in silence for a few minutes, both alternately staring into space, drumming fingers, doodling on various scraps of paper.

Finally, Very spoke. "Let's make notes, I mean, thinking type of notes. Pros and cons, for example, or a Venn diagram. Anything to move us forward on this. I know, a mind map. Start with Mouse in the center, then add suicide, and other ideas, sister, uh, uh. I don't want to write murder down on a piece of paper, I can say the word, but putting it down, writing it, is too creepy. Skip that. How about a time line? We can start with one year ago, for example. Like this." Very took a clean sheet of lined paper from her notebook and wrote at the top "April."

"We can start with this. A year ago, she was working, had a car, her own apartment."

"She was seeing a therapist for the purpose of exploring her troubled past," Darrell added.

"Well, that is something of note, but that had been going on for a while." Very wrote it down. Then she added May, June, July, Aug, Sep, Oct, Nov, Dec, one to each of the following lines. "Anything else happen in that time frame? Anything change?"

"It was February that she quit her job, the end of the month."

"And it was at the same time, give or take, that she stopped seeing her therapist. Now, I had just assumed that it was money problems that caused her stop seeing her therapist. It happened out of the blue, according to the woman she was seeing, just a phone call to say that it was the end. It was my impression that the therapist didn't care much. If Mouse didn't have the money to pay, then she was happy to let Mouse go. When I said it was something of note to say that she was exploring her troubled past, I meant it. Can't all of us spend many, many hours in a therapist or a psychiatrist's chair scrutinizing our previous sufferings? Doesn't everyone have a boatload of anxieties from their not-quite-forgotten former life to complain about? 'I was picked on by bullies,' 'my sister was prettier than me and everyone would comment on it,' 'my nose has always been too big and so I was never able to get girlfriends or boyfriends or whatever.'"

Darrell's hands flew to his nose and covered it protectively. His eyes fluttered to Very's face and revealed fear and self-loathing.

"Darrell, I wasn't talking about you! There is absolutely nothing wrong with your nose. It is the perfect size, it is a wonderful shape, it is the epitome of masculine beauty and grace." Very leaned back and rolled her eyes exaggeratedly.

Darrell slowly lowered his hands and made a moue, twisting his mouth in a vain attempt to lessen the size and alter the shape of his proboscis.

"See what I mean? A perfect example of someone who could spend ages and ages with a therapist, trying to right a perceived wrong. However, Mouse had something that wasn't in balance. Something about sexual harassment. On the other hand, show me a woman who has never been harassed by some dirty old man, had some guy expose himself to her, had a heavy hand on a shoulder, or worse. We have all had it done to us; we don't like it, but we mostly move on. Mostly." Very stopped. A youthful brush with a neighborhood boy had upset her, but she moved on. Did not forget, but moved on.

"Mouse forged ahead. She quit her job, stopped seeing her therapist, bought a notebook, started writing poetry. She was making changes, striding ahead. That doesn't sound suicidal to me. Does it?" Very turned to Darrell.

"Something happened to her, it was either murder or suicide. It couldn't have been an accident."

"Murder." Very said it, tried to feel the weight of it. "I've never seen a murdered person. It doesn't happen very often, does it? I've known a few, but the actual dead person, no. I believe that I have been trying to prove she didn't commit suicide. And it just keeps coming back to…suicide. So, now we need to rethink and try out the murder angle."

"We've tried asking about enemies or who would have wanted her gone and keep coming up with nothing.

She didn't have enemies. So, a casual encounter? An opportunistic attack?" Darrell mused, tapping his pen on the side of the desk, as if the sound or the motion would stimulate thoughts.

"How do you drown yourself by suicide?" Very's mind wandered away from the topic at hand. "I remember seeing a Victorian movie where someone sewed rocks into the hem of her dress and she walked into the sea. Just kept walking. I don't see Mouse sewing rocks into the hem of her jeans. Wait, what were the marks on her body? A huge hole in the back of her head, strangulation?"

"The autopsy report is not available, but what we do know is that there were signs of bruising, probably from rocks in the river, and that there was water in her lungs, a sign of drowning. But the rest of it? Unknown. Remember, she had been in the river for three days. That is, of course, if she went in on Saturday."

"So, she parks her car at the little parking place. There are some big rocks there, aren't there? Like a shelf." Very looked at the ceiling, trying to picture the place. "The current is very swift there, because the river narrows a bit."

"And the water is very cold. She could have jumped into the river and opened her mouth. She could have let the water carry her away."

"Don't," Very said, shivering. "I don't really want to think about it." She rubbed her arms where goosebumps had risen.

They both stopped and listened to the traffic outside on 17th Street. The humdrum stop and go of cars was soothing, mundane and everyday.

"Javi said he saw her, he was pretty definite. The kids were hesitant, not sure. Javi said he saw her in the late afternoon, walking away from the river. He was looking for Maria then. We know that the tape was where it happened. Well, moderately sure. I mean, what else could it be but the place where Maria and Hector went into the river? I forgot to ask if he was with Hector. Oh no, I didn't forget to ask. I couldn't ask. You should have seen his reaction to Hector. He spit on the floor and wiped it out with his foot, like squashing a bug. But maybe they were together, looking for Maria. And then they saw her, needing help. And Hector went in and drowned and Javi couldn't save him."

"Why didn't Javi drown too?" Darrell asked.

"Because Javi could swim, presumably Hector couldn't. You remember, Hector was from LA. They don't learn how to swim. No place in East L.A. But Javi was in the Navy, he could swim, and he told me they could all swim in his family. They still have swimming lessons in some pools in Bakersfield. But if the water was really cold, it wouldn't take much for a young girl to get in trouble and drown. But…"

Darrell looked at Very's face where sadness had come over it.

"What if," Very started. "What if Mouse and Maria were together? What if Maria wanted to go in, to prove something and Mouse tried to dissuade her, but Maria went anyway? What if…"

"But you said that Javi saw Mouse walking away, walking towards her car. Why would she have done that if there was a girl drowning in the river?"

"Okay, okay, you're right. Let's get back to the timeline. Mouse was turning over a new leaf, she was looking for something new. Maybe she was just exploring a lot of different options. Let's look at this map again." Very spread out the map of Hart Park on a corner of her desk. She took out the notebook that Mouse had left on the front seat of her car, along with the copy of the torn-out piece of paper with the suicide note. Then, Very got out her own notebook and the jottings she had made of the interviews she had done. "Look, she is here," Very pointed to a place on the map close to where they had found the log and place to sit that matched the scribblings in the notebook. "Okay, here is the place. When is the time?"

Ten minutes later, she threw up her hands. "No way to tell exactly when she was there. Late afternoon."

Darrell said, "The alarm was raised at 5:05pm. All hell must have broken loose after that. Presumably, she left before then, otherwise she wouldn't have been seen walking to her car, it would have been…something else. Pedro Hernandez made the call. He said it was a possible drowning, but he didn't say who or how many."

"Pedro called, not Javier?" Very stopped and inhaled.

"Javier had been in the water, maybe was still in the water. Perhaps he told Pedro to call. It was later that they began to look for two people. Or maybe by the time the sheriff arrived, they had decided that two people were missing. You know, the whole episode was messy." Darrell sighed in frustration.

"Aren't they always? One minute the person is here, the next they are gone. Who was doing what, who saw what? You did say that there is ongoing investigation about these drownings?"

Darrell drew a deep breath and exhaled. "I really didn't want you to get involved with this Hernandez family. I know it looks as though they have given you some information, but there is a gang element in this."

"I know," Very said. "Pedro, the eighteen-year-old dropout, has a '13' tattooed on his arm."

"And Hector, the cousin, is from LA."

"Darrell, are you seriously going to tell me that Hector, the cousin, the poor guy who drowned in the Killer Kern, is a gang member, just because he's from LA? Of the millions of people who live there, how many belong to a gang? Half of one percent, less? Really, Darrell, why do you want to tar and feather him? Poor guy."

"Just saying."

"That relationship. Javier, Hector, Pedro, Maria. But, what does this have to do with Michelle? We need to go back to the scene, we need to check it out again."

"Can we have coffee first?" Darrell pleaded.

"Okay. Hart Park is not going anywhere. Caffeine first."

They sat in companionable silence while the coffee brewed. When the smell filled the air, Very ostentatiously breathed deeply. She collected the cups and left to wash them in the sink in the ladies' room. When she returned, she found Darrell with the door of the tiny fridge open and a look of consternation on his face.

"No cream, no milk, only sugar, I'm afraid."

"Sugar it is."

Very and Darrell shared the task of preparing the cups of coffee and then sat in silence while they drank. It was nice that neither felt the need of conversation during the break and was a strange bond that weirdly, brought them together. They could sit quietly, work or whatever, and not feel the need of mindless chit-chat.

When they had finished their coffee, Very gathered the cups and maker and went off to wash them. Darrell cleaned the office surfaces of that day's and previous day's round mug stains. When Very returned, Darrell announced, "I'll drive."

They drove up Chester to 34th Street where Darrell turned right, then left onto Union Avenue. He followed the wide street and eased off on the right-hand side, gaining altitude and curving around to Panorama Drive. To the left was Panorama Park, the thin strip of ground at the top of the bluffs that was the most popular walking path on the east side of town. Already, cars were lining the north side of the street, and by six in the evening, it would be full, no more parking. Very shuddered as she remembered her last trip over the edge of the bluffs to the river below. She had been chased by a drug-addled killer who had made the mistake of confessing the crime. At that time, Very had outrun him, but it had a cost. Even though she lived only a block from the park and had walked the footpath for daily exercise, she had not returned to the park in seven months. She looked at the path, some new landscaping, and the crowds. Maybe it was time to return, overcome the fear, put the past behind her. Maybe.

At the corner of Mount Vernon, Darrell made a left turn onto the precipitous drive down to the base of the bluffs. Very tried hard not to say anything, but she pressed the floor with her right foot, trying to slow the car down as it swooshed down the hill. Darrell had to brake near the bottom as the accumulation of speed and daring-do had finally unnerved him. Very let her breath out.

The roller-coaster ride out to the park was more fun, Darrell maintaining a fast pace, but not dare-devil. The hillsides had already turned golden as the heat had dried up the winter green of the grass. Global warming had become local. This was not even June, and already summer had come to the Valley. Even though there had been a late rain, it had not dropped enough moisture to force new growth before the inevitable dry of summer. Even the winters were warmer. Tule fog rarely invaded the city any more, and there were fewer days of frost. It was as if the desert was attempting to reassert itself and reclaim the dry land.

It was a welcoming sight of green grass, tall trees and water as they entered the park. Darrell dutifully slowed to twenty-five, but rapidly gained speed as there seemed to be absolutely no one in the park. Darrell drove to the far side and stopped the car half on and half off the grass near the place where they thought Mouse had been.

They walked to the river through the brush where they had figured Mouse had been sitting, writing in her notebook. They were soon out of sight of the road, or any other paths. This was an isolated spot. They found the tiny beach, just a few yards across, where the police tape hung in low arcs. The beach had been disturbed, even more than before, as deep scuff marks and half footprints could be seen. The water had receded and it was easy to see the quick fall off in depth just a few feet out into the water.

"This is it, this is where they went in. Mouse later had to drive her car up the river, so I can't see her going in here. But with the tape and the description in Mouse's notebook, this was it." Very put her own footprints on those already there.

"Maria could have gone in first. By all accounts, she was anxious to get in the water." Darrell joined Very on the tiny beach.

"With or without her clothes. It's such a sheltered beach, maybe she felt safe shedding her clothes. Do we know if she was found with clothes on or not?" Very asked Darrell.

"Don't have that information. Maybe Mouse saw her here and decided to leave her in peace to swim, or just play in the water."

"But then, where does Hector come into the picture? He tried to save Maria, so maybe he came later, after Mouse had gone. Remember what she wrote in the notebook, 'someone coming.' She might have left as Maria came. And that's when Javi saw her, walking back to her car."

Very left the beach and walked back the way they had come, Darrell trailing behind her. The car was parked less than a hundred yards away. Even if Mouse had parked further away, the walk to her car would have taken only a few minutes. Very's mind raced as she tried to duplicate Mouse's movements. Javi said he had seen her walking towards a car. How did Javi know this was where Maria had gone to go swimming? It was isolated. Not visible from the road, or the picnic area.

"No, no, no. This scenario does not work. Mouse couldn't have been with Maria when she went into the river. If she had seen her go in, and get into trouble, she would have been screaming or crying, calling for help, surely?" Very turned on Darrell. "She would never have left a young girl to drown in the Killer Kern."

Chapter Nineteen: Mouse's Friend Karen

"Lunch?" Darrell asked meekly. This question was accompanied by a rumbling stomach growl.

"Sure. Chinese? How about the Rice Bowl this time, spread around our custom?" Very sighed. Although she was concerned about where her next meal was coming from, who doesn't, she had to laugh about Darrell's need for reassurance at every turn. Or was this a male thing? No, no, she knew women who were just as anxious about food.

They got into Darrell's car and made the ride back to Bakersfield. The green island of Hart Park, that seemed so divorced from the city, was just a short ride away from the downtown concrete. The city fathers had chosen wisely. It was far enough away to be a destination, but close enough that almost anyone could reach it, given that almost everyone owned a vehicle hereabouts. And if they didn't, their cousin did.

As they neared downtown, Darrell softly asked, "Are you sure you don't want to go to Panda Express? It might be faster?"

"Local, we need to go local. The people who own their own small businesses need us to support them. Don't you agree? As a small business owner, don't you want locals to patronize you?" Very asked in a righteous voice.

"Whoa, whoa, I was just thinking about faster. Yeah, we need to go to the Rice Bowl, local business."

Darrell found a spot in the parking lot. The two restaurants, Bill Lee's Bamboo Chopsticks and the Rice Bowl, sat across the street from each other. Not a rivalry, just one then the other, or "we always go to…" kept them both in business. The menus were similar. The prices comparable. Although, and Very knew from experience, the Chinese patrons in town gravitated to the Great Castle. She didn't care, and if Darrell wanted Panda Express, it couldn't be said that he was a great aficionado of Chinese food. Very liked it all, even Panda Express, if pressed.

Inside, they were seated promptly and chose quickly. Very asked for chopsticks in Chinese, but the waitress looked at her in horror. Very glanced up and then realized that the waitress wasn't Chinese, but Hispanic. "Sorry," she said, "I'd like chopsticks, please." The waitress scurried away.

Darrell gaped at Very. "You speak Chinese?"

Very smiled enigmatically. "There are a great many things you don't know about me."

Soon, the table began to fill with soup bowls, packets of oyster crackers and a pot of tea with tiny tea cups.

Very turned again to the waitress. "And oh, bring a pair of chopsticks for my friend, he needs the practice." Very smiled an evil jester grin at Darrell.

"I was in Hong Kong at a small restaurant and I had to share a table with a local family. The parents were used to eating with the sticks, but the kids were a bit rusty. I took out my chopsticks and did this," Very broke the chopsticks in two and quickly rubbed them together, using the edge of one to detach any rough edges. "There were some shelled peanuts on the table. And I did something like this." She quickly stuck her pair into a packet of crackers, gently detaching one cracker and deftly threw it into her mouth. While chewing one, she grabbed another and tossed it in with the first. The third wobbled briefly, but Very quickly readjusted her leverage and managed that one as well.

Darrell looked at Very as he was presented with his own pair of Chinese cutlery. He mimicked Very's pre-treatment and then confidently stuck his two sticks into his own packet of crackers. They quickly crossed one another. He readjusted them in his hand and tried again. After ten minutes, he had still failed to get even one cracker into his mouth without help.

Very laughed quietly. "It's not easy to do. Even the father of the family had trouble; the kids were laughing too hard at the failures of their dad to do much more than make half-hearted attempts. Only the mother could do it. You know, Chinese use giant chopsticks to cook with, so I think she had more experience. They were all so impressed that I could not only use chopsticks artfully, but pick up peanuts."

Darrell was about to ask about Very's experiences not only with chopsticks, but her seeming fluency in Chinese, when the rest of their food appeared. Darrell groaned with pleasure at the sizzling plate and the mounds of food.

"Sweet and sour, my favorite," Very said, serving herself a generous helping of the bright red globules of chicken.

"No, my favorite is this one, with the thin slices of beef and veggies." Darrell piled it on his plate along with a great mound of fried rice.

They didn't speak again until they were asking for boxes to save the rest of their meal to go.

"Fortune cookies," Very said, taking one and pushing the other on the small dish towards Darrell. "Oh, get this. 'You will have a chance meeting that brings good luck.' When have I ever had a chance meeting? I never do anything without planning; it's part of my persona."

"Don't you think coming to my office with your request was good luck? Our initial meeting turned into a fruitful partnership, didn't it?"

"That wasn't a chance meeting. It was deliberate. And besides, that was in the past. This is for the future. So, I'll just wait and see. What does yours say?"

Darrell broke his cookie into two pieces and carefully extracted the small piece of paper. He turned it right side up and read it silently. He put it down on the table.

"What did it say?" Very demanded.

She reached over to grab it, but Darrell was quicker. He snatched it off the table and stuck it into his pants pocket.

"That bad? You are a dark horse, Darrell. Can't even read a silly fortune out loud." She leaned over the table and stared at him. "You do know that it is all nonsense? They are written in the back rooms of the bakeries, just made up silly sayings. Don't worry about it, your secret is safe with me. Another phobia, fortune cookie fortunes."

They each put some cash for the bill and as they finished their tea, Darrell mused. "I wonder how many Hispanics are working here? All the wait staff, but what about the kitchen?"

"I think almost all, if not all, of the menial jobs are done by Hispanics. They do make up half of the population of the area. In the beginning, I'm sure everyone working here was Chinese. The idea was that it was a place where you didn't have to know English to find a job, and the whole family could work, and that meant that it was a good job for newly arrived immigrants. Asians are much better educated these days. I'll take the food, no matter who serves or cooks it. Although I do think the head chef must be Chinese."

Very lifted her tea cup and glanced towards the swing door from the kitchen which opened wide at that moment. A tall white hat emerged on the head of a short Hispanic man, whose eyes swept the dining room. The lone waitress approached and they exchanged a few words. Very strained to hear what language they spoke but gave up as the clatter of dishes overwhelmed the quiet of the lunchroom. "I think even the cook crew isn't Chinese," she said.

As they walked out, Very apologized for not coming back to the office with Darrell. "I have two contacts that I need to check in with. It's easier and quieter to do that at home. I have my notebook, so just drop me off at my car." They sat in silence for the four minutes it took to reach the spot where Very had parked. "Thanks, see you soon. Let me know if there are any more developments."

"In which case?" Darrell asked.

"Any or all! Bye." Very got out and gently closed the door.

As she got in her car, she decided to go home the long way and take a short trip around downtown Bakersfield. There had been some newer developments in the past few years, but it appeared hit or miss. The old Fox Theater had been renovated and restored, but other blocks had been left to the weeds. She drove towards home, through neighborhoods of houses that had been turned into small businesses. As one house became a tax preparer, the tenants in the house next to it wanted out, and so that house became another business and so on. Who wanted to live in a neighborhood where the other homes were not occupied, except during the day?

A dust devil swirled in the street and this brought up thoughts of Dorothy from Kansas being swept up in a tornado, the big brother of these tiny, intense wind storms. Was it possible to call a big one down on Bakersfield? Flatten these homes, make way for development of a proper downtown? Just then, a small dog ran out into the street. Very braked and a woman came out on the porch of a nearby house, yelling at her dog to come home. No, some people still made this neighborhood their home. Every city needed a neighborhood of cheap rents, even though they had tax preparers as neighbors.

When she reached home, she first checked on the backyard pool. Sticking her finger in the water, she reacted to the coolness. No, she needed to wait a few more weeks for the temperature in the pool to rise. Like the river, the pool was in no hurry to warm up. Her mother's cat came up behind her and rubbed her ankles, asking for a pet. Very bent down absent-mindedly and stroked the cat, speaking softly to her.

The cat's purrs turned to meows, which grew louder in volume as Very fussed on the patio, sweeping leaves into flower beds. Finally, the cat sat and screamed in displeasure at Very. "Okay, I'll feed you. But I'm not leaving it out here, like the old lady did. I don't want the raccoons to think I'm feeding them as well." She went inside as the cat scooted in right behind her, somehow or other making it inside before she did. Very filled up the bowl with kibble and smacked it down on the floor. The cat immediately dug in, crunching the food in a show of appreciation, or was it showing off? Very didn't care.

She found her phone and the number of Karen, a friend of Mouse's. Deborah had found the details in a phone book and recognized the name as someone who had known Mouse for years. When she reached Karen, they arranged to meet at a local Starbucks, not far away. Neither seemed eager to invite the other home. Very described herself, "I'm a little older, gray hair, tall."

"I'm sure I can find you," Karen said and hung up.

Does not do unnecessary small talk, she concluded. Neither does Very.

Twenty minutes later, Very entered the coffee shop. Looking at the menu, she rejected the caffeine-laden coffees and asked for a chai. When she turned away from the counter, a well-dressed younger woman waved at her. Very was dressed in Bakersfield casual, her usual since she retired. But now, she reconsidered her profession and choice of clothes. Should a PI wear casual, especially crop pants and cotton tee shirts? Then again, she had been to the park and played at the tiny beach. Didn't that call for casual? Retirement brought liberties and some of those were the rejection of hose, heels of any height, and form-fitting bras. Younger women could suffer.

Very took a seat opposite Karen. She smiled and formally introduced herself, "I hope you feel comfortable talking about Michelle."

"Yeah, Mouse. Even when I knew her, she called herself Mouse. I feel comfortable talking about Mouse, now that she's gone. I knew her in high school, a little. She used to revel in being called Mouse, she thought of it as cute, something different; it made her stand out and that made her happy. So, yes, Mouse."

"And recently? I thought that you were close, always."

"No, we reconnected when we both finished college and came back to Bakersfield. She was never a close, close friend, if you know what I mean. We went out with the gang sometimes and met for coffee, talked about work."

"Men?"

"Me and men, yeah, but she couldn't seem to find the right type. When I met her in high school, she was confident, cocky even. She was going to conquer the world. But she changed. I am not sure when, but when I met her as an adult, she had lost that head-held-high bravado. It was subtle, but I couldn't quite connect with her like I thought I would. When she was young, her mother died and that hit her hard. We all rallied around her. But, like stupid thoughtless teenagers, we didn't keep up the closeness. We couldn't say over and over again that we were sorry or laugh too much. Or here's one, we could never complain about the latest stupid thing our mother had said to us, made us do, or in any way put down mothers. Things like saying, 'I'm never going to be a mother.' We would forget and then she would go all red or sad or run away. So, again like stupid teenagers, we would exclude her. It was thoughtless and

I think quite cruel. But we had to get on, make our way in the world, and we couldn't afford to hang back in the past. We just didn't know what to say. It was sad.

"But when we reconnected later, I felt as though I couldn't apologize and eventually, it wasn't necessary. I think she understood. I did mention, more than once, that teenagers could be thoughtless and cruel and she just nodded. It turned out not to be all about her mother's death. She told me, in strict confidence, that she had had an episode of sexual molestation or assault. But she wouldn't go into detail and I thought that she had pretty much put it in the past. I knew that she had started seeing a therapist. I mean, if there was assault, real assault, like rape, well, that stays with you. And it can lead to lifelong trauma. I know, my dad was in Vietnam. It took all of us years to understand that it had changed him. He was angry, he drank, he was miserable to live with. And therapy, no, that was for wimps and he wasn't that. So, he struggled; we all struggled. I can see a glimpse of what Mouse went through. She said that she and the therapist were working on it. I said I supported her and we never talked about it again. But it was there, all the time. She had trouble with finding a good man, and I know there were trust issues. But then she told me that she was quitting her job and was going to look for something else. I never saw her again after that. I got married a couple of years ago, and then I had a baby, so I hadn't been able to keep up with her much. I didn't see her; it was just a phone call. But of course, I wished her luck and all. She was not very warm towards my daughter the one time she came over, didn't want to hold her. I tried not to be offended, gave the little one a good sniff to make sure she wasn't poopy, but she still didn't want to even look at her. Brought a gift and all, but it wasn't going to be a reconnect, that's for sure."

"Some people don't like little squalling babies. I don't. When they get bigger and can talk, then I'm okay. But definitely not the fragile poopy ones!" Very admitted.

"She did apologize for not being able to stay. Maybe she did have something to do, but it seemed forced."

"After she quit her job, did you ever get back to her? Talk with her again?"

"No, she said she was going to quit, but I didn't know if she had or not. I never talked to her after that last phone call. I have no idea what was going on with her."

"So, if I told you she had committed suicide, what would you say?"

Karen sat back in her seat and played with her honey striped hair, making curly strings around her face. "Not at all surprised. I don't know if she had ever tried suicide, but she talked about it a lot. It was the way she was going to die, she was sure. Oh, maybe not that day or the next, but at some point down the road, that was the way she would go out."

Chapter Twenty: What About Murder?

Very drove home along the bluffs. In an attempt to clear her head, she got out and walked with the rest of populace. She watched the late afternoon sun slowly dip towards the west. The filthiest air in the country, Bakersfield wins again, and that meant that glorious colors were a daily gift at sunset. When there were clouds, it could be one of the most exquisite sights, worthy of a calendar. What would that be called, the twelve months of grubby air and splendid sundowns?

Very had not been out at the park walking since the day she ran from the crazed killer, the homeless addict and former drug dealer. Being mixed up in the final stages of discovering what had happened to the body in the orchard had put her off coming to the walking path for her daily exercise. But now, it was time to be brave, face the memories and put them in their place. She strolled and nodded to others on the path, dads with kids on bicycles with training wheels, groups of medical personnel, still in their uniforms. Just a bunch of friendly Bakersfieldians, out for an evening stroll. Lots of people, nothing to fear.

A dog and jogger loomed ahead, on her side of the path. Very tried to decide whether to head off the path to her right, or nip over a little to the left. She stopped and then stepped off to the right, laughing as the two whooshed past. The blue-eyed husky wore bright blue running shoes on all four feet. The jogger wore matching blue running shoes. The harness jingled as they went past. "Great shoes," she called as they ran down the paved path. Interesting jogging buddy.

She found a vacant bench and sat. She looked out towards the oilfields as far as the murky atmosphere allowed. Pumpjacks, pipes, storage containers, fields ruined for anything other than the pumping and refining of the black liquid that was the foundation of Kern County prosperity.

She whispered to herself, "Murder." Not a thing she was fond of. At times, she believed that was what had happened to her Frankie and she felt immeasurably sad. At other times, she convinced herself that he was still out there, having run from the mess that had killed Danny, living a life in hiding. But with Mouse, she had trouble thinking that's how her life had ended.

She opened her notebook and found a fresh page. She labeled it, "Who would want to murder Mouse," and began to write. She noted that the coroner had not been conclusive as to the cause of death as the body had been battered by the rocks and debris in the river. The lungs were full of water, so that indicated drowning. But that didn't mean that it was on purpose, or accidental. There was the note, the casual suicide note, which pointed to other than murder. But could the murderer have forced Mouse to write the note? Deborah had certainly thought that it was unlike Mouse, although she did admit that the note was in Mouse's handwriting. That part was genuine.

But if Mouse didn't commit suicide, who murdered her? Who were her enemies? Very's pen hovered over the page. She had no clues about anyone who would want her gone. Look at it another way. Why did someone murder anyone? Greed, money, revenge, jealousy? Mouse didn't have any money, or did she? She certainly did not live the life of someone who had dollars to spend. Revenge? A jealous wife? There were mentions of a boyfriend, Karen didn't have any real clues as to whether this was current, past, or even real. Thirty-somethings can still get crushes and think there was something there, when in fact the feelings were not reciprocated. Maybe it was the other way around, maybe it was an unrequited lover, someone no one knew about? How would Very find out about someone no one knew?

She reached into her bottomless bag and rummaged. She found the notebook, Mouse's new notebook, with all of her writings. Very flipped through the pages, trying to spot a man's name, a description of a romantic feeling, a change in attitude, anything. And what about this old sexual assault? Was she still bothered by it, in fear of someone? Was it still eating at her? Very had seen nothing in the notebook about sex, romantic or traumatic. The light languidly faded.

Very stood and looked over the edge. Just months ago, she had scrambled up this very hill with a crazed druggie on her heels. She had never run so fast in her life as she used all fours to dodge grasping hands and outcroppings of Bakersfield cactus. It was an event not to be repeated. "I have learned my lesson, take someone with you." The other lesson learned was not to listen to confessions of murder, it was a dangerous occupation. While it might be satisfying at the moment to extract the intimate details and confirm suspicions, in her case, it proved extraordinarily precarious. After hearing the confession, she needed to be silenced. Thus, the chase.

And Father Sullivan heard the other man's confession, the one who was complicit in the murder of Danny Harger. But the two were dead, and they took any knowledge of Frankie Monroe to the grave with them. Two of them, dead in a cell in the jail overnight. The guard had said it, "Truth is stranger than fiction." It was an episode that should have been over, closed and shut up in her memory. But she still had no idea where Frankie was. Dead in a grave in an orchard, or buried in a field not far away from here? Was the body in the bank that of her runaway fiancé? If it was, he was not so much a runaway as a murder victim.

Very sat and watched the sun fall below the clouds and the sky turned orange, cantaloupe, carrot, coral and then crimson followed by a fading into rose, carmine, magenta and could it be? Vermilion? The entire sky participated in the changing colors and drama of the setting of the sun. She had seen it many times, and each time was a gift of theatricals and melodrama.

Before she left her front row seat, she sat and contemplated one more of the myriad dramatis personae of her previous adventure. Father Sullivan had played a key role in helping her locate the drug dealer and had been involved in the final stages of his and his friend's deaths. He had known all of them, with the exception of her fiancé. He had denied knowledge of Frankie Monroe. But why was he here again, involved in this mystery?

It wasn't in connection with Mouse, but with the Hernandez family. Therefore, he wasn't connected. Unless Mouse had gone to him for spiritual advice. It was entirely possible. The man of the cloth was a well-known person around Bakersfield and Very had known plenty of non-parishioners who had dealings with the charismatic cleric. Clarence "Killer" Sullivan was a local boy made good. Sissy may have gone to school with him, or was it his brother? The "Killer" nickname was a holdover from days on the gridiron in high school. And now he was a rising star in the Catholic Church. She should ask him about the connection. After all, wasn't curiosity a strength in detectives?

She drove home, just a few blocks away. She dialed Sissy's phone, but once again left a message. She waited too long to add the additional note about Father Sullivan and the automatic machine cut her off. She then called Mouse's sister Deborah, also leaving a message along the lines of, "You need to give me a list of her enemies."

She also tried to contact Joey's son who had gone to school with Mouse. Realizing that she didn't have his number, she called Joey to get the phone connection. When Very called the number Joey gave her, the wife answered. Very mumbled an incoherent request to consult with her husband on this case of the suicide. The wife was a bit snippy with Very, essentially telling her that her husband did not play around and to quit bothering the busy father and husband. What did the woman think of Very? They had known one another for years. The getting very-long-in-the-tooth old maid school teacher and librarian, after her husband? An old friend of her mother-in-law? Knickers in a twist? She needed to settle down.

Very redialed Joey and got her son's cell number. A civilized conversation then took place in which Joey's son, the classmate and former friend, denied the knowledge of any enemies. "She was sweet and kind to everyone. I don't think she changed over the years, so it is unlikely that she made enemies later in life. She was the kind of person who would be sweet and amiable to an ex-boyfriend's new love or be besties with a new boyfriend's ex. She couldn't make enemies. That's not to say that she didn't get in the way of someone, learning something she didn't know she knew. Knowers of information, especially if they are unaware, can be threats, or seen as threats, even though they aren't. Does that make sense?"

"Sure, thanks. If you think of anything later, let me know. And apologize to your wife. She seemed a tad defensive and not as kind as usual. Anything wrong?"

The answer came with a belly laugh. "She got on the scales this morning and found she had gained five pounds. So, she hasn't eaten all day in some bizarre attempt to shed the offending weight immediately. Also, she feels ugly, neglected, tied to screaming children, denied her creative outlets and is likely to bite anyone's head off."

"Flowers, jewelry? No chocolates, although the serotonin and dopamine might be the best cure for what ails her. Take care of the kids all evening, cook dinner, comfort food and salad. Surreptitiously call a friend and ask her to call? All of the above?"

"Wow, how do you know so much about it?"

"I'm the friend. I've heard it all. By the way, thanks for the info on Mouse. Oh, one last question. Is there any connection between Mouse and Father Sullivan?"

This question was greeted with another belly laugh. "That old goat? Do you think that she is one of his, his…"

"Conquests? I don't know. But you know the rumors."

"Father Sullivan is a good guy. The rumors that swirl about young boys, young women, married women, married… Never mind. Vicious rumors."

"What about the idea of where there is smoke, there is fire?" Very countered.

"I'm one of his supporters, don't talk to me about his detractors."

"But you called him an old goat?"

"That's a nickname for himself, poking fun at himself, before anyone else can get a name or another accusation in."

"And the church funds?" Very threw in another one of the many other allegations made against the sainted priest.

"Whoa, enough. As I said, we're all supporters here."

"Take care of your wife! Thanks for the gossip." Very hung up. She had forgotten to ask why Father Sullivan was at the Hernandez house. The most likely answer was that they were his parishioners.

Very sat on the darkened patio as early mosquitos buzzed around her. She sprayed her legs with insect repellent and hoped that would be enough. Patios were not always the most inviting places in Bakersfield in the summer, but could this be summer already, in late April? Nasty little biting things.

She fell into a fugue. What should she do with her mother's things? She hadn't dusted, or even opened, the cabinets full of glassware and pottery collectibles. Her mother had died more than a year ago. Was it time now? She'd been buried and mourned; the condolence cards had been tossed in the trash, the name on the utilities changed, but the final distribution of assets was still pending. Still waiting for Very to decide what to do with the house and contents. They were hers to distribute, as Sissy had gotten her portion of the life insurance policies and the house had gone to Very. What did she want of her mother's? What was important for her to take with her on the journey of the rest of her life? Mementos, tokens of inheritance, signs of heritage, but not the small things of her mother's life. Not her clothes, not her china figurines, not her private collections of trinkets, not her intimate life. But those things that represented the heritage of her mother's and her father's families? Yes, those. How to distinguish? How to choose? The weight of choice created a feeling of an unwanted burden.

Cassandra. What about Cassandra? Of course, there was no direct relationship between the two of them, just that they all believed that she was the biological daughter of Very's fiancé. If her baby had lived, Cassandra would be the half-sister of Very's child. So, what kind of relationship is that? Very liked Cassandra. Maybe she could give some of the keepsakes her mother had accumulated to her, to pass on to her children? Would that be appropriate, welcome, or an imposition? Very needed to ask. Gently. Speculatively. And after Sissy had claimed what she wanted. The leftovers, then? Why bother? Sell anything no one wanted and give Cassandra money? Tacky, definitely tacky; that's what her mother would say.

Maybe, before Sissy got to things, Very could choose one or two nice pieces to give to Cassandra. A token, but one from the heart. Frankie wasn't here to connect the two, but he still made a connection.

Her mother's cat suddenly appeared and rubbed against her ankles, mewing and demanding attention. Very reached down with one hand and rubbed the cat's head, cooing and mumbling sweet words. The cat purred and chirped in appreciation. Then she was gone, slipping into the shadows of the night, preparing herself to pursue the real or imagined animals that frequented the back yard in the evenings. So easily pleased with life, pets were.

What about the body found in the bank? Had Very forgotten that this body might be that of Frankie? All indications supported that it could be: the time frame, the gender, the location. All similar to the body in the orchard. Very's hands clenched into fists. When could she expect some sort of answer? And what answer could that be?

Chapter Twenty-one: Revelations About the Body in the Bank

Ding, ding, ding, ding. Very's phone chirped, again and again. She was not a millennial, so she did not sleep with her phone and half awake, she stumbled into the kitchen where she had plugged in her phone. Just as she picked it up, it went silent. Damn, it must have been important, so early in the morning. Very looked with bleary eyes. Joey. She pushed the call back feature, or what she thought was the call back button, but former messages started playing at her.

She started all over and tried to call Joey. Busy. She gave up the telephone tag game and made coffee. As she listened to the burble of brewing coffee, she sat at the breakfast table and inhaled deeply. Did caffeine float in the air? Maybe the deep inhale collected enough to jump start the brain, or was it just the anticipation?

While the coffee finished, Very collected the newspaper. When she returned, she discovered that Joey had returned her call. She waited until she was securely seated with milky coffee at the ready before she pushed the automatic redial again.

"Ah, Very. News about the body, the unidentified one. You need to go to the sheriff's office yourself, and they can give you the information that is available to the public."

"Do you know, can you tell me?"

Joey sighed, "Just go. Ask for Bobby." She hung up.

Very raced to the shower and then tried to find some decent clothes. She had blouses, skirts, slacks, nice sandals, and even, if really called for, pantyhose. But she thought that just decent was good enough for the sheriff's office. She grabbed a favorite pair of beige slacks and a colorful blouse that hadn't been worn in a year. No time for fussing. Very slapped make up on her dry, freckled skin and wiped lipstick over her cracked lips. A brush through the hair revealed more grey than she had previously noticed. Who cared?

Her drive to the Kern County Sheriff's Office on Norris Road was swift. The traffic was light and the office situated in a part of town not given to heavy traffic. It was a lonely office, but there was room for expansion, unlike the other downtown offices of the city and county. She looked, but wasn't able to find a parking place in the shade that would last for more than twenty minutes. She shrugged and pulled the eyeshades out of the trunk and fixed them under the visors in the front seat. Proving the additional shade made any difference to the temperature in the parked car was difficult, but wasn't it a pleasant thing to position the colorful shades and pretend they were useful?

After security, she approached the front desk. "I have come to speak with Bob… Sanchez, uh, Robert Sanchez." She knew that everyone, but everyone, called him Bobby, but this was his place of work. Robert it should be.

She sat in the waiting room, full of Bakersfieldians. One elderly man strolled in front of her. His back was stooped and he walked slowly, placing one shit-kicker clad foot in front of the other, as if he would fall over if a wind should spring up. His jeans were so new they were the original deep purple-blue indigo color and gave a crunching sound of stiff denim as he walked. His shirt was classical Western, with snaps of faux mother-of-pearl and matching color piping. An outsized leather belt encircled his small waist, and a huge buckle threatened to pull him over. Gleaming metal horses, rearing and bucking, graced either side of an old-fashioned oil derrick. Cowboy oil roughneck. Only in Bakersfield. For being in the office of law enforcement, he walked with great dignity, as if he had just come from gracing one of the west side oil towns annual parade as grand marshal. As he walked majestically past Very, he turned to give her a smile. A huge turquoise sat at his throat and the twin tails of his bolo tie swung with the gesture.

Across the room lounged a large woman wearing a yellow and green muumuu. Did anyone still wear those things? Comfortable, easy to care for, hid all kinds of bad choices in lifestyle and diet, perfect for Bakersfield weather. At her feet lay a large bag of colorful design and unknown origin. Out of the top snaked two strands of multicolored yarn. A large crochet hook was wielded at warp speed, and a hat started to form as Very watched. What was she doing here? Was this one of those places, like the public library, where people came to sit out the heat of the day or the blustery winds of winter? Or did she have business with the sheriff and his company?

Against the back wall lined with chairs, a woman and three young teenagers waited their turn. Her brown face was suffused with anger, mistrust, loathing and fear.

The three boys sprawled across as many chairs as they could manage. Their hair was sculpted and shaved into words and symbols that Very couldn't read from far away. None of the three had buttoned their shirts and the thin fabric flapped at the waist. Faces turned a blank look towards the world, young men trained to be tough and devoid of humanity. They stared back at Very when she glanced their way. She had seen that look among the boy-men in her library but much less seldom in her English class.

If they were of average intelligence, they knew that life held little promise of riches. If they had some talent, musical, artistic, physical agility, did they even know where to turn to develop it? Very's words of praise and encouragement in high school often fell on deaf ears and minds that were unable to comprehend the kindness behind the words. They had heard those words before: study hard, do your work, fit into the mold and you will succeed. But there was so little evidence they would do better than their brothers, cousins or fathers, that they turned to easier ways to make themselves into stars on the local scene. So, what were they doing in the sheriff's waiting room? Their mother's anxious face predicted it was not a casual social call.

She was called by the clerk and ushered into a room back in the bowels of the building. Waiting at the door to a small room was Deputy Sheriff Robert Sanchez. His uniform was ironed with pleats that threatened to cut the hand that dared to smooth them down. His thick brown belt held the belly that, at home, protruded as a sign of the good living he enjoyed. His hair was cut to perfection, short back and sides. Small wisps of gray spread at his temples, otherwise the shock of thick black hair showed the smooth lines of the comb that kept it in check. Bobby stuck out his hand and Very took it, shocked that she had never before shaken his hand. She had seen him in his uniform, as well as at work on his job, but she had never before been in the situation of greeting him as a county officer of the law. What a handsome man, what lovely manners, what warm hands that matched his voice.

When they were seated, Bobby leaned forward and asked, "What did Joey tell you?"

"Nothing, only that you had something to tell me. Have you identified the body? The remains, that is?"

"No, not yet."

"Then why am I here? Why tantalize me with non-information?"

Bobby produced a folder that Very had not seen him carrying. "I just wanted to tell you what we have so far. You know that DNA analysis is too expensive. But we did have enough money to get a good guy from LA to look at the body, particularly the skull. You know that different races, if there is such a thing, have different parameters. Longer or higher craniums, heavier brow ridges, jaws that are heavier or lighter. And there is a marked difference between men and women. Well, we were very certain this was a man from the beginning, and the second look confirmed that assumption. So, then we had him look more closely at the… Very, are you okay?"

Very had felt her blood pressure drop and a buzzing sound penetrated her ears. She had put her head down and was gulping for air, trying to stifle the rising feeling of dread. And then her stomach flip-flopped. Oh no, not enough breakfast. Only a cup of coffee, too much caffeine. Buzz, buzz.

"Here," Bobby's voice cut through the noise in her head. "Water, have a drink of water."

Very gulped down the tiny paper cup full of tepid liquid. As it slipped down her throat, she willed herself to be calm. Anxiety had never been a problem before, why now?

She sat quietly for a full minute, breathing normally, head down, eyes closed. Then she drew in a deep breath and looked at Bobby. "I'm ready now."

"I'm sorry, I should have prepared you better for this. But I thought you'd be disappointed, so I was trying to do this gently. But I think I have misjudged you." He reached for the folder again and opened it. Very followed his motions with her eyes, her breath suspended.

Bobby handed her a charcoal drawing of a face. The man was looking directly at her, his features clear and precise. Very gasped, "This is NOT my Frankie. No way."

"No, it isn't. But we wanted you to see this anyway."

"He's African, pure African," Very said. The artist had even darkened the skin to show what the man would have looked like when alive. Short, dark curly hair grew on his head, heavy lips and a broad nose completed the portrait. "When I spent a summer in Tanzania, I met his brother, or someone just like him. That's why I said he was African, because these features are the exact ones that the men I met there had. But he is definitely not my Frankie."

"Now that we have this, and a better age range, 30 to 45, we can start looking for a missing person."

"And what will you do if you don't find any? And what do you do with the body, or rather the bones, if you don't find a missing person to match?"

"We keep them for a while, we'll take a sample for DNA, if that is the only way to identify him and then…"

"And then what do you do? With the remains?"

"There's a section of Union Cemetery that we use. Respectful." Bobby reached his hand out and tried to take the sketch from Very's hand.

She clung to it for a few more seconds, studying the face of the man that might have been her long-lost fiancé. "Please let me know, keep me informed. I really need to know what will happen. I want to know who has lost this poor soul. It's because it isn't Frankie. Because Frankie may still be out there, stuck in some orchard or lying in a shallow grave in someone else's godforsaken part of some rural area. Buried and forgotten, like this. I want to know about this one, who he is and what happened to him." Tears trickled down Very's cheeks. It wasn't a gusher, just a definite ooze of salty wet.

Bobby handed her a box of tissues and Very pulled two out with a rip. She daubed at her eyes, then sat bold upright in her seat. She parted her lips in what she thought was a smile, but turned out to be more of a grimace of pain and despair. She stood and strode out the door.

As she pulled into the driveway of her mother's house, two dogs came bounding out and swerved around her car. The pit bulls snarled and barked as they headed down the middle of the street. Very recognized them as the troublesome pit bulls that belonged to someone down the street and around the corner. Very cautiously parked the car in the carport. The back gate hung open and Very immediately went through to investigate. Had she left the gate open, unlatched? She slowly entered the patio and looked around. The tables, chairs, the potted plants, all looked undisturbed.

Then she saw the bundle of grey fur. Her mother's cat lay sprawled on the bricks, a trickle of blood in her fur. Very gasped and bent over the small cat, reaching her hand to touch the animal. The cat was still warm, but did not respond to Very's touch. She was dead, murdered by the dogs in her own yard.

Very stood and screamed. It was a prolonged howl of rage and sorrow. She ran out the gate and into the street. The murderers had escaped, disappeared, and were now beyond the arms of Very's righteous anger. She returned to the back yard and bent over the dead cat. As she touched her a second time, the disgust at the feel of a dead body rose within her. How could something be beloved one minute and be an object of offense the next?

Very began to cry, tears welling and falling unchecked down her face. While she cried, she also became pragmatic and searched for a shovel to dig a grave and something to wrap her cat in. A shroud for a cat? Better to find some newspaper, it disintegrated faster. Who wants to find the body of a buried pet, especially someone else's buried pet's bones, while planting petunias?

She found the shovel and grabbed an old newspaper from a pile on the porch. She scanned the back yard for a suitable gravesite. In the corner was a square patch that her mother had often used for vegetables. Last week, Very planted some tomatoes, but in the intervening week had forgotten to water them. The plants had died, but the soil was soft and disturbed. The shovel went in easily and within minutes Very had dug a two-foot hole. All the while, a rivulet of tears ran down her face, dripping into the grave.

Very continued crying, occasionally choking and coughing. At one point, she sank into a chair, bent over and let a torrent of tears, mixed with snot, run onto the bricks. Who was she crying for? The cat had belonged to her mother and Very had fed and watered her, taking her to the vet for shots and when she got an ear infection. But this animal had no hold on her heart. Perhaps it was the connection with her mother? Very had shed few, or was it no, tears when her mother had departed this mortal life. She had spent so much time in the last few years caring for the woman in her declining years, that it had been a relief when her Mom had claimed her heavenly reward. Were these lamentations, finally, for her mother?

Or was it for Frankie? Was it the shock of finding that the body discovered in the bank of the Killer Kern had not been that of her fiancé? Was she mourning him? Or mourning the loss of the knowledge of his fate? For years she had pushed the thought of his whereabouts away from her conscious mind and lived her life as if the events of the past were finished. She knew better, but she had avoided facing the truth, avoided the quest for the answers, avoided the entire episode as if it hadn't happened. Were these tears now for Frankie?

Or were these tears for herself, her lonely life, her empty bed, her lost opportunities, her sterile existence? Could she have had a more robust life, full of friends and family? She howled with frustration at finding some reason for these copious tears, this outpouring of grief for the small animal.

She took the newspaper and spread it out on the patio bricks. Gently, with more care than she had ever shown the cat during its life, Very arranged the body in the middle of the doubled sheet and folded it over, carefully making sure no clods of dirt would touch the kitty's fur. When she had made a careful package, she bent over the grave and placed the cat's corpse in the ground. "Ashes to ashes, dust to dust," she murmured. She took the shovel and bit into the pile of dirt piled to the side of the grave. She let it dribble onto the neat bundled shroud.

She stopped and looked at the newspaper covering the body. She bent over and gently wiped the dirt away. In full color was one of those local stories that the newspaper loved to run on the front page. Children gathered around a priest, fully kitted out, who held a cross. All around were pet rabbits, cats, cages of birds and well-behaved dogs. It was the St. Francis Day for the Blessing of the Animals. Father Sullivan smiled as he made the sign of the cross over his parishioners and their precious pets.

Chapter Twenty-two: Planning a Return Visit

Very sat in Darrell's office on Friday morning, filling in her partner about the findings of the body in the bank. She sipped her coffee quietly and shifted uneasily, stretching and massaging her painful muscles. She explained that she had spent the previous afternoon cleaning her mother's house, or rather, cleaning and boxing up items to dispose of. She kept to herself the death of the cat and subsequent crying jag. She kept a bright smile on her face, the muscles there aching as much as her thighs.

"I had put too much hope in that body. It was stupid of me, I know. I had so much bottled up and invested in this being my Frankie."

"It's okay to have a meltdown," Darrell commiserated. "Big expectations, big letdown."

"I suppose anyone would. Everyone does now and again, don't they?"

Darrell lowered his eyes, "Well…"

"Don't tell me you've never had a total, raging fit? Or are you the manly-man type that never lets a single crack in the façade."

Darrell met her gaze with a look of fear.

"Oh, you don't have to tell me. I'm not going to squeeze it out of you. But what was it? When the dog died?" Very smiled in jest.

"No dog, my brother."

Very sat wordlessly, appalled by her misstep.

"He had a serious illness, my older brother. He spent years in and out of the hospital, treatments, tests. He lost weight, his hair, his mind. My parents had no time for me. They loved me, that wasn't the problem, it was just that they had no energy left over for me. Finally, he went to live in a care home because my parents were too tired and couldn't care for him. Finally, he died. It was very, very sad. But I couldn't cry, I had used up all of my tears for him on myself. I've got no more heart."

"Don't worry Darrell, you have a heart, you're not like the Tin Man. Do you want a heart? Do you want to care for someone so much that it hurts you if something happens to them? Don't worry, your secret is safe with me. You can hide your pain, you can pretend that you never cry. It's okay."

Very stood and patted him on the shoulder as she stepped over to put her coffee cup on the table. His shoulder relaxed at her touch, but Very pointedly did not meet his gaze. She felt his shoulder lean in, as if he wanted more. Like the cat, coming up to Very's chair and rubbing against her leg. Even if Very had given the cat a pet, she always wanted more. Did Darrell want more shoulder rubbing? More petting? Darrell as a cat? Didn't see that one coming.

Very sat down, picked up her notebook and opened it. She looked at the pages full of notes of times and places, people she had spoken with, what they said. "If Mouse didn't commit suicide, then it was murder.

Agreed? She couldn't have had an accident. So, murder. But who, how and why? I started making some notes, but couldn't come up with anything. I guess I didn't ask the right questions, or ask the right people."

"Ummm." Darrell sat staring ahead, at a spot on the wall. What can of worms did Very's questions pry open?

"Darrell, if, just if, now god forbid this ever did happen, and I found you in a similar situation, who would want you murdered? This is all hypothetical, as yet. Who are your enemies?"

Darrell leaned back in his chair and shifted his gaze to a spot closer to the ceiling. Do enemies lurk in the walls, out the window, or are these other answers or questions Darrell is exploring?

Very leaned back in her chair and listened. There was silence in the office, but noises from outside in the street came rumbling in through cracks in the window. The traffic rumbled by, then slowly died down. The light had turned red and the traffic had stopped and was waiting to resume. When it did, Very could hear the cars, a different sound for trucks and then occasionally, the deep throated whine and screech of a large semi or massive engine of a garbage truck. The rhythm was soothing and Very reached into the calming space as she tried to reorient her mind to the task at hand. Hard to do when the task was murder.

"Who would want to murder me, is that the question? I've never thought of it in those terms. There are the criminals that I have helped put behind bars, quite a few, but most spent a few months and then they were let loose. White collar crime doesn't have the same stigma as violent crime. Everyone thinks that those poor accountants, or managers, or executives don't deserve to be in the same place as those who hit people over their heads and steal their money. Stolen money all the same. Doctors, those are the worst. As if they don't make enough money legally and they need to bilk the government out of more. They write too many prescriptions for drugs that are dubious at best, and then they get kickbacks from the pharmacies. One or two of those might want me out of the way. Oxycontin, who ever needs that stuff? But, I can't imagine that any of them would go out of their way to kill me.

"Murder is a desperate act. It takes some drastic twisting of ideas, a firm belief that one will never be caught, that taking someone else's life is okay. War, maybe. But revenge for getting caught writing dubious prescriptions? That is dire. So, what could Mouse have done that would have caused someone to plan the ultimate?"

Very took a breath and opened her mouth, but Darrell wasn't finished with his ruminations on murder. "There was this one character. He tried to get worker's compensation for a bad back. There was no doubt that he had hurt his back and there was no doubt that he was not a person that others would like to work with. But he was doing yard work and I verified that. However, just because someone looks after their plants and mows the lawn does not necessarily mean they can do other heavy lifting. There was a big court fight, the worker lost and was very sore at me. He didn't pay his mortgage, hoping to get a big payout, and he lost his house. It was a series of sad events. I actually felt sorry for him. But would he have murdered me? Would that have gotten his house back? Would it have changed anything? No, I think murder belongs to a higher level of hate, not just dislike and being pissed off."

Very listened to Darrell's story and tried to imagine what Mouse could have done to get as far as pissing someone off, let alone engendering a murderous rage. "To have killed Mouse, someone would have to have followed her up the canyon, forced her to write a suicide note and then killed her in a spot that was visible from the road, or at least the parking area. At that point, there is not much room for another car to park and evade notice."

"Maybe they came on foot." Darrell scribbled on a notepad, drawing a little picture of the parking space and the river. "This is the area that they found the car. Just a little turnout. Let me show you on Google maps." Darrell turned to his computer and within a minute had a full screen of Highway 178. As he dragged the mouse, he showed Very the Turbine House where Mouse's body was found. As he followed the winding road up into the mountains, he turned the view to satellite. "Here's the Turbine, and here's the road. You can see the river and all the rocks. If you follow the road up, the curves are deep and there are so many of them. But here, about two miles or so up the canyon, there are a series of little turnouts. Just big enough for one car, maybe two. But they are exposed, all visible from the main highway. If there had been more than one car, someone would have noticed. They did notice Mouse's car. It was called in at least twice before someone could get off their backside and check it out. Not until Sunday. It was someone who lives in Kernville and who commutes all the time. He noticed the empty car twice, and called the second time he saw it. That was the first one. The second call was from someone who stopped, just barely, at the same place because it is so small. They looked around the area, but didn't see anyone. They walked down to the river and looked around. But see, here it is rocky, really rocky. You don't even leave foot prints in the gravel."

They looked at the computer screen, making the area bigger, then closing in for a fuzzier but closer view. Very tried to lean in without coming too close, not wanting to repeat the action of a few minutes before. Finally, she leaned so close that she lost her balance and put her hand heavily on Darrell's shoulder to steady herself. "Sorry," she muttered. "Can't see."

Darrell sat very still, not breathing, allowing Very's hand to press on his body. After a good look, Very stepped back. "I see what you mean. It's such a strange place. Do we need to go look for ourselves? No, I think we wouldn't be able to find out anything more. Great thing, Google maps." She sat down.

"The note, it keeps coming back to the note," Very said after a pause. "She wrote it, didn't she? No doubt about it. But it could have been written under coercion, agreed?"

"I think so. I could imagine someone standing over her with a knife or a gun and telling her what to write. She wouldn't really understand how final it would be. It's hard to think at a time like that, you get confused. Maybe she thought she could talk her way out of it, or escape or whatever."

"I've never been at the other end of a barrel, so I wouldn't know how it feels. I don't know what I would do. When presented with a threat, I ran, and I didn't even know he had a gun or a knife, or any kind of weapon but his drug-crazed mind. What would you do, if someone stood over you with a gun and wanted you to write a suicide note?"

Darrell looked at Very with a frisson of fear. "Never happened to me. I do not know, I truly don't. Write, I think. Fear is a powerful motivator."

"And what about the fact that there was no blood, no signs of a struggle, no fingerprints from some unknown person? What about Locard's principle? You know, the idea that every crime scene has an exchange; the criminal brings something and leaves it and that he also takes away something. Both of these can lead us to the criminal, connecting things. What was left, what was taken away?"

"I hate to point out that the scene wasn't really treated as a crime scene as such. I mean they must have noticed blood or dirty fingerprints, boot prints, marks of a scuffle? Nothing like that in the report that Mouse's sister let me see. Just the note. Car keys in the ignition, purse shoved under the front seat totally invisible, and notebook on the seat, along with the note."

"Yeah, the note. It all keeps coming back to the note." Very stood and took two paces before she encountered the end of the room and when she turned back, Darrell had swiveled his chair to obstruct her pacing. "I'm missing something." She sat down.

"You've looked at reports, you have talked with her sister, her former friends, classmates, her therapist. What more?"

"The Hernandez family. They didn't know her, but they were probably the last ones to see her, or notice her. They saw her, or at least Javier did, the older brother. But I don't think they are telling the truth. I think there is something they are not revealing. I'm going back, one last time, to see if I can get something more out of them."

"Very, they are in mourning. They have had a double tragedy. Do you think that is wise?"

Very looked at Darrell with a stare that dared him to question her motives or movements.

"Okay, okay. I will go with you."

"No need," she laughed. "They are very nice people. I don't need a protector. Besides, I may run into Father Sullivan again."

"Again?"

"Yeah, do you know anything more about him? Why he was there? I keep running into him, and it makes me nervous. Just saying."

Very stopped by Dewar's on her way home. She nodded to the animal heads mounted on the wall and walked to the counter where they sold the chews. She ordered a variety, not being sure what everyone liked. But wasn't that the point of chews, small pieces and a variety of candy, so that no one needed to eat the only kind available? She had also learned how her favorite candy, peppermint chews, was made when she was young and in the Girl Scouts. The troop had gone on a field trip to the back rooms of Dewar's and watched the making of candy. Rows of chocolate were being dipped and marked with a squiggly design that identified each flavor or filling.

The chews were the most fascinating part. On one end of a long stainless-steel table sat an enormous peppermint chew, pure white nougat in the center and thick ropes of red candy pressed into its sides. The long table was needed as the giant chew was reduced, gradually and gently, by pulling it into one thin rope, which was snipped by a pair of scissors and wrapped swiftly in a square of wax paper. Clouds of powdered sugar swirled in the air, as the monster chew became hundreds of small ones, ready for Christmas stockings.

Now a stash of peppermint chews nestled in the bag along with peanut butter, Sissy's favorite, and lastly caramel. Almond seemed too much like peanut butter. Very gulped as she paid the price, but there were literally a hundred of pieces of candy, enough for the entire neighborhood if it came to that.

Very headed home, ate a quick lunch and stretched out in the back patio, a gentle breeze trying to lull her to sleep. She lazily heard a wind chime from a neighboring yard and the quiet hum of a car heading down the street. A heaviness lay on her chest. The body in the river, killed and stuck into the ground not far from the flowing waters, was not Frankie. This investigation into Mouse's death, suicide or not, was going nowhere. Lassitude swept over her like the tide in shallow water.

"Meow, meow, MEOW!"

Very's eyes flew open. Where was that cat? She looked around the yard until the weight of truth fell. The cat was gone. Had another cat, a stray, already claimed the territory? Very got up and strolled to the grave. She had found a large rock and written in indelible ink, "Cat" and the date of death. She hadn't known the date of birth; it didn't matter now. Only death was important.

Chapter Twenty-three: Return to the Hernandez House

Very carefully put her large purse and the bag of chews on the front passenger seat and got in. She slowly backed out, stopping at the end of the driveway. She could see cars coming up the street, but a row of shrubs and the curve in the street prevented her from seeing if traffic was coming down. She had ridden in cars that had back-up cameras that had the ability to see in both directions from a position closer to traffic than the driver's seat. She needed one of those. Maybe in her next car she could make sure to get the latest safety technology.

She inched out into the street, trusting to oncoming traffic to notice a bright red car slowly backing into the street. She turned and then put her car into gear. As she drove down the street, the houses, the trees, the bushes, the flowers, and the sidewalks all were familiar. Too familiar. The house that she lived in was one her parents chose almost 45 years ago. At that time, they had two girls and the other homes on the street also had children.

But now, all of the children had grown up, moved away, and sold the houses. There were no longer youngsters playing basketball in the driveways, hopscotch on the front walkway or hanging out around a car full of members of the opposite sex. All of the children had gone except her. There were a few older adults, those that were her mother's age, and many her own. But now it seemed more like a retirement community than a street on which families occupied the homes.

She quickly drove to the street in East Bakersfield where the Hernandez's lived. She slowly cruised past their house and then five doors down to find an empty parking space. It was just after quitting time and the street was filled with parked cars, as if there were no garages or driveways in which to park. Very eased into the large space. She and her mother had argued about the definition of a parking space. Her mother had insisted that it was two cars length and that it was impolite to park too close to either the car in front or the one behind. Very maintained that one and a half was sufficient. If one had lived in a city, or a place with limited street parking, one learned how to parallel park in much smaller spaces. Very argued that in cities, parking was at a premium and drivers parked where they could. Her mother had insisted that in Bakersfield, two car lengths was the standard and it behooved polite, cautious drivers to be generous. "We have the space, use it," was her motto.

Very retrieved her two bags and walked back to the house. Nothing had changed in this neighborhood, not in two days, or two months or twenty years. It was dry, dusty, full of neglect or lack of care. Tenants were unlikely to own their homes, so why should they put too much work in? Even those who owned their homes, and tried to shower some care and attention, were likely to be shamed into letting it go, so as not to show up their neighbors. If you had enough money, there were neighborhoods that welcomed the rising middle-class homeowners. It was an ambition shared among many on this street. Get out if you can.

She walked up the short walkway and knocked on the door. Gabby answered. Her eyes lit up when she saw Very. They became big when Very held up the bag that declared it was from Dewar's. "I brought chews this time. I hope that's okay?"

"For me, all for me?" Gabby teased brightly.

Very laughed, "What do you think?"

"Come in, everybody's here. Petey, you know, Pedro, came back."

"Oh," Very breathed in quickly, as she sidestepped the screen door that opened out. "Do you think I could talk with him?"

"Yeah, sure," Gabby assured her with a confidence that felt questionable.

Gabby grabbed Very's arm and dragged her into the living room. The room was small, and was full of people. Mr. Hernandez, father, stood in the kitchen doorway. An older sibling who stood facing the couch was a taller, older version of Carlos, but Very noticed the family resemblance. Carlos stood behind his mother, who sat on the couch, along with an older woman, likely the grandmother. Very hesitated to enter as the atmosphere was heavy with animosity, disappointment and fear.

Gabby still held her hand and tightened her grip when Very attempted to back out. Gabby announced their visitor. "Miss Very came back and she brought candy." Gabby grabbed the bag and held it up triumphantly, as if she had asked, or willed, the candy into the household.

Mrs. Hernandez immediately took the bag and murmured a quick, "Gracias. Thank you." She shoved her husband aside in order to get to the kitchen. She returned with a large glass bowl. Silence greeted the tearing open of the bag and they all listened to the "ping, ping" as chews fell into the improvised candy dish. Grandma hauled herself to her feet and took over as hostess, walking around the room, handing out candy to all. The older version of Carlos shook his head, but Grandma persisted, shaking the bowl under his nose until he reached in and took two chews. Very heard a murmured "Thanks" flung in her direction. The sound of papers being torn off the candy filled the air and muffled the tension. After all, it was hard to yell with a mouthful of sticky candy.

Was this the abuelita who impressed upon Javier that, "Sweets take away the bitterness?" Very's eyes followed the older woman around the room and Very made sure to take one from the common bowl, even though she had brought them. There were plenty left and no doubt they would make their way out the door so that the neighborhood could also assuage the collective bitterness of death on the street. The little voice that had told her not to be a cheapskate was right. What difference did a few dollars make to her bank account in contrast to the possibility of participating in this family's grief in a small way? After all, she wanted something from them.

Gabby, her mouth stuck together with what looked and sounded like two chews, grabbed Very's hand and pulled her through to the small alcove next to the kitchen. Carlos had moved and now sat there, already chewing a candy, the paper discarded on the table next to his books. How did the candy migrate to his hands and then to his mouth so quickly?

"Thanks, Gabby, but I really want to talk with Pedro, if that's possible?" Very found herself pushed down into a chair, or rather, an uncomfortable little stool.

"Yeah, yeah," mumbled Gabby. "I'll get him." She left.

"Hi, Carlos, how are you?" Very said.

He mumbled a reply, obscured by the inability to open his mouth. "Bluh, bluh, good."

Gabby returned with Pedro in tow.

Very stood and extended her hand, "Hi, I'm Very Blew. You're Pedro, right?"

Pedro, a surly expression on his face, stared at the outstretched hand and then at Very's smile. Neither the hand nor the smile wavered and finally Pedro took the proffered extremity and squeezed, hard. Very squeezed back.

Pedro let go and stood, waiting for Very. Gabby ran out and returned with another small stool, squeezing it into the cramped space like an expert in setting an extra place at the table. "Here, sit down Petey, make yourself comfortable."

Very sat and turned to Pedro as he too, sat down, with an awkwardness that showed his reluctance to have this conversation. Once again, Very spouted the usual words of being sorry for the loss and apologies for interrupting their time of mourning. Very waited until Pedro accepted the platitudes. He could hardly do otherwise with little sister Gabby sitting next to him waiting to pounce and remind him of his social duties to visitors.

"I came here because I need some information. I am so glad I found you. They told me that you had seen her." Very bent to her purse to get the photo.

When she looked up, she saw another expression on Pedro's face. Dread, bordering on terror. What caused that? What ailed this young man, so fearful of a simple question?

Very held out the photo to Pedro. "I know that she was there, at the park, on the afternoon of the drownings. They," she nodded to Gabby and Carlos, "said you might have seen her."

Pedro crossed his arms and looked at the photo, studying the face, the hair, the figure carefully. "What kind of car was she driving?"

This time Very was prepared. "A white Toyota Camry, 2005. Just normal looking."

"Yeah, I saw her. She was walking towards her car, or one just like it."

"Where was the car? What time did you see her?"

"It was parked on the road, you know, just half on and half off, like everybody parks. She was heading for it."

"When, when did you see her? In the afternoon? When..." Very stopped, biting her tongue. She needed to let him tell her, not put words in his mouth.

"Yeah, in the afternoon, when we all went looking for Maria." He looked down, his shoulders slumped as he said her name.

"So, were there a lot of people around? Was she alone?"

"Yeah, alone. Not many people, just the family, trying to find...her."

Very clenched her teeth. Try not to tell him what to say, just let him say it for himself. "What was she like, right then? Happy, sad...?"

Pedro's eyes slid sideways and he hesitated. He fidgeted, turning his arms inside out, exposing the tattoo, the "13" tattoo. "She was crying, or at least that's what it looked like. I didn't pay much attention."

"Did you speak to her?"

"No, of course not. That would be rude, wouldn't it? Don't talk to strange girls. She looked okay, just upset."

Very scrambled to keep him talking. What else could she ask? "Was she carrying anything?"

"Like what? A gun?" Pedro looked disgusted.

"Oh, no. Did she have a gun?" Very blurted out. A new twist to the saga?

"No, of course not. She didn't have anything, maybe a purse. I don't know, what difference does it make?"

"She drowned that day too. I am trying to find out about it." Very said calmly, trying to keep the conversation going.

"Isn't that what the police are supposed to do?" He waited for her answer and then said, "We're done here. I don't know anything, do I?" He leaped up from his seat and left the alcove.

Gabby and Carlos looked at each other and then at Very. No one said anything. The kids chewed their candy.

"Look, I'm sorry he couldn't tell you anything else." Gabby stood and removed the tiny stool and indicated Very could sit in her chair, the more comfortable seat. "But we're glad to see you again. How have you been? Well, I hope. Are you getting any further on your investigation? I hope so. Don't mind Petey. He just got back. We weren't sure where he'd gone and it didn't feel right. The police were asking about him as well. He didn't have anything to do with anything, but at least he came back. We were getting a little worried, to tell you the truth."

"Especially his girlfriend," Carlos added. "She's pregnant, for sure." He gestured a baby bump.

"Yeah, she was mighty unpleased with Petey," said Gabby.

"Pedro, call him Pedro." Carlos threatened to stand, but there was no room for the gesture, the chairs and table were too tight in the space. "She was really pissed. She thought he had left her for good. I think she was thinking wedding bells."

"Oh, a wedding would be nice, don't you think? But in any case, she wanted him to be around, to say he was the father and at least let the kid know he had a father." Gabby wound down and looked at Very for confirmation that it was the expected thing to do.

"Yeah, that would be nice, I know that," Very put a thoughtful look on her face.

Gabby came closer and whispered, "Why do you know that? Is that what somebody would do? Get married? They're old enough."

"I know that because it happened to me too. A long time ago. It's water under the bridge now, but I know how it feels."

"What happened?" blurted Gabby.

"Got pregnant, was going to get married, but he left the night before the wedding. Never said anything, just disappeared. I still don't know what happened. But there, abandoned."

Gabby leaned in close and whispered, "What happened to your baby?"

"I lost it. Didn't even know whether it was a boy or a girl. Just lost, gone. It was a long time ago." Very sat, trying to avoid any more revelations.

Gabby and Pedro looked at Very. She looked at them, one silent tear crept down her cheek. What did they think of that? This gray-haired old lady, with a story to tell. A teacher, someone too old to have ever been young, left by her man, left with a baby, who then died. The saddest story ever.

An eruption from the front room interrupted the museful interlude. Spanglish flew back and forth. The English part consisted of choice curse words and the Spanish from the older women, soothing murmurs. Very cocked her head and tried to make out the topic and the speakers.

Gabby leaned in, "Oh, he's made trouble for everyone."

Chapter Twenty-four: A Chat with Javier

Amidst the tumult in the living room, Very leaned over to Gabby. "Do you think I could talk with Javier again? I want to ask some more questions. Is that possible?"

"Yeah, he's here, out in the back, I think. He's avoiding the Petey question. Wait here until I check, then I'll take you there. Better than here." Gabby got up and headed out through the kitchen.

When Gabby had gone, Very turned to Carlos, "What are you studying? What's your favorite subject?"

Carlos quickly became shy and hung his head. His answer came in a whisper. "I like studying animals and the weather, you know, natural things. But not biology or chemistry and stuff like that, they're too boring. And too hard for me. Just the animals and things."

Very was about to reply when Gabby reappeared. "Yeah, he's here. C'mon."

Very turned to Carlos. "Study hard, and stay with it."

She followed Gabby out the back way. No one was in the kitchen, which seemed strange this late in the day.

No food preparation was visible. Things must be awfully hot and hectic that food was being forgotten. At least the women were there, in the living room, in the midst of the discussions. They might bring some coolness to the atmosphere.

Gabby bounced down the two steps to the backyard and turned to Very. "He said he'd talk to you because you were sensible. That's what he called you, sensible. Does that mean that you make sense? Boy, I wonder if he'd change his mind if he found out you got left?"

"Well, Gabby, I didn't leave, I got left, it's really different. I didn't do anything, I think. I was abandoned. So, I know how Pedro's girlfriend felt."

"I don't think they are yelling about Petey's girlfriend. It's about the other thing. And I think Javier likes you because you like his motorcycle. He told me. He said you 'admired it.'"

Suddenly, the dog surged from his doghouse and set up an unholy growling and howling. Gabby squeaked in fear and tried to step back, bumping into Very, who also stepped back. The dog barked, throwing spittle on Gabby's feet. She screamed in terror.

The door to the garage flew open and Javier stood in the doorway, shouting curses in Spanish at the hound. It took twenty seconds of barks, howls and curses to stop the noise. Javier approached the dog with a raised hand and the now hang-dog hound backed again into the doghouse. Javier kicked his food dish off into the corner of the yard, a clear signal of who was alpha in their relationship. Very feared the dog, and she also feared Javier. Which did she fear more?

"Sorry about that. He doesn't like all the yelling that's been going on around here. Gabby, go back inside. Let me know if anyone comes, right away. Got that?

Anyone. Keep a low profile, girl." Gabby quickly backed up and disappeared inside, letting the screened backdoor slam. The dog stuck his head out and a low growl emerged.

As Very followed Javier into the garage, she noticed how late it had become. The sun had gone down, disappearing into the low hills to the west. The entire sky had become suffused with a soft pinkish-orange light. The natural rhythm of the earth did not care about the puny concerns of a few of the animals that dwelt there. Arguments, fear, barking dogs, greedy children, these were small concerns to the changing of the day, which inexorably marched on.

Javier's shoulders sagged and Very saw the unshaven face which was unable to hide the lines of tiredness and tension. "He'll shut up once we're inside and close the door. Basically, he's a coward. Just likes to hear his own bark, like some others around here."

Once inside, Javier reached for a small towel and wiped his face, twice. He threw the towel into the corner as small beads of sweat continued to form on his forehead, threatening to run down into his eyes. His shoulders slumped even more as leaned against the gym equipment.

Very looked around for the chair that had been here, but she couldn't see it in the dim light. She really wanted both of them to sit. It's wasn't good to discuss these things standing up. There was a kerfuffle in the main house, so it would be best if there was as little as possible here, when Very hoped to get more clarity on the situation about Mouse.

Very stood, holding her bag over her shoulder, looking around. Javier finally noticed the darkness and lack of seating equipment. "Sorry," he said, stepping behind her to flip a switch that brought light to the garage. Then Very saw the chair. They both reached for it and their hands touched on the back. Very shied away from Javier's touch, as she felt the heat of his emotions. "Sit," he said. A man of few words, to a guest or the dog, a simple command. She sat. He took two steps and sat on the unmade bed. This was a distracted man.

Very tried to use quiet as a balm. Then she started the conversation. "You must be happy that Pedro has come back."

Javier snorted. "Misguided youth."

"How do you mean?" She wasn't going to mention the pregnant girlfriend or the tattoo.

"You know about the tattoo." It wasn't a question, it was a statement. "Do you know what it means?" Javier's eyes closed to slits as he squinted at her.

"It's a '13', the 13th letter of the alphabet, M. I don't know which gang, but it is a sign of gang membership. Right?"

"Stupid young kids. They never learn. Even when it stares them in the face. Or sleeps in the next bed."

Very waited for more of an explanation, or for herself to figure it out. Then she thought she understood. It wasn't about Pedro's girlfriend; it was about the cousin. "Hector?"

"Did you ever wonder why he was here? I didn't know at the beginning. My stepfather's brother-in-law's kid, that's who he was. He was sent here, supposedly to get away from the gangs. He was in trouble. Down in LA. So, ship the kid off to Bakersfield. That's supposed to help? We have no gangs here? No one will snitch on him? Really?"

"I know there is a lot of gang activity in Bakersfield. And you're right, the gangs here are probably all related to LA gangs."

"Not all, some are Nortenos, from up the valley, Northern California. But they all are in contact, a lot through the police department. Crooked cops. But how did they think him being here would get him away from gang activity? It's like finding a poisonous snake. You don't take him out of one snake hole and then put him into another. It's still in the snake pit. All the other snakes know who you are and where you are. You're still a snake."

"But Hector's..." Very sputtered.

"Dead? Yeah, but the evil stays on. The venom, it gets from one to the other. You sleep with snakes, you get bit."

"Is that why you're out here?" Very asked.

Javi looked at his unmade bed and tried to smooth the sheets and tuck in the thin blanket. "Yeah, trying to get away from the evil snake."

"But what about Carlos? And Pedro?"

"I tried with Carlos. I warned Hector off. I threatened him about Carlos. But Pepe, I don't know. Don't get me wrong, I don't think Pepe is evil. But he's been exposed. Like the flu. It's catchy. You have to take precautions."

"Is it serious?" Very looked over her shoulder.

Javi laughed, a tense sardonic snort. "It's not your problem."

"No, it isn't. Sorry for the intrusion. But..." Very saw Javi's jaw clenching and unclenching, along with both fists.

Should get on with it. Questions needed asking. But then, get out of here. This place was itching with an infestation of fleas, or was it bigger, rats? Don't forget the snakes.

"Pedro told me that he had seen my friend, Michelle. And he also said that she was upset, crying. He saw her when she was walking to her car. Does that fit with what you saw?"

"Yeah, maybe she was not happy, upset, crying a little. I'm sorry I didn't tell you that. But what was I supposed to do about it? I couldn't, DO anything. I was looking for her."

"For Maria?"

"Yeah, that snake Hector." Javier stopped and looked out towards the alleyway, cocking his head like a dog trying to pinpoint a sound.

Very also looked out the wide-open door of the garage. The sunset had almost played out. The air vibrated with the last of the colors that tinged some leftover clouds to the south, like puffs of cotton candy.

"So why was she upset?" Very asked.

"I don't know. It wasn't her business and if she had seen them, she should have said something." He shook his head. "No, it wasn't up to her, it was up to me."

"Michelle saw Maria? Do you think they were together?" Very remembered the conversation from the previous visit that unearthed the speculation that Mouse and Maria had somehow or other been together.

"Not together. But maybe your friend found them. I should have stopped it all much, much sooner."

"Found them?"

"Hector and Maria. I should have done something. She was my sister. I knew he was bad. Bad for this whole family. But very, very bad for Maria."

"Hector? What did he…?"

"What didn't he do? They told you about the quinceanera? How she was practicing her dance? She was a little girl. She was only fourteen. She had no business throwing herself around like that. She didn't understand what message she was sending." Javier shook his head and then put his hands on either side of his cranium, squeezing it in frustration. "You see, she didn't know who or what he was. She was like a deer in the headlights or a tiny mouse being hypnotized by a deadly viper. He was like that, sneaky and rotten through and through. Oh, you know what the fancy psychologists would say, 'He had an unhappy childhood.' Hey, he wasn't the only one. My dad ran off, left me with my mother and two very unhappy grandparents. They took it out on me. By the time he came along, I hated all men who were bigger than me and could beat the shit out of me. He's not bad, he tried, but it always came out in the end. They were all his, I wasn't." Javier stopped and caught his breath. He was sweating profusely and breathing quickly, the turmoil in his head seeping out through his pores and now, his mouth. "But he did try and make me graduate from high school, get into the Navy. He's not all bad, but he's NOT MINE."

"Mr. Hernandez? Not your real dad? But that's not his fault. You said he tried. We can only do so much in life. We cannot go back and change the clock, change someone else's behavior. We can only do what is here and now." Very sat quietly, waiting for Javier to expend his bile and become more rational. She needed him to keep to the point.

"So, what was Maria doing that was so bad, so out of whack that you thought you had to intervene?" Very finally asked.

"I caught them once," Javier answered calmly. "She had been 'practicing' her dance. I could hear the music. And her laughing. Then it went quiet. That's not good. He was in her room and she had half her clothes off. And she was high on something. I got mad. Really mad. She was a little girl. She was his cousin. He was supposed to be looking out for her, not trying to get her into bed. Like I said, a snake. An evil, good-for-nothing parasite."

"What did you do?" asked Very quietly.

"I threatened him. I told him off. I told her that she had to watch out for men like this. She just laughed at me. So did he. Maria didn't understand. She didn't understand that he was going to get to the point where he would take what he wanted, whether she liked it or not. She was so stupid and he was so, so…"

"That day, that Saturday. What happened?"

"Maria wanted to go swimming. Everyone said she shouldn't, that she wasn't dressed for it and it was cold and she shouldn't go. So, she at first said okay. Then she disappeared. She could be really sneaky. I was trying to get the barbeque going, so I wasn't paying attention. Then my mom was going to go and so she wanted to check on everybody. But she was missing. So, then we had to decide what to do. Pedro volunteered to go look. But I was busy. Anyway, I said I would go. Everybody just scattered around. Dumb. We should've organized a search, not just everybody go everywhere."

"When was this?" Very asked. "Before or after you saw Michelle?"

"Just about that time. I went looking, nobody but me went that way, at first. I thought she would go where no one else was if she was going to swim in her underwear. She was kinda silly that way. One day she shows it all and the next, gets shy and says no one can see her, her…"

"So, you went to look for her, off to the south, to the little beach?"

"Yeah, I didn't see Maria, but I did see Hector, the snake, go that way. I knew he was following her. So I tried to follow. That's when I saw your friend. She was walking away from that place, that beach, and she was crying. Now I realize that she had probably seen them. Seen Hector try…"

A flash of insight hit Very like a slap in the face. She gasped. It suddenly became clear to her, now that she knew what Mouse had probably seen. Definitely she had seen. Maria and her cousin Hector, the snake pursuing the prey. Mouse had been sitting quietly, a little hidden and there, in the river, in the bushes, or on the beach, she had seen the older man. Maybe he was being nice, maybe he was flattering the young girl, maybe he was trying to persuade. Or maybe he was trying to do worse. Maybe the vile man Hector was finally carrying out his nefarious plan, to sexually attack his young cousin.

Mouse had seen it. And tipped her over the edge, sent her crying to her car. Mouse had committed suicide and Very knew why.

Chapter Twenty-five: The Gang

"Michelle saw Maria and Hector." Very said.

"I guess so. I saw her as I was coming to the little beach. I stepped off the path to let her go by. I didn't want to ask. It's scary for women to see me. In a place like that. Alone. So I just let her go by. That's when I noticed her crying. I watched as she went towards her car. I don't think she saw me. Distracted, like. And then I heard Maria scream."

"Michelle saw them, Maria and Hector, together?"

Javier stood, turned to pace, but found no room. It was too cramped, with the motorcycle, the gym equipment, Very sitting in a chair and his own bulk. He sat back down, but twisted his hands together like he wanted to strangle or contort something. "See? Did she see them? I don't know. I only know what I saw."

Very sat waiting, sitting still, taming her racing heart. This was Javier's story now. He needed to tell it. Tell it in his own way, with his own words, his own version.

"She was there, on the little beach. She had taken off her shorts. But she still had her little blouse thing on. But

I saw him do it. He grabbed and ripped. Like an animal. She screamed. I heard her scream. Like a bird when the hawks get them. You know, aawwwkk." He imitated the high-pitched screech of a red-shouldered hawk as it hunted for prey. Slightly off-kilter, the prey and the predator reversed, but the effect was dramatic, as intended.

Very leaned forward and opened her mouth, wanting to ask for more details. She stayed like that for five seconds, then snapped her jaws shut. This was Javi's story. She sat back.

The glow from the overhead light was the only illumination now. Night had begun. As Very turned to watch, the shadows in the alley merged until everything was black outside, like a shade coming down on a window, shutting out everything. The noises from the street crept into the alleyway, but it was quiet here; no one was using the narrow pot-holed alley to go anywhere. They were only two here. The teller and the listener.

"Okay, okay. I'll tell you. You might as well know it all. Someone needs to know my story. Needs to know the truth. They might say anything, but only I know all. I know the real story. I'll tell you. Then someone will know. You will know. You can tell it like it came from me."

Very did not move. Her bag slipped off her shoulder and came to rest in her lap. She let it stay there, fearing to break the thread.

"I've got to tell you now. It can't wait any longer. It's my only chance." Javier looked around again, listening for something. He shook his head. He began to sweat again. What frightened this man? He could crush just about anyone but a giant. Who could scare him like this?

"You see, Hector had been doing it for a while, making eyes at Maria. She thought she was Selena. She said she was channeling the great, glorious, and very dead Selena. You know, you can find her in Youtube videos, all of her videos. She thought she would be a princess, if she just had the clothes, the moves, the…you know, the look. She flirted like a little whore. She didn't know better. She was, like they say, naïve.

"But Hector knew what he wanted. What all men want. But Hector knew that it would cause problems in the family, and he wanted that as well. He chased her. He texted her. He flattered her. He told her she was just like Selena. He stalked her, just like those filthy old men. I tried to explain it all to Maria, but she laughed. She thought it was funny. She said she could handle it. I warned her." Javier sat down again and caught his breath.

Very wanted to ask what happened, when Javier went on.

"That Saturday, Maria said she was going swimming. My mom said she couldn't go in her clothes and she had no swimming suit. Sparks flew. It was like dragging metal on the ground. Bang, bang, bang. In Spanglish, all the bad words that both of them knew in both languages. It was funny. I thought it was funny then. I laughed at them. Then Mom left. She had to go to work. Did she think that was going to be the end of it? Maria knew it wasn't. She disappeared. She just wandered off. I didn't see her go. I wasn't paying attention. I didn't want to get caught up in that drama. Mothers and daughters. Drama queens.

"But then I saw Hector walking away. He was a man with a mission. I saw him, but I didn't think about what it meant. Then I asked Gabby about Maria, where she had gone. Gabby was sassy. Said, 'Mary will do what she wants to do.' Said she went to the bathroom. Then she changed her mind and told me that Maria went swimming. She was going to go to a place by herself, so no one would see what she was, or wasn't, wearing. That made me a little scared. Gabby said that she had asked to go with her, but Maria told her to stay and watch that no one went after her. Gabby was beginning to get scared about then. She knew it wasn't a good idea. Then I remembered Hector.

"Hector the snake. I know that he was following Maria. I left the barbeque, someone else could do that, and I went after him. I tried to follow which direction he went. Because then I knew that he was following Maria. Stupid, naïve, little Maria."

"What were the others doing? Did they all realize that Maria was gone?" Very leaned forward. She strained to keep up with the story, trying to follow the sequence of events and the persons involved. Javier's emotions robbed him of coherence at times.

"Yeah, they all began to panic. They just rushed around, yelling for Maria. Some went to the bathrooms, trying to find her. I knew which way she went, but I didn't say anything. I knew that Hector went that way too. He was following her. So I just took off and went that way. I went towards the bushes across the road. But I couldn't see or hear anything. I couldn't really follow anybody. I spent way too much time, just crashing through the bushes and going up one walking path and then another. They all kind of dead-ended and I didn't know. Then I heard something. I thought it was Maria, or Hector, but it was your friend." Javier gestured at Very's purse, which he knew contained the photo.

"And she was walking towards her car, crying? Isn't that what you said?" Very asked, happy to get back to her point of what happened to Mouse.

"Yeah, I tried to ask her, but I told you. I scare people. I was going to ask if she had seen Maria or Hector, but I thought that she wouldn't tell me. I stepped back into the bushes, to get out of her way. So she wouldn't see me. Then I watched her go towards her car. Then I went the way she was coming from. I wanted to see what made her upset. But I think I knew."

Javier stopped here and sighed deeply. Very waited for him to go on. He said he would tell her everything, so she needed to wait for him.

"I thought maybe Hector had been bothering her. I wanted to ask, but you know, I'm big and I'm like some hulk-thing. But I went that way and then I saw. I saw Hector. He had his hands on Maria. They were there, on the edge of the water, at the little beach. I just saw red. Really, honestly, it was like blood came over my eyes and my head pounded. I just ran at him. I pushed him into the water and I grabbed him. I don't know what happened. It was so fast. Everything was so fast. And hard. Punch, pull, smack."

"And where was Maria?" Very whispered.

"I don't know. I didn't see where she was. I thought it was just me and Hector. I didn't care about her. I didn't see her. I was punching and hitting and dragging at Hector. I thought she got out of the water, that she ran back. I didn't care about anything. I pushed his head under the water and I squeezed his neck. When he didn't fight back any more. I let him go. God, that water was cold and I got out. I was shivering and I didn't care.

Hector just went away, down the river. And Maria? I couldn't see her. I…"

Javier had just confessed to murdering his cousin Hector. Very held her breath as long as she could, then let it out slowly. What was he going to do now? He should've thought about that before he confessed.

"And when I got out, I saw Pedro, my brother Pepe. I didn't know then what he saw. But now I do. He saw everything. He stood there and watched everything. He watched Hector try to rape Maria. He saw me kill Hector. Why didn't he try to save Maria? I don't know. I didn't get a chance to ask him. He just ran. He left then. He is a coward. I am a killer, but he is worse. He is a coward who watched his sister die, then he left."

"And now he's come back," Very said.

"Yeah, he's come back. And what has he brought with him? He brought the ugliness back with him. He didn't even try."

Javier's face twisted into a bright red ball of pain. "No, it's not all his fault. It's mine. I let Maria drown. I let her die. I was focusing on Hector. I wanted to get him. I wanted to kill him. I wasn't going to let him get away with anything. It was all about me. All about what I wanted. I didn't think about Maria. I forgot her. I forgot that this was about that poor stupid little girl and that she couldn't defend herself. That was what it was about. Not me. Not me and my big hands and my anger. It should've been about Maria. And I let her down. I didn't try to save her. I forgot about her. That's the worst thing about this. It's not that I killed Hector. I killed Maria. She died because of me. I could've saved her. But I didn't. I was selfish. I killed my little sister."

Tears now began to fall from Javier's eyes. "Maria, Maria." He murmured her name. "I let you go down the river and I didn't even try."

A noise came from the street.

They both turned towards the sound. It was muffled by the garage and the closed door, but they both knew what direction it came from. Cars and trucks were gunning their engines, out in the street, in the front of the Hernandez house.

"What is that?" Very stood.

"They're coming for me. They don't know or care anything about you. You have to go."

"Who's coming?" A flicker of fear crept into Very's voice.

"Hector's gang. Pedro told them. He knows, or he guessed about Hector. How Hector 'drowned'. So, now, Hector's gang has come for me."

The garage door flew open just then. Gabby, wild fear etched on her face, stood at the door.

"Get out. Go. Gabby will take you." Javier turned to Gabby. "All safe? Like we talked about?"

Gabby nodded vigorously.

"Take her. You know the way, the back way. Careful of cars in the alley." Javier's voice was steady. "It's better this way. They only want me. Go!"

Gabby grabbed Very's hand. Very felt the sweat and stickiness from the Dewar's chews. They went out into the darkness of the alley. Very turned to look at Javier. His shoulders had relaxed and he casually leaned against the magnificent Harley-Davidson. He turned his face towards the open doorway. The dog had begun to set up a low howl at the noise. Javier leaned over and doused the light.

Very let herself be guided into the alleyway beside Gabby. The night was dark, with no moonlight or street lights in the alley. No cars cruising the back roads to light their way. Gabby tried to pull on her hand, but Very hesitated, waiting for her eyes to adjust to the little light from the sky.

"Miss Very, we have to go. They are bad men and they won't hesitate if we're still here. They will hurt us."

"But what about Javi? Can we just leave?" Very's voice had dropped to a whisper, even though the noise from the street continued at ear-splitting volume.

"It's Javi they are looking for. They don't care about the rest of us. We need to leave."

Very still hesitated, torn between saving her own skin and trying to protect Javier. What kind of person was she to just creep out the back door and leave someone there alone, facing danger?

A shout was followed by a gunshot, close at hand, probably at the back door.

Very allowed Gabby to take her hand and pull her deeper into the dark alley.

Chapter Twenty-six: Escape

Very felt the tugging at her hand, but she could hardly see anything. Young things, with their super eyesight, they needed to take the lead. Very took her bag and slipped it across her chest, bandolier-style, giving herself two hands to feel with. Gabby still had one hand firmly gripped, but Very used the free hand to feel the sides of the garage and then the next yard's fence. She looked across the alley and heaved a sigh of relief. She could see the fence just fifteen feet away, a white painted wooden fence. She blinked and more came into focus. Gabby whispered and pulled at her hand again.

"Let's go this way," Gabby said, heading east towards the unseen hills, towards Hart Park, towards the river. "Your car is this way."

"How do you know where my car is?" Very whispered back.

Gabby giggled, a bizarre reaction to the tense situation. "I have eyes in the back of my head. My Dad says so. I watched you. It's red, your car is red. And new, it kind of sticks out a little on the street."

"And who are the people in the street? Where did they come from?" Very burned to know the answers to the questions that bubbled up.

"They are Hector's gang. They come from LA. They are here for him. For Javi. Like he said, it's only him they want. But we need to get out of here. It's revenge time. That's what Petey said. And we can't be here. Just hold my hand, I know the way."

Very let the twelve-year-old lead her down the alley. They had gone only one house down when a flash of light blinded them.

Gabby pulled on Very's hand and pushed her towards the side of the alley. Very, startled by the gesture, lost her balance and fell on her left knee. "Ohhhmph," she said.

"Quiet, quiet," Gabby said. Then she pulled Very close to her and they moved up behind some large beige garbage receptacles.

Very rubbed at her knee and her hand came away with muck and gravel. At least her slacks had not torn.

Gabby poked her head up cautiously, until the car's headlights lit up the top of her head. "Oh," she squealed. She pulled Very down, behind the garbage cans. "Don't move."

Very crouched down and waited. Her legs began to cramp in the squatting position she had taken. "Ooooooh," she complained quietly.

"He's not moving. Just a lookout. How can we get past him?" Gabby said. "I want to see, but I don't want to get up."

"Even if you could get up, the light would blind you. Just stay here," Very shifted her legs and got some relief, but she, too, had to resist the urge to look.

Suddenly, there was a noise from behind the car. Car doors opened, slammed shut, voices shouted. Very quivered with fear. Then the car slowly backed out of the alley, its lights swiveling and illuminating the fences and trash in the alley. It returned to the street and drove away.

As soon as the alley was dark once more, Gabby pulled on Very's hand again. Very stood, but realized that her height was against her; anyone could see her if she stood. She bent over and tried again to follow Gabby's lead down the alley.

The noise from the street the Hernandez family lived on continued unabated. Rumblings from cars, shouts and then, banging on a door. Very listened for more gunshots, but there was only the one that she had heard in the beginning of the melee.

Just as Gabby and Very neared the end of the alleyway, yet another car entered, this time from the opposite end of the block. Gabby ran for the nearest cluster of plastic refuse cans. Diving into the center, Gabby grabbed Very's hand and then pulled the three different colored bins around them, creating a barrier. The beige one, garbage, stood sticking out into the center of the alley. The green, garden waste only, protected them on the left and the last one, blue, the recycling bin, blocked the view towards the headlights on the car. In the center of the putrid plastic place of refuge, Very crouched. This time, she had the good sense to be afraid.

Raucous music blared from the car's speakers as the car began a slow procession along the alley. At the midpoint, just feet away from the Hernandez's garage, the car stopped. Shouts emerged and then the lowrider car began to jump up and down. The hydraulic system caused the car to bounce, the lights rising wildly, then coming down. Very peeped around the edge of the blue can she hid behind. The music, the shouts, and the wildly bouncing car was a circus act performed by the out-of-towners. The locals stayed inside.

Then the car stopped the wild gyrations and proceeded down the alley. Very and Gabby pulled inside their refuge, listening as the car processed down the tiny back street.

Suddenly, the engine roared and the car picked up speed, blasting past them on its way to the street. The car clipped the outermost plastic can and the whole light-weight beige bin went flying, landing with a crunch and a splat on the far side of the alley. Both Very and Gabby sat, exposed to whoever looked.

But no one looked. Very had been crouching so long, she had developed cramps and so released the tension in her thighs by sitting on the ground. She immediately regretted the action as she felt wetness seep through her slacks. The smell of one-week-old garbage, that had been sitting in the sun in a closed plastic bin, with all kinds of thrown-away items fermenting together, rose up from the dirty alley to assault her. "Blah," she cried, shooting up from her position.

"Have they gone?" she asked in what she thought sounded like a normal voice, although significant wavering in the throat accompanied the croaking sound.

"Shhh. Yes, they've gone, but there are more. Let's get out of here." Gabby grabbed for Very's hand and jerked her forward.

Within seconds, they were on the sidewalk of the cross street. Very reached for a support as a miasma of uncoordinated shivers hit her. She felt a familiar light headedness and bent over, gulping air to force her oxygen levels up. Gabby dropped her hand and turned back to look at Very, now bent double and rasping loudly. "Are you okay?" Gabby said softly.

"Yeah, yeah, just a minute. I just need to catch my breath," Very gasped out.

Gabby inched backwards towards the fence that enclosed the backyard at the end of the block. Very allowed herself to be led until she felt the fence at her back. Slowly she stood upright and inhaled deeply twice more. Fainting here was a very bad idea, but so was standing at the end of the block, exposed to all who cared to look.

It was then that Very noted the absence of light, even the porch lights had been turned off. "Why is it so dark?"

"Pttt. It's always this way. C'mon. Your car is just down here."

They scampered down the sidewalk, which ended abruptly at the Hernandez's street. Very saw one porch light on, just up the block, otherwise the street was bathed in shadows and obscurities. Houses loomed on all sides and the street was littered with silent cars, with the exception of those in front of the Hernandez house. The headlights were off, but the roar of the cars was like the trumpeting of elephants before a charge. The lowrider car had stopped in the very middle of the street and was gearing up for a repeat of the alley show.

Her car was there, in front of her, exactly as she had left it. She bent down to hide herself and edged around the car, trying to keep her body low and obscured. When she reached the driver's door, she shifted her bag to the front and sucked in her breath. This lockless entry had always worked. This time it was crucial; her life might depend on it. Whoever invented this was to be praised or damned. Just make it work.

Very reached up and tried the door handle. A small beep reached her ears as she quickly glanced down the street. No one was obviously looking in her direction. She moved as swiftly as she had ever done. She opened the door and slipped inside. She closed it shut behind her. She slunk down into her seat and tried to douse the automatic inside lights. But they went off before she could figure out which switch or button to press.

Then she saw Gabby, face pressed against the passenger door, frantically trying to open the door. "Help," she mouthed, "let me in."

Very hit the button to unlock the door. She couldn't hear the click for the racket behind her, but the door opened and Gabby jumped inside, pulling the door shut behind her.

She checked the rearview mirror. No one was paying attention to the red Prius five doors up the block.

"Go, go, go fast." Gabby blubbered urgently.

"No, no. We go slow, very slowly."

"But we have to hurry. Get out of here quick." Gabby's tears began to surface as emotion wracked her body.

"We need to get out of here unseen. We need to be silent, as quiet as we can." Very touched the ignition button. She grimaced in fear as the car gave a quiet hum, then went quiet.

"Shh," Very warned. She released the brake and let the car find its own setting. She stretched her foot onto the gas pedal, giving it the slightest nudge. The car began to move forward, silently.

"Wow," breathed Gabby. "How did you do that? How is this car moving and no sound?"

"It's a Prius, a hybrid car. The electric motor is running now. If we go really slowly, we can be almost silent."

No one had parked in front of Very, so she stayed in the far right of the street. She cautiously looked in the rearview mirror. The clamor and noise continued behind her and now, she could see figures exiting the cars and streaming towards the house.

"Keep your head down," Very warned Gabby. "Don't look, don't make any movement."

Very drove quietly. As she neared the end of the block, she slowed and tried to see if anyone else was coming. With no lights, this car was a sitting duck; a big, dark moving beast in the road. She pressed on the accelerator and the car whirred into life and picked up speed. Very punched on the lights and went faster.

Behind her, the sounds of chaos exploded. Car horns blared. And in the background of that, gunshots, lots of them. Very peeked into the rearview and saw bursts of light. She stepped on the gas and the car roared, leaping down the street.

"Stop, stop." Gabby screeched beside her.

"No, I've got to get us out of here. We can't stop now."

"But we're here. Stop, here it is." Gabby tried to open the door. Very punched on the brakes, screeching to a stop in the middle of the street.

Gabby grabbed the door handle and pulled, then she threw herself out of the car.

Very looked and saw a dark, quiet house. The front door slipped open and in the rectangle of light that poured out into the yard, Very saw figures. Suddenly, the screen door opened and a familiar-looking body threw itself out onto the cement walkway.

"Wait," Very yelled out the open door. "What? Who?"

Gabby waved at the figure standing illuminated from behind by the light from inside, then turned back to the car. "It's okay now. They're all safe, and so am I. And you too."

"But whose house is this? Who are they?" Very called out the open door.

"Oh, this is aunty's house. It looks like they are all here. Thanks for the ride," Gabby said before closing the door. Very recognized the slight figure that rushed to greet Gabby as her brother Carlos. He grabbed her arm and pushed her towards the house. The group of people at the front door waved. Mom, Dad, grandma, and maybe aunty as well. Very waved back, not sure she could be seen.

Behind her, no longer visible as a group of cars with guns blazing, the scene lit up. The sound wave of the "boom" broke over the car, compelling Very to step on it. She raced up the street as porch lights now blazed on and inhabitants spilled outside, craning their necks to see what was happening behind her.

A dust devil, one of those little tiny tornadoes, blew up from the street behind her, swooping her up into the wind vortex. Very stopped and squinted as the dust and debris hit the windscreen, pinging and scratching the glass. Damn, the dust had baptized this windscreen. This car was not very old, but now, and forever, it would bear the mark of the desert. A car of Bakersfield.

The mini-whirlwind had left behind debris that clung to the windshield wipers and caught under the lip of the hood. Tiny white papers, dozens of them, crinkled and sticky. Very leaned forward and read the teeny labels. "Dewars." More of them came swirling past.

Dozens, hundreds and hundreds, came racing down the street, caught up in the wind. Very had not brought this many chews to the Hernandez's house. Where had they come from? Why was the air so full of these papers?

Very drove through the flying debris until she reached a familiar street name. She turned left and sped up the hill, to her mother's La Cresta neighborhood.

Chapter Twenty-seven: Escaping the Gang from LA

As her head cleared, Very's driving became steadier and she lowered her shoulders that had been bunched up by her neck. She had escaped. But what had she left behind? And what knowledge did she take with her that could be useful? To the police? To Javier?

As she swung into the street to her house, her mother's house, she noted the lack of street lights here as well. Just like the poorer neighborhoods of East Bakersfield, as this, too, was an island of county in the midst of the City of Bakersfield. No sidewalks, no street lights, no police services; only county sheriffs ever bothered with this enclave.

She pulled into the driveway and immediately doused her car lights. She sat for a moment and then unbuckled her seat belt. Wait, how did it get buckled? Who did that? When? She breathed deeply, then fished her phone out of her bag and speed-dialed Joey.

After only one ring, the phone was answered. "Very," said Joey in a breathless voice. "Where are you?"

"Whoa, lady. I'm okay. At home, where would I be?" Very hunched her shoulders in anticipation of the next question; which would be about where she had been.

"Are you alone? Safe?"

"Alone, of course. Why do you ask?"

Very got out her keys and was just about to insert them into the back door, when Joey hissed. "Stay where you are, don't move. I'm coming. Or rather, turn off all your lights and wait for me."

"Joey, what is it that you are not telling me?"

"Very, what is it that you are not telling me? You need to duck and hide. Are you inside? Do you see anything?"

Very, backed away from the door and hid behind her car. "Joey, what is it? Am I in danger?"

"Honestly, Very. Are you okay? Where have you been?" Noises of getting into a car, shouted instructions for someone to watch a little one, a barking dog, all intruded upon the conversation.

The silence on Very's end prompted Joey to give up some information. "The shooting in East Bakersfield. At the Hernandez house. Were you there?"

Very peeked out into the street. This part of the La Cresta neighborhood was as quiet as the cemetery just around the corner. The chaos of a few minutes ago was far, far away. "Yeah, I was. I was there when a lot happened. I don't know what exactly."

"Ok, listen to me, Very. Are you inside the house?"

"No, not yet, I just got home. I'm in the driveway, hiding from the boogeymen of my lovely upscale neighborhood."

"Listen carefully. Is your house locked up tight?"

"Yeah, as far as I know." Very inserted her key into the lock and cautiously opened the door. "Door carefully locked. Quiet inside, no lights. No movements."

"Don't turn on any lights. Just pack a small bag, you're coming here, at least for now. Yeah, yeah, put it in the trunk."

"Joey, put what in the trunk?"

"I'm not talking to you. Just be ready for me. No lights, creep around like a thief."

Very heard the trunk slam and Joey start the car. "Be as quiet as you can. I'm coming."

The tone of Joey's voice was enough to turn Very's rapidly beating heart into a thunderous pounding. The violence at the Hernandez house hadn't followed her, had it? She had left it in the neighborhood where it had started. End of story.

Nevertheless, Very crept like a criminal into her own house. She stopped at the fridge and slipped a hand into the door and extracted a bottle of water, which she drank greedily while crouching below the window level. It was then that she noticed the smell. The garbage, she had forgotten to take it out. And now, it had taken over the kitchen, the stench of rotting vegetables and…

Very knelt and turned around. She took a hand and touched the back of her slacks, still wet with putrid goo from underneath the garbage bin in the alley. "Oh, no," she whispered to herself.

Slipping off her shoes, which she left in the kitchen, Very couched down and darted towards the bathroom. Once there, she slipped off her clothing of the nether regions and threw it in the dirty clothes bin. As soon as she had done this, she regretted the hasty action. Those slacks needed to join the glop that clung to them in the dump, not in her clean house. The lid to the dirty clothes hamper had closed and the stench had significantly lessened. Need to deal with that later.

She darted into her bedroom and in the dark, slipped on fresh clothes and gathered the few things she needed for a night away. She reached into the bottom drawer and blindly felt for the travel anywhere, anytime bag of cosmetics, creams and shampoo. "Gotcha," she said triumphantly, hoping that the small vials and plastic bottles had not been depleted from the last trip. When was that? Certainly before her mother's death a year before. She grabbed nightgown, underwear, a light sweater, stuffing them into a small overnight bag.

Still clinging to her purse, she retraced her steps to the kitchen. In the darkness, she dared a short look out into the street. Quiet.

Near the back door, Very reached for the door handle, but missed and knocked over a bag that sat on the counter. It was there waiting for Very to dispose of it, near the door where she wouldn't overlook or forget it. The bag fell and with a shattering splat, scattered cat kibble all over the vestibule near the back door. No time to pick it up; Very left it. She crunched over the noisy cat food as she made her way out the door.

When she had reached the carport outside, she stood and breathed deeply. The next step she took was with no care for the round, slippery kibble and as she fell, she realized that some had stuck to the bottom of her shoe, creating an effect like marbles under her feet. She tumbled sideways, banging her elbow on the cement.

"Damn," she said aloud. She rubbed her elbow, hoping any blood would not run down and ruin this shirt as well.

A car, its engine running quietly, crept up the street, slowing and stopping in front of the house. Very peeked out from behind her car and saw Joey get out of the car. Joey whispered, "Very, are you here?"

Very stood and stepped from behind the car, nursing her elbow. "Yeah, I'm here. Are we ready?"

"Not quite. Come and help me with this thing. It's in the trunk."

Very walked to the car, opened the back door and stowed her gear in the back seat as Joey struggled with something from the trunk. Very closed the door and went to the back to help Joey. "What in the world is it?"

"Bobby made me bring it. It's a car cover. For your car, so we can hide it from anyone trying to find you."

"Are they looking for me? How do they know me? Do they know where I live?" Was she surprised that anyone would care about her?

"Bobby says to put it over the car. C'mon, help me with this, it's too heavy for one person." Joey demonstrated by grunting when she tried to lift it out of the deep trunk. Very jumped to her side and the two pulled it out amid loud grunts and not-so-nice words. They carried it awkwardly to Very's car.

Despite attempts at silence, their grunts of exertion, sotto voce directions, and expletives when fingernails got caught or they dropped their end of the heavy canvas car cover created a small disturbance. Ten minutes later, they had managed to cover the car, and the license plate. The carport was open to the street, but the shadows of the night hid all.

Joey shook her head as she headed to the car, still sitting silently in the street in front of Very's house. She clamped her mouth shut as she drove to her own house on the other side of town. Very remained silent, contemplating what she would say. She knew that Bobby Sanchez would have some pointed questions for her and she wanted to rehearse her answers.

When they arrived at the Sanchez family home, it was like entering into the chaos of a mafia hit murder. Three sheriff's cars were parked in front, other cars littered the street parking, the front door hung open and music, along with the clink of bottles and ping of aluminum cans, arose from the backyard.

"Are you having a party?" Very asked.

"No, I'm not. But the men, well…"

At that moment, a small figure emerged from the front door and ran out to the street. "Grandma, Grandma." Clara wrapped her arms around Joey's leg. Then she noticed Very. "Ah, Aunt Berry. Come and eat dinner with us."

"Sounds like a plan," Very said brightly. "Let me wash my hands."

"Put your stuff in our bedroom," Joey said quietly. "We'll sort it out later. Don't know who's in which room and who might be sleeping. Babies, you know."

Very followed Joey and Clara into the house, but was waylaid by Bobby Sanchez, in full uniform. "This way, please," he said, indicating the den.

A huge TV screen adorned one wall, and deep couches, a huge lounge chair and footrests littered the rest of the space. Bobby indicated that Very should take a seat on the couch. Very looked at it. She had been there before. Once, she had thrown herself onto the couch and then sank miles and miles into the deep cushions. She had had trouble getting up from the half-reclining position the couch had put her in. Now, she hesitated.

"Can I sit in a chair? This is totally uncomfortable." She stood, rubbing at her injured elbow. "Or is being uncomfortable what you want me to be?"

Bobby left the room and returned with a kitchen chair, setting it near the couch. Very sat. "Oh, please do take a seat as well," she said, waving at the couch.

"I'll stand. He'll take notes." Bobby indicated a younger man, sitting at a desk in the corner. "Now, Very, if you know anything at all about this shooting, you need to tell us."

"Shooting? Me?" Very blinked and tried to smile. She would have batted her eyelashes if necessary. "Wait, why are you asking me? Or are you interrogating me? Is this official? Because if it is, I need to know. You have no right to just make me sit here and ask questions. So, what is it? Casual or…"

"Very, this is a shooting, as in people have been shot, presumed dead." Deputy Sanchez stood taller, spread his legs and crossed his arms. "This is now very serious. This is no longer PI Blew pretending to investigate a simple suicide. There is death this time, deliberate. Although this is not official, I'm serious now."

Chapter Twenty-eight: The Shooting

"I didn't see any shooting. So, let's start there. I didn't see anything. But I did hear what could have been gunshots, lots of them. But I also heard shouting, music, and hydraulic cars."

"Where were you?" Bobby pushed.

"Exactly? In the alley."

"What were you doing in the alley?"

"Leaving." Very crossed her arms in front of her chest. Surely, Bobby could read that bit of body language as he had practiced it himself.

"Very, if you know anything at all about this shooting, please tell us." Bobby turned a stern face towards her.

Outside the room, a squawking set up, official communications. Bobby looked over his shoulder, torn between extracting information from Very and finding out the latest developments.

"Like what happened? Or who did it? Or why?" The sarcasm in Very's voice belied the real questions she hoped could be answered. Just not by her.

The tug of inquisitiveness pulled Bobby from the room, followed by the sidekick from the corner. Very got up from the hard chair and heaved a sigh of contentment as she sank into the enveloping softness of the couch. She closed her eyes. There was no illusion about being able to sleep, just a moment to recoup some energy.

Five minutes later, Joey appeared, carrying a large glass of cola with clanking ice cubes and some cookies. "Sugar," she announced.

Very reached for the glass and drank. "Thanks, sweetie. Do you know what happened? Have they told you anything?" Before waiting for a reply, Very hurried on. "I mean, I don't know if I can say anything without knowing what was happening. I was there, but I didn't see anything. I was in the alley when all hell broke loose outside, but again, I didn't see anything. What can I say?"

"Answer the questions. What can I tell you?" Joey reached over and punched the remote. The TV flickered and came to life. Joey lowered the volume and flipped through channels. "Too early for the news." She pressed some more and then she found it.

A reporter stood in the street outside the Hernandez house in East Bakersfield. The reporter held a fuzzy microphone to his chest and a look of weighty austerity was directed to the camera. "Tonight, the tragedy continues. We are live at the scene. One brother has been killed and another badly wounded when gang members targeted the Hernandez family home. If you recall, less than two weeks ago, Maria Hernandez, aged fourteen, and her cousin Hector Fernandez, aged 25, both drowned in the Kern River while swimming at Hart Park. Tonight, a gang associated with Hector Fernandez, from East LA, invaded the Hernandez home and opened fire. Sheriff's deputies are at the scene at the moment. It appears to be yet another gang shooting with LA gang members invading the turf in Bakersfield."

The background showed lights, cars, neighbors gathering to gawk and a strong wind sweeping the street. "Wait, there's breaking news. Some gang members have been detained and are being questioned now. More news at 11."

Joey turned the channels, but there was no more news on this early in the evening.

"Ok," Very said. "Now it makes more sense."

"It makes no sense at all," Joey countered. "The guy drowns in the river and then his gang comes from LA and attacks the family? What's the sense in that?"

"Revenge. Where's Bobby?" Very asked.

"Here I am. Are you ready to talk yet?" Bobby stood in front of the couch.

Very looked up. "The reporter said two brothers were involved, one dead, one injured. Which one is dead?"

"The older brother, Javier, is dead. The younger brother, Pedro, is badly injured and is at the hospital. They think he'll live. Okay, now tell me what you know."

Very looked at her hands, holding the big glass of cola, now empty. "He's dead. It's hearsay, isn't it? No one on earth can touch him now. He's with the angels, as Clara would say."

"Angels? Pah, not that one," Bobby snorted.

"Oh, pardon me, did you know him?" Very struggled to rise from the depths of the sofa.

"There you are," said the newest arrival, Darrell. He pushed Bobby out of the way and knelt down by the sofa.

Very looked at Darrell's face, crisscrossed with anxiety. "How did you get here?"

Darrell held his breath, but over his shoulder, Very saw Joey, a guilty look on her face. She bit her lip and then mouthed at Very, "I called him."

Darrell said, "I should have gone with you. Trouble, you always find the trouble!"

"That's not fair, Darrell. Look, I'm fine, no harm done. Here, help me get out of this hellhole." Very struggled to get upright.

Darrell bent over Very and grabbed her under her elbow. A strange look passed over his face and he sniffed Very, like a dog trying to tell if a fellow dog is friend or foe. "Very, I hate to say this, but you smell funny."

"Shh, I'll tell you later. Just help me stand up." When she was standing, eye to eye with Deputy Sanchez, she said, "I will tell you what Javi told me. But I have no proof of anything and I doubt you do either. And you didn't know Javi Hernandez."

She turned to Darrell. "I solved the case. I am sure, almost 100%, that Michelle committed suicide, just like everyone, except her sister, said she did."

"Yeah, I heard from her sister. She said that she contacted a friend, someone that we didn't know about, who had spoken with Mouse, aka Michelle, or is that the other way around? Anyway, this friend spoke with her in the last few weeks of her life. Mouse was very depressed and spoke often of suicide. The sister was, understandably, unhappy that her sister hadn't confided in her. But, sisters, huh? Apparently, it was about an event that had happened a long time ago, some sort of sexual harassment as a teenager. She was having trouble coping with the memory." Darrell shrugged as if he did not quite get why someone would be unhappy years later.

"Exactly. That's what I figured out. So, is Mouse's sister satisfied?" Very's shoulders fell with the weight falling off of them.

"Yes, she is even going to pay us as promised. Why people do this, I don't know. Contact me, then solve their own problem. But, are you okay?" Darrell looked at Very with troubled eyes.

"Physically, yes. And I'll live."

Darrell touched Very's sore elbow and she squeaked.

Darrell jumped. "Sorry, did you get hurt?"

"Not much. I'll live."

"Come by the office tomorrow and we can sort all of this out. Late, maybe 10ish?" Darrell's face was not that of the boss asking the employee to come to work.

"Now," Very looked at Bobby. "I'll answer your questions. I went to the Hernandez house to ask about Mouse. And I found the answers I needed. I was just in the wrong place at the wrong time."

"Okay, okay. The rest of you, out. Very, sit down." Bobby swung his arm and indicated that the extraneous people in the room ought to leave.

Very sat in the kitchen chair. Bobby found another chair the same height and sat opposite her. Out of the corner of her eye, Very saw the young assistant had once again taken an unobtrusive seat in the darkish corner.

"First," Very started. "Can you tell me about the rest of the family? Are they okay?"

"Yes, all present and accounted for. Staying with relatives. No one but the two brothers were even in the house at the time."

Very took note of this tidbit of information and ran it through the timeline she was going to present. If Gabby wasn't in the house, then neither was she. She left before the gangsters from LA arrived. "How's the house? Was there much damage?"

"The house survived, but not the garage. And no other dwellings were damaged. A few psyches in the neighborhood were traumatized, I guess. But… Wait, you are telling me that you were there? Definitely, this evening. What did you see, what can you tell us?"

"I went there to ask again about Mouse, if they had seen her or not. And I found out the information that I was seeking. Yes, they saw her. Even Pedro, who I met just this afternoon, for the first time. And they told me that she was upset. Apparently, she had been there when Maria and Hector were near the river. Of course, all three of those people are dead, so I don't really know what happened. Just the reports of the others about Mouse." Very stopped.

"And did you talk with Javier?" Bobby pressed.

"Yes," Very answered. She hesitated. How much was too much information? After all, Javier was dead. And no one else knew the contents of the conversation they had.

"He…was, really, really upset. Almost in tears. He felt so guilty. He felt as though he was responsible for Maria's death. He said that he was too late to save her. The river took her away so quickly. He was in tears, so I couldn't really get all of it."

"And Hector's gang? What were they doing at his house?"

"You know Hector died too. Drowned. And Hector was in Bakersfield because of something to do with his gang, or rather some other gang. I don't know. I just wanted to ask about Mouse."

"And what did Javier say about Hector?"

Very hesitated. "Well, Hector was there, wasn't he? And I don't think he could swim. So, Hector was a sure one to go under. You know, Maria could swim, so could Javi. But if the river was too much for Javi, it must have been hell for a guy from LA who had never learned to swim. The Killer Kern isn't called that for nothing, you know."

"So, you were there? You talked with Javier, but you don't know why Hector's gang from LA would target Javier?"

"If you look for fingerprints, yeah, you'll find mine. Mostly in the garage, that's where we talked."

"The garage is gone."

"Completely? Everything? Including the… motorcycle?" Very looked down, trying to hide the pain that crossed her face at the mention of the destruction. She had not yet taken in the idea of Javier's death, but that the machine he loved was gone too, threatened to tip her over the edge. She gritted her teeth.

"Yeah, the motor's gone. Someone put a bullet hole through it, probably hit the gas tank and everything went. There's not much left. Sorry about that. It's hard to take in. Very, tell me what he said." Deputy Sanchez leaned in.

"He said," she hesitated. "This is just what he said, you know. Just his version of events. And I can't quote what he said, exactly. Can I? I was upset, he was upset. I don't remember exactly."

Bobby was silent, waiting for Very to get her version of events as straight as she was going to get them. The other side of the story was gone. He wouldn't be able to say whether Very told the story straight, or crooked.

"He said that he was a terrible brother, letting his sister die. He was full of anger at Hector, and he let that cloud his judgment. Instead of saving Maria, he took it out on Hector. For being a bad cousin, for being a bad man. Now, those weren't his exact words, but that is the gist. Maybe Hector's gang thought Javi had something to do with the drowning. But it was a tragic accident, wasn't it? Even I would hesitate to go into that river that day."

"And when did you leave? What time?"

"Oh, Sheriff Sanchez, that's a tough one. I didn't look at my watch. But Gabby and I left together, and I gave her a ride to her aunty's house. She lives just down the street. The aunt. I saw the rest of the family; they waved at me."

Bobby stared at Very. He had known her long enough to know that if Vermilion Blew gave a statement, that was it.

Very stood, "Are we done here? I'm hungry. I was promised dinner."

As Very headed for the door, Bobby spoke again. "One last little thing. We found some papers scattered in the street. All over the street, as a matter of fact. I just wondered if you knew anything about how they got there?"

Very looked startled, and guilty. "Oh, Dewar's chew papers?"

"Yeah, a lot. Hundreds. Maybe thousands. Those things aren't cheap. Do you know how they got there?"

"I brought some. But maybe a hundred, not more. I suggest we consult with Father Sullivan about the story of the loaves and fishes. Maybe there was a miracle?"

Chapter Twenty-nine: Mouse's Suicide

Very spent the night at Joey's house, as did a number of her extended family. There seemed to be a buzz all night long. She listened to the toilet flush, whispered conversations about drinks of water, and snores from various rooms. Very wrestled with her conscience about the lies, or omissions, that she had made in her statement. Was it better to cover up with saying she didn't know, or should she change her statement and say that she remembered? Remembered that Javier had confessed to murder? That was not going to fly. No, no one else knew what he had told Very, unless he had told someone, like the gang? His brother? Neither the gang, nor his brother, wanted any more complications. The best course of action was to let sleeping dogs lie. And then she slept.

Breakfast was a chaotic affair with multiple cooks and their favorite foods. Bobby Sanchez was pointedly absent and Joey told Very that she still might have to go down to the sheriff's department and be questioned again, more official this time.

"Question all they want. I have been traumatized and I don't remember much. As each hour passes, my memory becomes more and more jumbled." She heaved a sigh of consternation. "Joey, how do I get mixed up in these things? I don't try, I really don't."

"Hah! We can take you home and collect the car cover. That was Bobby's way of protecting you, by the way. He thought the gang might have seen you or something. He thought it best that your car and license plate were hidden, just in case they followed you. He was really worried that the gang could target you. If they knew you were there, then… Repercussions, maybe."

"I got that. Sort of. Overly protective, don't you think? Anyway, it's over for me. I need to get downtown to talk with Darrell. We need to wrap up this case, the Michelle/Mouse suicide case. After all my investigating, the sister comes up with another witness and my work seems superfluous."

"Oh c'mon, Very, you weren't superfluous. You helped with the Hernandez drowning case."

"Yeah, but I didn't know that was a case, did I? And I got mixed up with scary things. I had nothing to do with the drownings. Which reminds me, I need to thank Gabby for helping me get away. She was the lookout, by the way."

"So, you did know what was going on? You knew all along!" Joey said with irritation.

"No, I didn't. If I had known, I wouldn't have gone there. End of story. Let's get me home." Very went to gather up her overnight things.

When they were in the car, the back filled with grandchildren and their toys, Joey asked about the cat. "Did you leave food for her? I worried about her last night. You know, you usually are so conscious and considerate of the kitty, I just wondered if you had forgotten."

"No, I didn't. She's gone."

"She ran away? Oh no, Very, what will you do?"

"No, Joey, as in deceased. Murdered, by two bullying pit bulls. I buried her in the backyard. She even has a tombstone. It's funny, but she was the last living thing to connect me to my mother at that house. Without the cat, and my mother, there doesn't seem to be any reason for me to stay there. Maybe this is a sign that it is time to move on. You know, when the cat died, I cried, really cried. I cried for my mother, I cried for the cat, I cried for Frankie, I cried for all the lost souls in my life. Maybe I cried for myself as well. I think it is time to move on. Move, find a new house for myself. Maybe I'll move to the coast, where it's cooler. Cayucos or Cambria or San Luis. Out of this cauldron."

"Oh, Very, I'd miss you. I know it can get really hot in the summer, but you have air conditioning. And a pool. And your friends are here!"

"Yeah, a little like changing my name. Looking for something better. Besides, I hate the cold, and that coastal fog would drive me nuts. At first, I thought maybe working with Darrell and trying to find Frankie would keep me busy, give me a raison d'être. But now, I am not so sure. I think it's a bit too much for me. I am a woman of certain years and I should be enjoying my retirement. I should be taking cruises and enrichment classes, learning something new, like watercolor painting or knitting, yoga, mah jong, photography, screen writing…"

Joey laughed. "Listen to yourself, lady! Watercolor painting? Cruises? Nah, that's not the Vermilion I know." They pulled into Very's driveway. "Hey, anyone want to help us with the car cover?" she asked the back seat.

She was answered with a chorus of assent.

When the Sanchez clan had finally left, after a long tug of war with the car cover, a visit to the kitty tombstone, and a moment of silence, Very was left alone. She changed her clothes and headed downtown, to keep her appointment with Darrell. It was time to finish off the case.

As she looked for a parking place near Darrell's office, there was a flash back to the first time she had come here, last fall. She had come looking for someone to find her long lost fiancé, Frankie Monroe, but instead she had found a job. Time to end this connection. No Frankie in sight and the job had led her to more excitement than she wanted.

As she climbed the stairs, she laughed out loud. "Miss Wonderly, in the guise of Brigid O'Shaughnessy, entering the office of Sam Spade." She looked at the gold lettering on the glass door. "Darrell Pitts – Private Investigator." A throwback to earlier times, that look was outdated.

Before she could knock, the door was jerked open, and Darrell greeted her with a big grin on his face. "You're here," he said, backing inwards to let her enter. "I was thinking, it's easy to change the lettering on this door, you know. It's just store bought sticker things and they scrape off easily. We could change it to 'Pitts and Blew – Private Investigators.' Or we could use our first names, too. If you want. Whatever." He looked at Very's startled expression. "Whatever you'd prefer."

"Uh, Darrell, let's hold off on that for a while. Um, I may need a leave of absence, so I can't make any promises right now. I just came to tie up the loose strings from the case."

"And collect your pay. I did tell you that Deborah Smith has declared the case closed, and we have her money. So, this is your part." Darrell reached into his desk drawer and pulled out a check, made out to Very, for far more than she thought was owed. "She understood that we had done all of this in good faith, so she had good faith. Also, she inherits Michelle Malden's estate, so she can afford to be generous."

"I want details, and I will tell you mine, if they are of any interest, or use." Very sat at the extra desk, the Very desk that had been allocated for her use. The chair squeaked and the cushion squealed as she sat.

"Here, I'll let you listen to the recording. I recorded it, I thought that was the easiest thing to do. You ready?"

Very shrugged. Was making notes appropriate at this time? She needed to make a final report, but it could be very simple, just a few sentences, and it would be recounting what the Hernandez family had said. And her own conclusions. But now, given this new evidence, would much be needed about her ill-fated trip to East Bakersfield?

The urge to make a record got the better of her and she pulled out her notepad and a pen. Darrell hit the play button and Very listened to Deborah's story.

"…and then I contacted her. I didn't realize that they had become close in the last few months, but there it is. They had been close in college, but drifted apart, like we do. She told me that Michelle had tried to turn over a new leaf. She quit her job, she was trying to write, poetry and short stories, things like that. Her therapist had suggested it as a way to deal with the past, the present and to envision a better way to live. But Michelle, even though she looked fine on the outside, was still hurting inside. You see, it was an event from the past, sexual predation, when she was in high school. I knew that something was wrong at that time, that's when she came to live with me. But my life was rather stressful and I just waited for Michelle to say something. She never did, so, I forgot about it. But it still haunted her. That's what this friend said. Haunted her. Prevented her from diving deep into relationships. And if she ever felt like someone was getting too close, or was trying to manipulate her, she would retreat. In the last few months of her life, Michelle was deep into a depression, which she had been so good at hiding. Her therapist knew, but of course, she couldn't talk about it, being a professional and, you know, client privilege. When she quit seeing the therapist, this friend was a little afraid, but Michelle assured her she didn't need all the talk, talk, talk anymore. That she was handling it. But the friend said that it was obvious she wasn't. And, given the suicide note, and all the other things going on, it was just that. It was just what it looked like. Suicide. Michelle had finally chosen peace. So, that's it, I accept it. It doesn't make me happy, but life is what it is. Michelle was a tortured soul. She shall now find peace. I want to honor that memory by letting this whole thing go."

Darrell clicked off the recording. They sat there looking down, lost in their thoughts. Very had made a few notes, but she didn't need more. She had confirmation.

"I'll tell you the rest of the story, shall I?" Very said, finally.

"There's more?" Darrell was startled.

"Well, why do you think I went to the Hernandez house? Because they had seen her, Michelle, that day.

But it was only yesterday that I knew for certain what she had seen. Deborah talked about sexual predation, and that's what she saw, I'm certain of it."

"What did she see, did she write it down, did she tell someone?" Darrell asked.

"This is what she saw and what she did. Speculation only, but this explanation makes sense, the only one that does. Michelle is depressed. She has lingering nightmares and depression about an incident from her girlhood, high school. It has to do with some incident about sex, about forced sex, whether it was one time, repeated or whatever, she has never gotten over it. She is at the park. She has her notebook and she is trying to get in touch with nature, writing poetry, whatever. She goes off towards the river on this hot day and tries to find a quiet place by herself. We were there, at that seat, that log and it was quiet, and hidden, sort of. She may have been seen, but it doesn't matter at this point. And then, two people, a young girl, high school age, and an older boy, man, appear. Maybe they were already there, at that little beach. The older man is harassing the girl, maybe Michelle even witnesses an attempted rape. What can she do? She can't stop anything, she's a small woman. She's alone. It brings back memories, of the things she has been trying all her life to forget. This is a replay of what happened to her. Maybe not exactly, but close. She panics and runs, in tears, to her car. What she may or may not know, is that a couple of people have seen her.

"She then drives up the canyon and pulls over near the river. How long she is there, we don't know. But she takes her notebook and writes a suicide note. Not long, not elaborate, but she knows that it is what she should do, write a suicide note. She gets out of the car and throws herself into the river. Even if she could swim, that water was cold, and fast. It wouldn't be painless, but it would be quick and probably fatal. Witnessing the harassment is the trigger, I believe, to her suicide. Remember what everyone said, that they were surprised she lived so long. She had been a tortured soul for at least half her life. Her sister said it, let Michelle rest in peace. Requiem aeternam, Mouse."

Darrell sat, speechless. Finally, he managed to form the question that needed to be asked, confirmed, if possible. "How do you know she witnessed a rape?"

"I was told, by someone else who saw the attempted rape. It all makes sense, that's what I'm saying."

"Don't you think we need to tell Deborah? Just to confirm?" Darrell said.

"I have no confirmation, so no. I think we need to close this case. Let's just say that we don't need to let the cat out of the bag. Deborah has accepted the suicide, so shall we. The End."

"So, where do we go from here? Get a new sign? How do you like the Pitts and Blew idea? I can have it done by tomorrow. And we need some new advertising, a new business card. And then, I have some more ideas about where we can look for Frankie Monroe. You know, the Facebook thing is getting really big. Now, I think we can create a page and have a call for action or something like that."

"Wait, wait, Darrell. I'm not so sure I'm ready for this. I haven't cleaned out the house, I still have my mother's old clothes, and my grandmother's, come to think of it. This is the time, now. It's getting hot out there and I need to stay inside and clean. Clean out a lot of things. So, this new partnership? Well, I'm not sure I'm ready."

Darrell's face fell and he began to bite his lip. Very recognized the look, the prelude to tears. Darrell wouldn't do tears, surely. But she needed to stop the thought of tears, not let him down.

"Not that this can't be in the cards in the future. I never said that. I just said, not now. Hey, listen. Let's do it this way. You can play around with the names, we can think of first names, that's good. But maybe it's too long, they may get a bit crowded on the door. You just work on that one and when you're ready, you just let me know." Very reached over and patted Darrell on his shoulder. He lifted his head and looked into Very's face. She smiled her very best warm and fuzzy grin. He smiled back.

Very turned to the computer and put in the password. She found the document that contained the notes for the Michelle suicide case. She spent ten minutes typing in the last few sentences. It was perfunctory, not what she would have liked. But the details needed to stay in the graves of those who had passed.

Darrell had also turned to his computer and had gone silent. When he sensed Very finishing her work, he turned around. "Lunch?"

"Sure, I'd like that. Need to fortify myself for the tasks ahead."

They discussed their destination as they descended the stairs. Out on the street, Very remarked on the mild weather. "Last gasp of spring, I think. The hot weather awaits. I wonder, you know, this whole thing started with drownings in the river, 'the Killer Kern.' But they weren't drownings, were they? None of them. The River spit them out, but it didn't kill them. I think we have been too hard on the old Kern River, giving it such a bad rap."

Chapter Thirty: Burials

Very stood at the back of the crowd, just as she had done in the church. The families, the neighborhood, the gawkers; they had turned out in force. Very had wanted to remain inconspicuous and had arrived late, hoping to slip into one of the back pews unnoticed. She had not needed to worry; the church was full and others, later than she, stood on the side. Father Sullivan had been resplendent, tall and authoritative, decked out in the best, the shiniest robes, for the funeral. His voice thundered and rolled in the church, sad at the deaths of the young people, sister and brother, and angry at the way their lives had been snatched away too soon. No mention of gangs, revenge, the Killer Kern, or any other tangible reason for their early deaths.

When the last "Amen" had rolled through the church, Very sneaked out before anyone else and hurried to her car. Fearful that some of the gang members might be here, or someone might recognize the distinctive red Prius, Very had parked down the street. Because of that, she was not early to the cemetery. She watched the two hearses drive into main gate and watched their procession to the single canopy pitched near the graves. Very walked quietly across the manicured lawns, arriving at the same time as the family.

Gabby, decked out in an ill-fitting black dress, much too old for a child of her age, looked around as she walked to the gravesite. When she spied Very, she opened her mouth and looked as if she would run to Very's side, if she could. Very smiled and nodded, hoping Gabby would understand the gesture as one that Very would wait and speak to her after the burials. Carlos walked with Gabby and he, too, acknowledged Very. He hung his head and smiled shyly. He took Gabby's hand possessively and pulled her to stand next to their parents.

Very watched from afar, not listening to the prayers at the graveside, but looking at all the guests and estimating the number of the crowd. This wanting to know how many was a holdover from her father's day. Whenever anyone went to a function, of any style or purpose, the first question he asked, upon a wife's or a child's return, was how many had been there. Was the house, auditorium, restaurant table, backyard pool gathering, church service, whatever, well attended? How many, then who? Very learned how to rehearse the answers to these questions. Her mother never cared much, but had asked out of habit. Now, Very began her crowd estimate and stopped at 300. And still they came. They filled in the space between her and the family, now huddled together nearest the grave. She turned and stepped back, allowing the mourners to get closer.

She noticed, on the edge of the cemetery, a group of people holding signs and a simple banner. "Mothers against gang violence," it read. They respectfully stayed on the periphery of the events, but everyone leaving would pass by the small group. Who were they and why were they here, today? Very had never heard of them, but in a town that was known for its gangs, it wasn't a surprise that someone in the community thought it was high time to organize. She made a note to ask Bobby; he'd know who they were.

Very waited in the back of the crowd as Father Sullivan finished the short ceremony. Then a guitar appeared and a young man led everyone in a hymn. A few uniformed men approached and presented Javier's mother with a folded flag. The sound of the bugle drifted across the cemetery as everyone stood at attention. The crowd was silent until the high sweet tones drifted away on the wind. Veterans' funerals were always full of emotion. The thought that the vet could have died, but rarely had, during war, was there. The sacrifice of time, youth, perhaps a better paid job than Army or Navy, could not be forgotten. She would never have joined up, but she appreciated and gave a nod to those who did.

Very casually started to drift to the back of the crowd. Suddenly the 300 parted and the family processed to the cars parked on the edge of the lawns. Heads bowed in dignity, wrapped on the arms of those who were stronger, the family headed straight for Very. She did a side step out of their way and backed into the crowd.

But Gabby had seen her and detached herself from the others and approached Very. She stood in front of Very, her head down, her voice well-modulated as she said in a serious tone, "Thank you for coming. We are glad you could make it."

"I couldn't stay away, for Maria, or for Javier."

"Oh, I am so glad I saw you. It is wonderful that you are here. It was sooooo nice of you. And besides," Gabby lowered her voice, "I have something for you."

Very had visions of Dewar's chew papers, but steeled herself to be polite. "Yes, what do you have for me?"

"It's Javi's. You know, his motorcycle was blown up, nothing left of it. But my uncle, he went looking through all the junk, the stuff left, and he found this." Gabby opened her hand and in the palm lay a piece of metal, the two wings a little worse for the accident, or rather, attack on it. In the center, the words were still clearly etched, "Harley-Davidson."

"But how, how did this survive? I thought the garage burnt? Everything gone?" Very took the piece of metal and turned it over. It had been through the war. The gang war, the fires of war.

"My uncle did this, see, there is a hole here, for a key chain. He said, he said," Gabby choked up. "You know, Javi loved that machine. He really did, it was like a girlfriend, or a wife. He just loved it. And he was so happy that you liked it. He was surprised, he told me that. He didn't really understand it, and he didn't understand you. But he said that you were a person of honor and that you weren't afraid, of anything. He really liked you. And I know that he would be happy for you to have this. You can put your car keys on it."

"Thank you, Gabby. I am honored. I liked Javi too. And I know, for certain, that he was a man of honor. Remember that I said that, and don't let anyone ever try to tell you otherwise. Man of Honor."

"Come to lunch with us?" Gabby looked at Very.

"No, thank you. Say hello to your family. Tell them I am glad that you are all safe."

"Well, not everyone. Petey," she shook her head.

Very followed Gabby's gaze and then she saw Petey, Pedro, with his arm in a sling and a discreet bandage on his face.

"He's getting married and they are going to Colorado. She has relatives there. You know, it's far from here, which is a good idea for him. And my mom, ooooh. She's being really clingy, you know, like the wrap stuff. I feel like she is making me stick to her like glue!!!"

"That might not be a bad idea. Listen, Gabby, please keep in touch. If you ever need anything, this is where you can find me." Very stuck her hand into her bag, hoping that she could lay her hand on one of them quickly, and not make a fool of herself by upending her entire purse. "Aha, here it is."

She handed Gabby a business card. Firm, creamy card stock; elegant, classical font. Both full names, Darrell's first and then hers, followed by "Private Investigators." And a phone number.

"Oh, wow," Gabby said. "Look, that's your name." She looked up at Very and reached in for a hug.

Very allowed it and then gave her a quick kiss on her forehead. "You take care."

Gabby ran off to join her family. Very fought an upstream battle to reach the gravesite where Father Sullivan stood, exchanging words with mourners. Very caught his eye and they nodded in acknowledgement. Very stood looking at the coffins, about to be lowered into their deep graves. They were both the same size, and this confused Very until she remembered that there couldn't have been much left of Javier's body. She fingered the key chain token in her pocket, tracing her fingers over the wings, as she had done the first time she saw it.

"Selena, Maria channeling the dead Selena. And a Man of Honor," Very whispered. She turned to leave.

As she walked to her car, she knew she had done the right thing. Javi had confided in her, had told her the truth, because he was afraid no one else would ever know. But forgiveness was not hers to give. And the circumstances of the deaths meant that it should all be buried. All of it. Very was aware that death was never final and that this chapter may not have been over for this family. She would do what she could to make sure it was. Keeping secrets, she understood that.

It was a hot August morning and Very adjusted her sunglasses on her face. She sighed as she tried to find her way to the back of the cemetery, where the poor and unclaimed bodies were buried. She turned and scanned the cemetery, not willing to wait much longer for Cassandra. After all, this wasn't a formal thing at all. She clutched a bunch of flowers that she had managed to find in the garden of her mother's house, a few late roses and some brilliant zinnias.

"Hah," she said as she spotted the figure heading her way. She waved and then waited for Cassandra to join her.

"I am really sorry, I didn't know what to wear. I felt silly wearing black, so I compromised. You see?" She spread her arms wide to show off a black and white lightweight cotton dress.

"Perfect," Very said, giving Cassandra a one-armed hug.

"So, what's with the sling?" Cassandra asked with concern.

"Not much. Over and done with. You know the little fainting fits I used to have? Well, I needed a pacemaker and now I have one. A little computer in my chest to tell my heart to keep on beating. I get to take the sling off next week; then I will be a new woman, ready for many more years." Very gave Cassandra a brilliant smile to indicate that life moved on for her. "It's over here." She indicated a small section in the very back of the graveyard.

"Why so far away?" Cassandra looked around.

"Believe it or not, most of these other grave plots are claimed or paid for. The babies are here, they have smaller spaces," Very said, waving her arm to indicate the rows and rows of tiny plots, many decorated with plastic flowers and wind whirly gigs. "And here, in the back, are the unknown graves."

Arm in arm they approached one that had a newly installed marker. A small gray stone, plain but not low-cost, sat at the head of the plot. Together they read it. "Unknown man. Found 2014. Victim of the Kern River."

Cassandra was the first to speak, "But Very, we don't know he was drowned by the river."

"Oh, he probably wasn't. But he was a victim, he didn't bury himself. And so, this is the best way to put it."

"What do we do? Say a prayer? I'm afraid I'm not terribly religious."

"And what kind of prayer do you think we should say? Christian, Jewish, Hindu, Muslim? No, I think it would be nice to say it out loud, what everyone has been asking me. 'What are you thinking of, Very, buying a plot and burying these remains?' So, I'm going to say it."

"It's about Frankie, isn't it? About my dad."

"His bones are altogether, so if he is identified, he can be easily dug up and buried somewhere else. Maybe someone else, his own family, would like him to be buried in a proper place beside his own. I would rather there was some real identification, but in the future, maybe there will be. The authorities have kept some bones and a tooth. They will be able to get DNA from that."

"Who will bother?"

"I don't know. But that's what I want to say. So, here it is."

Very stood as straight as she could, inhaled deeply and bowed her head. "For this unknown man, I hope that someday you will be found. I hope that someday, your family can look for you and when you are found, you can be reunited with your loved ones. Just as I hope that someday…"

"Just as someday, someone may find my father and be unable to identify him. I hope that if he is not alive, but dead, and found in similar circumstances, that he would be treated respectfully. I've come today to honor, not this man, but my father. This man symbolizes that other man who is lost to me."

"For Frankie, wherever you are," Very said, laying the flowers on the grave. "We remember you."

The two women stood in silence for a minute, then turned away.

As they walked out of the cemetery, Cassandra turned to Very, "Isn't it traditional to eat after a funeral?"

"Yes, lunch, it is. Woolgrowers? Or? And thank you for coming with me today. I didn't know anyone else who would understand."

"And did you hear that there was another victim of the Killer Kern just last weekend? That river!

About the Author

Phyllis Wachob grew up in the Central Valley of California, loving to read and use her imagination. After college at UC Santa Cruz, she began a career of travel and adventure, studying for an MA in England, traveling by bicycle through France and Italy, and then busing through Greece and Turkey. While trying to settle to life in California, working at a desk in an office, she stretched even further during vacations to Asia and beyond. She then became a full-time traveler and writer, spending a year in India, followed by a year traveling in Africa. She has continued to travel throughout her life and has to date, traveled to 76 countries.

English teaching as a profession was embraced during a spell in China, where she fell in love with the wild scenery and peoples of Chinese Turkestan. She subsequently lived in Japan, Taiwan, Australia (where she earned a Doctorate of Education in Teaching English to Speakers of Other Languages), China, Singapore, Egypt and Turkey, teaching and traveling. These extensive experiences are reflected in her mystery novels in the Teachers Abroad Mystery series. She took her knowledge of the people, places, food and customs and wove fictional stories of mystery and murder.

She has been influenced by the great mystery writers, (although she started with the Nancy Drew mysteries), enjoying Sherlock Homes and Agatha Christie's books among others. She believes that characters and their vicissitudes form the crux of mysteries and the motivation to solve the whodunit is the driver of the story. The colorful, exotic, and unfamiliar should draw the reader into the core of the mystery, while the mundane and conventional hold the keys to the solution.

Currently she resides in Bakersfield, California where she was born. Her newest series, the Kern Kapers Mysteries, is set in Bakersfield and environs and features the characters who live there. She is a member of Writers of Kern and benefits from the connections of this professional writing community.

More information and blog posts can be found on the webpage: phylliswachob.com.

Questions for Reading Groups

1. In the first and subsequent chapters, Very thinks about her mother's life. She worries that she is turning into her aging mother. Do you ever consider, worry and/or reject becoming like your parent? Does this change your attitude or behavior? How common do you think this attitude is?

2. Very has a number of episodes of fainting. She is told, and she agrees, that she should see a doctor. But there is no movement on her part to do this. In the last chapter, she has finally acted, and is surprised by the result. How common is this attitude, especially as we get older, that the signs of aging are trifles? Have you seen it in yourself, or older friends or relatives?

3. Very discusses changing her name. She has had a lifetime of trying to explain it to others, but Clara, Joey's granddaughter, tells her, "You can't change your name. Your mommy gave you that name because she loves you very, very much." Have you ever changed your name, or thought you'd like to? How common is this feeling? How important is a name?

4. Much in this story hinges on sexual predation. How common is this? The #MeToo movement has brought this more into the limelight, but is the topic still taboo?

5. Hart Park is a major setting in this story. Have you been there? What are your memories of it? If you haven't, is there a similar place in your hometown that was a special place from your childhood? How important are these memories?

6. Very reminisces about her Barbie doll, the one she didn't get for Christmas. How important are these wishes for gifts of material things? Very concludes that it wasn't the doll, but the gift of unconditional love. How do we treat gifts in our culture? In other cultures? How do we teach children the meaning of gifts?

7. When Very meets the Hernandez family, she is confronted with a number of characters from this immigrant family in transition. Who speaks Spanish and who doesn't? Who wants to leave the culture and names behind, who wants a foot in both worlds, and who wants to embrace being American? Have you experienced, or known someone who has this dilemma?

8. When the cat is killed by the neighbor's dogs, Very mourns. Who is she really mourning? How do you know? What do you think is the outcome of this overwhelming sadness? Do events like this really push change, or is it just the straw that broke the camel's back?

9. In the end, Very attends two separate burial events, one is a large funeral, the other, intensely private. What are the purposes of funerals in our culture? What do you think of Very's choice to pay for the unknown body's interment?

10. Where is Frankie Monroe? Do you have any ideas? If you were the author, what would you do?

Notes: